MW00576079

The Shroomboat Adventures

The Architect's Notebook

Mark Lynn

1

The Shroomboat Adventures

The Architect's Notebook

By: Mark Lynn

Boll Weevil Press

THE SHROOMBOAT ADVENTURES: THE ARCHITECT'S NOTEBOOK. © 2023 by Mark Lynn.

All rights reserved. No part of this book may be used or reproduced in any manner whatsoever without written permission except in the case of brief quotations embodied in critical articles and reviews. For information, address Boll Weevil Press, 2 Camphor Drive, Newnan GA 30265, USA

Acknowledgements

To my loving wife. Thank you for loving me. All the good and the bad. Thank you for teaching me to love myself. To accept myself for who I am. Thank you for the sacrifices you've made and all that you've put off for me to pursue this dream. None of this would be possible without you.

To my family. Mama, and my two amazing big brothers, Amos and JJ. Thank you for letting me be as strange as I wanted, but always supporting and feeding my creativity. Without my mom's love and support and my brothers' creative influences I wouldn't be here today!

Thank you, Jeff for giving me a chance and going out on a branch for me! For letting me put this book out there the way I wrote it. I can't express how much that means to me.

To my two boys: my youngest, my little adventure buddy, thank you for always being up for wandering through the woods with me and helping me find the magic; and to my oldest, thank you for being unrelenting in being you -- you and your amazing mind, always coming up with ideas. There wouldn't be several characters in this book had it not been for you! The two of you keep me on my toes, and I can't thank you enough.

To Mitch. You were there at the beginning of the journey and all the way through. You were the creative mind I needed to bounce ideas off. Our back and forth brought life to so many things. No matter what life threw at me, you always pushed for me to follow a creative path and always had words of encouragement. Thank you for being such a good friend.

To many other friends throughout the journey, you have each been a piece of my puzzle. I am grateful for each and every one of you, for your love and your time.

Thanks to my dad. I know you're watching over me, and I know you've been with me every step of the way in this journey.

The Birth

At exactly 12:34 on the morning of August 16th, 1945 a peculiar young man was born. He was given the name Erik, after his father's childhood best friend. It was a good name, a strong name. Like Erik the Red, the great Viking warrior.

Erik's mother had given birth in her home. No one to help her. The father was across the sea, fighting in the Great War. She didn't know how long it would be before the soldier would meet his son. Or that he would ever have the chance.

Over the next few weeks, Erik's mother welcomed the cries of a newborn baby. The silence of the house over the last few months had nearly driven her mad. All she had to keep her mildly sane was a small green book she had since she was a child. It was full of old Irish folk tales and mythology. She soon began to introduce her newborn child to the wonderful world she had partially lived in most of her life: the world of Fae.

Much to the mother's delight, less than a month after her son's birth, the Great War came to an end, and the love of her life returned. But the man who came back from the war was nothing like the man who had left.

The letters of love and concern had stopped after the first year. Nothing followed. The next year and a half she sat and waited for any news. When the door to the little house opened and her husband walked through the threshold, her heart leapt bounds. He had been wounded in battle and sent home. Strangely, he didn't exhibit much emotion. He made love to his wife, but not with any passion. After only two months of being home, he was told he was going to be a father. At first the news seemed to bring him joy. He even managed a fleeting smile. It was only a week after the news that the man's seemingly warrior spirit called to him again. He rejoined the Army and set out to the Pacific, his wife left at home with the unborn child.

This time was even worse. He was quieter than before. Even more to himself. As he walked in, he was handed his beautiful newborn son. The baby felt so light and feeble in the hardened man's arms. The soldier could feel his lip begin to quiver. He wanted to smile. He wanted to cry tears of happiness. He wanted to turn and thank his wife for her love and for giving him the greatest gift in the world. Yet he couldn't. It was like he was watching it all happen through a pair of eyes behind his own. He saw what was happening, felt emotions and wanted to act upon them. Instead, he held the baby and stared at it coldly, almost mechanically. Then he returned Erik to his mother without a word.

He seemed to only grow worse. The deeper he dove into the bottle, the more he withdrew from his little family. He became angry and violent when he drank too much. He always had a far off look in his eyes, as if he were somewhere else.

While he was away, Erik's mother did her best to try and ignore the nightmare that surrounded her. She would sit and read her book to her child for many hours of the day. She, too, now seemed to live in some far-off place in her head. Only it wasn't as dark as her husband's seemed to be. At least not on the surface.

The Window

Now, in Irish lore all the fairies aren't of good nature. In fact, the fairy who claimed to be their king was an evil being. He was known to take small children from the real world and replace them with his mischievous changelings. Once he had lured the children into the fairy world he would eat them whole. He claimed the small children of the real world had a special power that fed his own.

One night, fast asleep in his crib, Erik awoke to strange yet whimsical music coming from outside his window. Erik pulled himself up to see where the music was coming from. The young child could see out the window as if it were midday. Green valleys ran for as far as he could see, covered in all sorts of clovers and beautiful flowers. Two tiny creatures, surely too small for the normal eye to catch, slowly began to open the window. The music grew louder. Even though it was midwinter, a warm, sweet-smelling breeze wafted into the room. Erik looked over to his mother, who was fast asleep in a chair with her book of fairy tales open in her lap.

The young boy quickly noticed the picture on the open page. It was that of an evil fairy king by the name of the Erlking. His mother had read stories of him and how he would lure children to the fairy world forever.

Though just a small child -- about three in age now -- he sensed something was wrong. The little creatures had now unlatched the young boy's crib. The music grew even louder, and the smell even stronger. The tiny creatures -- Erik assumed they were fairies! -- began to tug at Erik's nightshirt, trying their best to get him out of his crib.

Eventually, Erik made his way down and over to the window. There, he stood in amazement at the sight. A hand that seemed to be coming from nowhere began to reach out towards him. The sweet smell quickly turned pungent. Erik looked back at his mother and took a step back. The music began to fade, until there was only a sound so faint that it sounded as if it were coming from a music box.

When the boy turned back to the window, the green fields were gone. All he could see out in the night was one giant of a man sitting on a stump. The only light was from two fairies that flew around him like flies surrounding a heap of dung (which is also what it now smelled like, as well!). The smell almost made the boy sick. The image wasn't terrifying *per se*, but it was enough to make the small boy wish to recoil back into his crib. Erik wouldn't always remember what he saw, but he would always remember the awful smell and the feeling it gave him.

The next morning Erik awoke to the sound of his father's voice bellowing through his room. Though there was nothing new to his father yelling, this time was different. It seemed to be coming from a place of concern rather than a place of anger. He yelled at his wife for leaving the window open in the dead of winter and for the latch on Erik's crib being undone. This was the first time she had ever seen him take a real concern for their son, and the whole ordeal seemed to bewilder the mother. She didn't remember opening a window. Being someone who was always cold, it didn't make any sense for her to do such a thing, either.

The Cold Morning

      Erik didn't remember much about this day, other than it being one of his earliest memories. It was also one of his worst. The doctor came and went from the room several times. Erik could still remember seeing his mother through the crack in the door. She looked as pale as a ghost and was covered in sweat. He remembered making eye contact with her, but she quickly turned her head away from him, instead of giving him her usual, comforting smile. After the doctor was there most of the day, a strange ambulance drove into the driveway. Two men dressed in white stood outside the car, awaiting Erik's mother and the doctor. Erik's father sat him down in a chair and tried to explain what was happening. He knew the boy was too young to really understand him, but he felt as if something needed to be said nonetheless. He explained that the boy's mother had caught a horrible cold and was very bad off. He explained she was going away to her sister's for a while to get better. He asked if Erik understood him, and the boy shook his head. All Erik gathered from the conversation was that his mother was leaving. That would be the main thing that would stick with him from that day. It was the last time he would see his mother.

As his mother left, she stopped and gave Erik the biggest hug she could muster up. Tears ran down her face. She told him she was sorry and that she loved him more than he could ever know.

The door opened and a blinding light shone through, though Erik seemed to be the only one seeing it. At once his mother lifted off the ground and into the sky. She seemed to have wings carrying her up. Up, up she went. Then she was gone.

His father watched as the ambulance drove down the road. A single tear ran down his cheek. He had a feeling in the pit of his stomach that it may be the last time he would see his dear wife. He would be correct in thinking so.

The Beckoning Call

During the next two years, Erik's father raised the boy by himself - at least he was present and kept the boy alive and fed. He was cold to his son, refraining from all emotion. Some days there wouldn't even be a single word exchanged between the two. At night he would drink until he fell asleep. It was clear he was not happy with life, or with himself.

Erik was a very clever boy, and in his isolation from the world he began to teach himself how to read, even at a very young age. He would read everything he could. Every box, bottle, or pamphlet he could get his hands on. He quickly learned to read simple books. His favorite, of course, was his mother's little green book of fairy tales. He loved it so much that he kept it on him, in a small satchel, all the time. It never left his side.

He would spend all day playing in the woods, pretending he was in some far-off land surrounded by the Fae folk without a care in the world. In the evenings, he would return home and quietly eat supper with his father and go to bed. His nights were plagued with nightmares. He couldn't recall the dreams exactly, but he always awoke with the same strange taste in his mouth, and an uneasy feeling.

Some nights he would sit up in his bed and stare out his window into the dark. For some reason, he always half-expected for there to be something out there. One night, as he stared out in a daze, he saw a small light in the distance, no bigger than a candlewick, flying about to and fro. At first he thought maybe it was just a firefly. But as it flew back and forth, it seemed as though it were trying to get the boy's attention. Finally, Erik's curiosity took hold, and he stood up from his bed and made his way to the front door.

His father laid motionless on the couch with an emptied bottle of liquor on the ground close by. The boy easily slipped by him and out the door. Outside, the strange lightning bug waited for him. It was clear it wanted Erik to follow it.

It started to move through the yard and into the woods. Erik trailed behind. Farther and farther into the woods the light took him. He was mesmerized by the glow and didn't even realize how far he was wandering into the forest. Finally, there was an opening in the trees. The moonlight shone through and lit the open area quite nicely. Erik could see a circle of clovers on the ground. In the middle of the circle sat a large stump. Erik stopped in his tracks at the edge of the opening. Something about the stump made him uneasy. A strange feeling began to overtake him and an all too familiar smell and taste began to fill his mouth. He began to back away from the stump. Suddenly a deep voice spoke from behind him.

"Where are you going, little one?" the voice spoke.

Erik turned quickly, but no one was there. When he turned back toward the circle, a large man now sat upon the stump. His smell was undeniable. Two small lights flew around him. Erik couldn't move! He was paralyzed with fear. The giant man held out his hand for Erik to take.

"Come little one! My master has been waiting to meet you for quite some time!" the ogre spoke.

The man grabbed Erik's arm, but quickly let go with a shout. Steam rose from his hand as if he had just laid his hand on a lit stove! His eyes widened and he stared at the boy in confusion and amazement.

Just at that moment, Erik felt two arms grab him and lift him into the air. He screamed as loud as he could, and tears began to pour down his face.

His father held Erik in his arms. They were both shaking uncontrollably. Just as his father was about to

17

scold him, he stopped, for he could see the fear in his child's eyes.

"Erik! Erik! What's wrong son!? What are you doing?"

The boy didn't speak the whole way home. When they got back to the house, his father noticed red marks on Erik's arm that looked to be massive finger imprints. He asked what had happened, but Erik acted as if he had no recollection of the events.

The next morning, Erik found his things packed up in a suitcase by the front door. His father didn't say much. All he would say is that Erik was going to live with his grandmother. Erik asked questions along the way, but his father remained silent.

Erik had only met his father's mother once and was too young to remember it. He tried to imagine what the mother of such a cold and angry man would be like. Would she be even worse? As they approached the house his worries began to diminish. It was nothing like Erik was envisioning. It was painted a soft, inviting yellow with a big, blue door. Many potted plants hung from the top of the porch and along the stairs. It was a quaint little house. A lady with white hair and a flower apron stood on the front porch, waving as they drove up. She had an enormous smile and cheeks that glowed red. His grandmother greeted him with the biggest hug he had ever had. He seemed to melt into her arms. He felt so warm. So comfortable.

A New Friend

His grandmother was a heavier lady, with snow white hair. She had one green eye and one blue. She seemed to always have a smile on her face, no matter what. She seemed nothing like her son. Or at least, not the son Erik had come to know.

At first Erik was almost overwhelmed by all the love and attention he was getting. He had grown so used to being alone with his thoughts, trying to deal with all his emotions with no help.

One night, Erik had one of his recurring nightmares, and he woke up screaming. Usually when this happened, he would sit in the dark, alone, and stare off until he calmed down enough to go back to sleep. As he prepared to do just that, the overhead light came on and in walked his grandmother. She had a small teddy bear in her arms. She sat next to him on his bed.

"You have these bad dreams a lot, don't you sweetie?," she asked him in her sweet and timid voice.

Erik shook his head. He hadn't ever really talked about his dreams with anyone before. He had just learned to try and deal with them himself.

"It's okay, you can tell me about them. You know, when I was little, I had bad dreams, too. They always felt so real to me. One day my father went out and got this little guy for me. He told me that he was magic and that he would fight off any bad dreams that I might have. And you know what? It worked! I never had those bad dreams again!"

Erik looked up at her with tears in his eyes.

"You.... You believe in magic?," he asked.

She smiled and handed him the bear.

"His name is Teddy! He was my best friend for many years. May he protect you and comfort you as well as he did me."

She proceeded to kiss the boy on the forehead and wished him sweet dreams. Erik held the bear tight in his arms and was back asleep in no time.

The next morning, Erik awoke to the most wonderful smells. His grandmother had made a marvelous breakfast just for him. She had made eggs, bacon, sausage, and pancakes! It tasted even better than it smelled. He stuffed his belly to the brim. That was a wonderful way to start the day.

After breakfast, Erik's grandmother took him into her living room. She told him to close his eyes and stick out his hands for a surprise. She then reached up onto the top shelf of her bookcase and pulled down a yellow and green book and placed it into his hands. Erik opened his eyes and looked down at the book: *The Wizard of Oz* by Frank Baum.

"You know how you asked me if I believed in magic? This here is a whole world of magic!"

That night she sat and read with him, and they made it nearly halfway through the book. This became one of Erik's favorite memories.

Over the next year, Erik learned to read full chapter books, and to write. He wasn't the most social child, but he was honest and genuine. Every evening he would rush home from school to an afternoon of sitting on the porch, drinking sweet tea and reading the Wizard of Oz books. In the evening, after a hearty dinner, Erik and his grandmother would sit in the living room and listen to the radio. They would listen to mysteries and sci-fi stories. Nights when there weren't any programs on, they would dance around the room. She taught him how to be a pretty good little dancer before long.

Everything seemed perfect. What love he had been missing was repaid tenfold by his grandmother. He wondered what could have happened to his father for him to be the way he is. Everything with her was so easy. Every day seemed to run on a perfect schedule. He knew every day as he walked home that he would turn the corner and see his grandmother there on the porch waiting on him. Every time it reminded him of the first time he rode up - the day his life changed for the good. The day he started to feel what love really was.

The Kitchen

One day Erik was on his way home, as usual. He turned the corner where he would normally see his grandmother waiting. Today, for the first time since he had started school, she wasn't there. At first Erik didn't think anything of it, but the sight of a police car in the driveway quickly began to make him worry. Erik rushed inside. He was stopped only a few feet in by an officer.

"Whoa there. Let's go outside and talk for a minute, okay buddy?" the officer said as he put his arm around Erik and led him back out to the porch.

The officer asked strange questions, such as how Erik's day was at school. Erik didn't care for the small talk. He only wanted to know what was going on and where his grandmother was. After more mundane questions, the boy couldn't take it anymore.

"What's going on!? Where's my grandma!?" Erik shouted.

The officer lowered his head and took a deep breath. He put his hands on Erik's shoulders as he spoke.

"I'm sorry, son...," he started.

Erik didn't want to hear the rest. Before he could finish his sentence, Erik pushed by him and moved back into the house. As he turned towards the kitchen, he saw another officer standing with a notepad in hand. Past the man with a notepad, all Erik could see were two distinct feet sticking out from behind the counter. He would recognize his grandmother's flat-bottom shoes with flowers on the top anywhere. His heart sank into his stomach. He did the only thing he could think to do. He immediately turned and ran out the front door.

He had never known anyone to die before. Now, the person he loved the most in this world was gone. He felt even more alone than he had before. Where before there was nothing, now there was a hole. He felt sick and drained, yet his legs kept running. He kept moving forward, but his mind was still back there standing in the kitchen.

He ran for at least two miles before he finally came to a stop. He sat down on a fallen tree to catch his breath.

As his feet hung down from the log, he began to imagine he was sitting on top of a giant skyscraper with

his feet dangling over the whole world. He closed his
eyes and let the wind calm him. His heart began to
return to a normal pace. A shuffle in the leaves next to
him pulled him from his trance. A little groundhog
popped her head up from under the log where he was
sitting. They both sat unmoving and stared at each other
for some time. It was the strangest thing. What was
more odd than the stare-off with the wild animal was the
little creature's appearance. She had one green eye ...
and the other blue.

"Hi there. Don't worry, I won't hurt you!" the boy
spoke.

At this, the groundhog turned her head to the
side as if she could understand him. The groundhog
looked for a moment as if she were smiling at him. She
put out her tiny paw and laid it upon Erik's knee. The
moment only lasted a second, but there was something
comforting about it.

The groundhog returned to its home under the
log. Erik sat for a moment and collected his thoughts. He
thought how strange it all was. How off everything felt.

He turned and began to walk back home. As he
approached the house, he could see the kitchen light on.
Maybe it all was just a bad dream! He began to picture
his grandma standing there in her apron with a hot,
delicious meal and a giant smile on her face. She would
pick him up and hug him tightly. Then they would eat
and sit on the couch and listen to their show together.
His pace began to quicken until soon he was in a full

sprint towards the house. He wanted so badly to just be in her warming arms and have all of this go away.

As he reached the porch, reality hit him like a freight train. One of the officers from before had fallen asleep on the rocking chair. Erik's eyes swelled back up with tears. He quietly opened the door and snuck by the guard. He walked into the kitchen and stared at the floor, unblinking. He couldn't place how he felt. He didn't know what he was supposed to feel. It was both an empty and a heavy feeling all at once. All he knew was that the person he had grown to love so much in this world was no longer here.

Into the Night

Erik ran up to his room and began shoving his belongings into a suitcase. To him, the essentials were his mother's fairy book and all the Oz books his grandmother had read to him. It made the case quite heavy and hard for Erik to carry, to the point where he had to drag it behind him. He inched his way down the stairs one step at a time, trying not to make too much noise. With Teddy in one hand and his suitcase in the other, he began to head out the back door. As he did, he stopped in the kitchen once more and stared at the spot on the floor.

He let out a deep sigh and wiped the tears from his eyes. He opened the back door and set off into the night. Luckily for Erik, the moon was full and high in the sky. He could see everything around him, yet the night felt uninviting and cold. He could hear all sorts of animals and strange noises in the distance as he walked down the trail. Even with the moonlight, Erik couldn't help but wish he had brought a flashlight or lantern. As heavy clouds began to cover the moon, his feelings intensified. It was as if someone had blown out a candle in a dark room when the clouds passed over. Suddenly everything was dark. He held out his hand and could only make out to the middle of his forearm. His hand was lost to the darkness. He closed his eyes and clutched Teddy tight in his arms. He prayed the clouds would pass quickly. He slowly began to open one of his eyes to see if the darkness still surrounded him. Instantly both eyes shot open, and his breath immediately left his body. Erik couldn't move. There before him stood his living and breathing nightmare.

The giant man stared at him with wild eyes and a mostly toothless smile. He now wore giant gloves like those of a blacksmith. He stood towering over the boy. The only light came from those two pesky fairies that seemed to follow the ogre. As the portly man reached down toward Erik, all the boy could do was close his eyes and await whatever fate may befall him. A loud ROAR filled the air.

Erik opened his eyes just in time to see the giant man slung into a nearby tree! The clouds had moved on and Erik stared in amazement at his defender. Next to him stood a massive grizzly bear. He stood on his hind legs with his arms forward as if ready to strike again. The two fairies and the giant man retreated into the woods and disappeared back into the darkness.

The bear returned to four legs and began to nuzzle his head into Erik's hand like a dog would do for attention. Erik began to pet the bear gently. He soon realized the bear was a friend, and he hugged the great beast as best he could. Due to his massive size, Erik's arms were still several feet apart. The boy thanked the bear over and over.

They walked a bit more before Erik began to voice how tired he was. It wasn't long before the boy had found a pile of leaves and made a bed among them. The bear laid beside the boy. The small child was barely the size of his belly. Erik nuzzled into the grizzly and was fast asleep in no time at all.

Morning After

The next morning was as surreal as the night before. When the boy awoke, he was in a hospital bed. He looked around the strange room. He had no recollection of how he got there or what was going on. He began to listen to the nurse and the doctor talk just outside of the room. They hadn't yet noticed he had awakened. From what he gathered, they said he had a severe asthma attack while running through the woods and passed out. Apparently, one of the officers who had been looking for him had finally caught up to him, after following a trail Erik had left from dragging his suitcase.

Nothing of this story had any resemblance to what Erik remembered. All he could recall was the bear.

After he was treated and seemed to be okay, one of the officers from the night before entered the room.

"Gave us all quite a scare."

Erik didn't respond. He tried to ignore the officer and look out the window. He felt as if he were in some sort of dream he couldn't wake up from. It only grew worse with each passing moment.

"Good thing you like to read so much. I might not have found ya if you didn't leave me a trail to follow!"

The officer tried his best to get a smile out of Erik, but it was no use. The boy remained silent, staring out the window.

"Hey kid, I know this is tough on you. I can only imagine what you're going through. I know you loved your grandma. We all loved your grandma. She was a great woman. A loving woman. All that said, unfortunately she's gone now. We gotta figure out what to do with you. You keep running away, like last night, and it ain't gonna turn out so good for ya. They'll try to put ya in an orphanage. Ain't none of us wanna see that! You just sit tight while we keep trying to get ahold of your father."

Erik looked down to his feet. He didn't want to go back with his dad. It was cold there. Silent, gray, and dull. He had been so content, so happy.

"What about my mother?" the boy asked.

The officer took a deep breath and thought a moment before he spoke.

"Well, son. Unfortunately, we looked into that... Records show she passed away nearly two years ago. I'm so sorry."

Erik's vision began to blur as he stared off towards nothing in particular. The officer kept speaking, but Erik didn't hear any of it. Eventually, the officer patted him on the leg and Erik came to as the officer was saying his goodbyes.

"You get some rest. I'm gonna do everything I can to get ahold of your dad," the officer said with confidence as he left.

Erik didn't share the same enthusiasm. He figured if his dad didn't want him before, then why would he want him now? He let out a sigh and laid back into the hospital bed. He felt so alone. So lost. He began to imagine life by himself. It was a sad and scary thought to him, indeed.

He began to count the tiles in the ceiling over and over until finally his racing mind slowed down. He closed his eyes and drifted away.

A New Beginning

The next morning, the officer returned to the room. His eyes were darkened and deprived of sleep.

"Well son, I got good news, and I got bad news. Which one do ya want first?"

Erik was sure he already knew the "bad" news. Though to him it wasn't so bad and very expected.

"You couldn't get ahold of my dad?" the boy scoffed.

The corner of the officer's mouth curled up in disappointment. It broke his heart to hear the boy talk the way he did. He shook his head and continued.

"Well, I reckon you were right about him. But the good news is, I did find some family members willing to take ya in."

"Who?" Erik asked.

"Your aunts. Your mother's two sisters. They've agreed to take you in. They seem like real sweet ladies. I talked to them for quite some time early this morning. They're about a four-hour drive from here. Now, I can take ya there if ya want. Or if you want to wait and see if we can get ahold of your dad, then we can set you up in a temporary home. It's up to you."

"No, you won't reach him, and even if you did, he wouldn't want me. So, yes sir, I'd like to go to my aunts' house please."

The car ride to his aunts' house was quiet. He rode with his head propped on the window, looking out. The two people he had loved most in this world were gone forever.

He didn't remember much about his mother. If he thought really hard, he could sometimes picture her beautiful face smiling at him. Her voice was the main thing he recalled. Sometimes he would close his eyes, and he could still hear her reading to him. Even though he was beyond happy at his grandmother's, he had always dreamed of trying to reconnect with his mother one day. Now, that wasn't possible.

The plains they drove through perfectly resembled what Erik was feeling at the time. Nothing. Miles of emptiness and unknowing. He felt bad that he wasn't more sad, but truth be told, he was nothing. Just empty.

"Here we are," the officer said as they drove up to the house.

His aunts' house was one of the biggest houses he had ever seen. It looked to be older, but well taken care of. Giant pillars lined the front of the house and a porch wrapped around on all sides. A few rocking chairs sat in the front. Erik thought to himself how much his grandmother probably would've loved to rock in them. A tear began to swell in his eye as the officer opened the door.

Only one of the aunts had come outside to greet Erik. She was a taller lady of medium build with wild, curly red hair.

"Oh, you sweet thing, come here!" she said as she pulled him into her with a giant hug.

Erik was amazed at the amount of sincerity her hug had. She held tight and rubbed his back softly. It was if she knew the pain he was feeling and how badly he needed this hug!

Erik could feel the warmth coming from her body. An energy almost. As he stood in her embrace, he couldn't help but feel that everything was going to be alright.

The officer said his goodbyes and headed out. He had a good feeling about the situation, as well.

They walked inside the massive house and the other aunt sat in the entrance awaiting them with a grand smile. She was clearly the older of the sisters. Her hair was short and shiny white and silver. She sat in a wheelchair, but Erik was soon to find out that wouldn't slow her down one bit! She leaned over and gave him an equally warm hug and kissed him on the cheek.

"You look just like your mother," she said with tears in her eyes and a smile on her face.

The Sisters

Erik's aunts' names were Angela and Brenda. They were both amazing people. Brenda was always joking and making Erik laugh. Meanwhile, Angela would listen to anything Erik had to say, no matter how silly or serious. She was always Erik's shoulder to cry on and ear to listen.

They told Erik all sorts of stories of when they and his mother were children and all the trouble they got in. One story about a milk jug and a bully resonated with Erik for many years to come. It seemed as if Angela had truly been their big sister. Always protecting them, looking out for them. But even after she wasn't able to stand anymore, she remained so strong. Erik would always marvel at the will his aunt showed.

Angela began to see Erik's creativity and started to teach him how to paint and draw. It came quite naturally to him.

Angela and Brenda didn't know much about the world of Oz, other than the movie. They also surprisingly didn't know much about Irish folklore, either. It was Erik's mother who lived with her head in the clouds and her nose in a book.

The aunts were much more practical and uniform than he was used to. They liked everything to be a certain way. Everything had a place and most things had a time. Still though, he loved them, and he loved living with them.

He still slept with Teddy close by and read the fantasy books every chance he got.

One night while Brenda was straightening Erik's room, putting away books, she was struck by an idea. The next morning, she went out early into town to the local bookstore. When she returned, she handed Erik two little red books: *Alice's Adventures in Wonderland* and *Through the Looking Glass*.

"I thought you might enjoy them! I remember your mother reading them almost as much as that green book you've kept safe all these years!"

She was right in thinking Erik would like them. He was instantly in love.

During Angela's painting sessions, he would often paint wild worlds such as Wonderland and Oz. Angela was always taken by the things Erik would come up with. He would take the landscapes she showed him how to paint and add all sorts of whimsical elements and wild colors! Any outlet Erik could create in, he enjoyed. If he wasn't out "playing pretend," he was drawing, painting, or writing stories. He hoped that one day he may be able to create a world of his own.

Angela and Erik would paint or draw together at least twice a week. Their usual spot was inside the sunroom in the back of the house. It was a delightful glass room full of plants and fountains. Late in the evening when it would cool down, Angela would take two easels into the room and set them up. Eventually, she ended up making a spot just for them, right in the middle of the room. She would simply take a picnic basket of paint back and forth. Erik would come to cherish those afternoons - always full of creativity, laughter, and good conversations.

Brenda and Erik had a bit of a different relationship. Whereas Angela was sweet and calm and had heartfelt moments with Erik, Brenda was witty, playful, and sarcastic as hell. She and Erik spent a lot of time together. They didn't have nearly as many heart-to-hearts, but in their day-to-day interactions they always joked and laughed. Even so, she was usually the main one to discipline him. Brenda would end up being the closest thing to a mother Erik would ever have.

Friends

At school, Erik was a bit of an oddball. He never talked about his personal life and was always doodling. He was polite and caring to everyone he met, and he did his best to not make enemies or have spats with people. Even when bullies tried to poke fun at him for being strange, he would always reply with a snarky comment or simply ignore them. He lived by the term "kill them with kindness." Even if his actions weren't reciprocated, he continued on.

Erik had many acquaintances, but only two people he truly considered to be his friends. They were a little odd themselves, but nothing to the degree of Erik. Their names were Christian and Samantha. Christian was friends with all the "popular" kids and played lots of sports. Looking at him, one wouldn't think that he would have much to do with an oddball like Erik, but they were the best of friends. Christian was always wanting to "play pretend" and see what wild things Erik would come up with, whether they were playing as army men or cowboys or detectives. There was never a dull moment with them.

Samantha was Erik's other close friend. Her hair was always tangled and dirty. She was blonde, but at first glance you could hardly tell. Being the tomboy she was, she refused to be called Samantha and would only answer to Sam. Now Sam was by far the toughest of the trio. She was always ready to fight and wasn't afraid of anything! If the trio got in any sort of trouble, you could bet she was the source of the idea that got them there.

When they weren't in school, the three of them would stay out in the woods playing until the sun went down. From time to time, Erik would sneak over to one of their houses in the evening and watch television. His aunts owned a little TV, but Erik wasn't even sure if it worked, because he had never seen it on. Christian's family, meanwhile, all seemed to be glued to it most of the time when Erik would come over.

Erik may have had an unconventional home, but he preferred it to what he saw at his friends' houses. Yeah, they had TV and all the new cool things, but Erik always felt something was missing when he was at their homes. Christian's family seemed to be a house of zombies; they were always doing the same thing every day. Even when they weren't in front of the TV, they were hardly talking. They would even seem somewhat surprised whenever Erik would try to strike up any sort of conversation with them.

Sam's house was more lively, but not in a good way. They didn't go to her house much, and even Sam tried to steer clear of it as often as possible. Almost every time they would go to her house, Sam's father and mother would be screaming at one another. From time to time, things would even be thrown across the house. If the fights weren't too heated, it could be almost entertaining to watch the two go at it. Still though, Erik couldn't imagine living in such a home.

Lucky for him, he couldn't really remember that he had lived a similar hell as an infant.

The Hermit and the Lake

One day the trio were playing in the woods (as they normally did). On this day, however, the sense of adventure overtook them. They had played in the creek near Erik's house many times before, but as they hopped from rock to rock they began to make their way down the creek, farther than they had ever been before.

They could see ahead through the brush as the woods opened into a field alongside a creek that ran into a beautiful pond. As excitement began to fill them, their pace quickened. Just as they were about to breach the treeline, they heard a voice call out.

"Don't even think about it! You step one more foot on my property, and I'll fill ya full of bird shots! Kids or not!"

Erik and the others froze in place, looking around for the source of the voice. Not too far from them stood an old man waving a gun overhead.

As soon as they saw the gun, they turned tail and high-stepped back up the creek as fast as they could.

"That guy is crazy!" exclaimed Christian once they had returned to familiar grounds.

Sam smiled a mischievous smile. "Yeah, but did you see that pond! Imagine swimming in that big boy! Way better than our spots in the creek or down by the river." It was as if she had brushed off the fact they had just had a gun waved at them.

When Erik got home, he told his aunts of the crazy man downstream. Angela and Brenda both burst out laughing and shook their heads.

"That's just ol' Luthor. He wouldn't hurt a fly. He's down there all alone, surrounded by his animals. No one hardly ever sees him in town unless he's getting food for them. The gun probably wasn't even loaded. He more than likely just saw you and your friends and wanted to scare you off... which clearly worked! I wouldn't worry about him. Now, that being said, I also wouldn't go that far down the creek anymore. He likes to keep to himself, clearly. Y'all leave the man alone, okay?"

Angela gave Erik a stern look as she said it.

Erik nodded his head in affirmation.

Over the next few weeks, Erik couldn't get the old man out of his head. How lonely he must be, he thought. To him, being alone seemed like the most terrible thing imaginable. He had not yet learned the importance of solace. Still though, even when you are fine with your own thoughts, it can be a lot when it's all you have. Erik had an overwhelming feeling, almost a gravity pulling at him from down the stream. He couldn't shake the feeling that he was supposed to talk to the old man.

Well, whereas Erik couldn't get the old hermit out of his mind, Sam couldn't get the lake out of hers.

"Summer's almost over, and I want to go swim in that lake. I say we just go down there and ask him if we can. What harm would come from it!?"

"My folks say he's a loon. He only comes to town once every two weeks. He goes to the feed store, then goes and sits at the diner for like an hour and drinks coffee. He never says a word to anyone. Pete Mars's dad said he thinks the old man is a killer. That he's got a beautiful garden and he keeps it that way by fertilizing it with dead bodies!" Christian spoke up, excitedly.

"Well, my aunts don't seem to think he's crazy. They said he's all alone and likes to keep to himself, that's all," interrupted Erik, slightly offended on Luthor's behalf. Sam put her index finger and her thumb to her chin.

"Hmmm..... either way, I think I may have a plan." She paused for a moment. You could see the wheels turning.

"Your parents said he goes into town for a few hours every two weeks, right? That's our chance! We can figure out when he leaves and go swimming while he's gone."

Though Erik was a bit hesitant, they all came to the conclusion that it was a solid plan. Luthor's bi-weekly trip happened to fall just a few days later. The three children lied and waited by the road where they could see the man leaving. They didn't have to wait long. The old pickup truck came puttering by, headed towards town. The trio ran across the road and jumped over the fence into the old man's yard.

The hermit's house was nothing like any of them had expected. While they had heard that he had a beautiful garden, the stories did it little justice. Bushes of flowers ran along the driveway, all the way to the house. Tomatoes and all sorts of vegetables grow in small fields in the front yard. The house was quaint and looked to be very well kept. But as they approached the house, a sight of horrors befell them. A massive pack of dogs ran toward them at full speed! Christian and Sam both turned and ran back towards the gate. Erik, on the other hand, stood in place. Soon he was engulfed by the wave of dogs. Sam and Christian screamed from the other side of the fence in horror. That was until they began to hear Erik laughing. As he laid on the ground, covered in dog slobber, he was certain they were harmless.

The children picked some apples from one of the many fruit-bearing trees and sat and played with the dogs for some time.

Remembering that they were on a time crunch, Sam quickly snapped to and grabbed the others, heading towards the lake. She had waited all summer. She was going to swim in that lake!

The time had finally come. Sam and Christian ran to the end of the dock and dove in. Erik, admittedly not being the best swimmer, hesitated and began to wade in from the shore. Over and over, Erik's friends ran onto the dock and jumped and flipped off of it. Meanwhile, he paddled around in the shallower water.

Finally, Sam swam over to him. She could see the disappointment in his eyes.

"It's okay, ya know," she said to him, trying to lift his spirits. "You can't be good at everything, silly."

"I know, I don't expect to be great at it. But I can barely keep afloat. It just looks like so much fun," he said, lowering his head.

"Well, then try it! You swim well enough. Just head straight back to the dock and grab hold of it when you come up."

After some thought, Erik decided to take the leap. He got out and walked to the edge of the dock and looked down into the deep water. His heart began to beat faster. Sam and Christian called to him from the water. To ease his tension, Erik imagined he was a pirate out at sea and he was being forced to walk the plank. He did things like this quite often when he was uncomfortable or uneasy about something. Putting himself in an imaginary situation helped him complete tasks at hand.

So he stood on the plank and looked down into the shark-infested waters below. The wicked captain poked and prodded him further to the edge. Erik didn't want to jump, but he knew if he didn't, then the fair maiden would be forced to join him. She struggled to get free as two men held her.

"Go! It's you or both of you! You decide!" the captain shouted.

It had to be done! Maybe he could fool the pirates and jump off and climb back aboard, he thought. He smiled and jumped.

Erik's fantasy quickly began to fade. As he sank deeper and deeper, the light began to disappear. He could no longer tell which way was up. He swam towards what he thought was the surface, but to no avail. He wondered if he was swimming deeper into the depths. His chest began to tighten. He wouldn't be able to hold his breath much longer.

One tiny light began to swim towards him. Then another. It looked like the lights on the head of an angler fish. They bobbed their way toward Erik. One of the lights made its way to Erik's face. That's when he saw that it wasn't a fish at all. It was a strange little human-like creature! A fairy? The fairy began to smile, but it seemed menacing. At that very moment, a massive hand grabbed Erik's leg and began dragging him further down into the depths. He used what little breath he had to let out a scream, but the water muffled it, and it was of no use. The evil fairies poked and played with the boy's air bubbles as they floated up. Then everything went black.

Erik floated in this black nothingness for what felt like forever. He started to come to as the water's current quickened and began to empty into a room. The room was full of jewels and treasures. Erik laid on the ground, gasping for air.

He began to hear footsteps behind him and turned to see what approached him. As he looked up, he saw the man who had haunted his dreams for as long as he could remember, standing over him, dripping wet and laughing like a madman. He smelled even worse than Erik had remembered. It had been over two years since he had seen the ogre, but still he hadn't forgotten the fear the man instilled in him.

As he looked upon the giant man, the room around him seemed to start to drip away like water. Before he realized what was going on, Erik was alone, lying on a forest floor. As he looked around, nothing seemed familiar. The woods looked nothing like the woods near Erik's house. This forest looked old. Very old. The roots ran across the ground, making it look as if he were standing in a spider web. A hooded figure with a crown made of antlers slowly began to walk towards him.

Erik had never seen the hooded man before, but he seemed familiar, and he instilled a fear in him even greater than that of the putrid giant.

"Who...who are you?" the boy asked.

The figure didn't say a word. He merely moved at a faster pace toward Erik.

"Please! No! Stop!" Erik shouted as the hooded figure moved even closer.

Then, the hooded man was upon him. He stood over him, looking down. Erik could see nothing in the hood. Only darkness. The figure began to reach out with decrepit hands. As Erik saw the hands, a memory long forgotten began to surface. He had seen such a hand before in a far off dream, when he was just a small baby. These were the very same hands that had reached for him the night that his window had been opened. The boy's heart was beating so quickly he thought it was going to beat right out of his chest.

GASP!

Air rushed into the young boy's lungs. He opened his eyes to see Old Man Luthor hovered over him, soaking wet and out of breath himself. Behind him, Erik could see his friends, pale as ghosts, with incredibly worried looks on their faces.

It took Erik a moment for reality to fade back into perspective.

Luthor walked Erik to his house, bundled him up with a blanket, and sat him by the fireplace. In the meantime, Sam and Christian were sent to tell Brenda what had happened.

As they sat and waited on Brenda, Erik tried to strike up a conversation. He started by thanking Luthor for saving his life. Mr. Luthor stayed quiet, but nodded his head as if to say "you're welcome."

They sat in silence for a bit longer before Erik attempted again to strike up conversation.

"Your dogs are really sweet. It must've taken a long time to train them so well."

Luthor scoffed. "Meant to scare people off, not lick 'em to death. Poor job training him, if you ask me."

Erik continued, despite Luthor's lack of enthusiasm.

"My aunt tells me you have horses, too?"

"She'd be right. Surprised y'all didn't hop on them and take 'em for a ride while you were helping yourselves to the rest of my place!"

"I... I'm really sorry. We shouldn't have snuck onto your property. It was wrong."

"You all coulda got hurt! Hell, if I hadn't shown up when I did, you'd be dead!" he said angrily.

Behind the anger, Erik could hear the concern in his voice. He sat in silence for a moment before he spoke again. He was hesitant to begin the conversation he had in the back of his head. It was a pretty heavy subject, but being a child, he didn't think too much of it.

"Do you believe in Hell?" he asked.

Mr. Luthor stared at the boy with a puzzled look on his face.

"That's a pretty heavy subject to talk about with someone you don't know. Why do you ask, boy?"

"Well, I think I saw the devil," Erik said with a timid tone.

"You think you saw the devil?"

"Yessir. Just then, in the lake."

"What did he look like?"

49

"He wore a black cloak and hood. The hood covered his face where I couldn't see him. He also wore a massive crown that looked to be made of antlers."

"Sounds pretty scary."

"It was! I was terrified! It was one of the scariest things I've ever seen."

"Well ... to answer your question, I do believe in the Devil, as well as God and Heaven and Hell. That being said, I don't think what you saw was the Devil."

"What makes you so sure?"

"Well, I've seen the Devil. A few times now. He ain't too scary. Not to look at, anyways. See, they call him the deceiver. He's more likely to show up as someone or something you hold dear. Just to trick you. Always playing tricks, that one."

"You said you've met him a few times?"

Luthor let out a deep breath as if he were debating whether to continue the conversation or not.

"More times than I'd like to admit. He'd come to me as my wife sometimes, other times as my children. For a while, I welcomed him. Then they began to ask me to join them. I thought long and hard about it. Almost did. Then I realized they would never ask me to do that. Not in a million years."

"When you say join them...?"

"First thing you need to know is that this town wasn't as accepting as it is today, especially for a black man like myself. Many people reee-ally didn't like the fact that a white woman was with me, and hated even more that we had mixed children. Many people around

50

here even see it as a sin of sorts. Anyways, they were driving home one night, and a truck full of drunken monsters had followed them from the store. They were driving next to them, shouting profanities and hitting the side of her car. It was raining like crazy out and the roads were slick. In a panic, my wife sped up. As they came upon the bridge, there was a car broken down in the middle of the road. My wife tried to miss the car and overcorrected. The tires on the slick roads slid, and she lost control... On my way into town every other week, I'll stop and talk to them a bit."

"I've seen the flowers by the bridge. I had no idea that... that that had happened. I'm so sorry."

"That was a long time ago. I was still a young man then. Didn't even have any gray hairs on my head. Now I'm old and just waiting for the day I get to see 'em again."

Loved Ones

Tears had welled up in Luthor's eyes. They quickly dried as a knock came at the door. Luthor opened the door to a fuming-red Brenda! She glared at Erik but didn't say a word. She thanked Luthor for saving and taking care of Erik and grabbed up the boy and held him tight. She was shaking. Erik couldn't tell if it was because she was mad or scared. Or maybe a bit of both. The whole ride home, Brenda stayed silent. Erik had never seen her so mad. When they got home, she immediately went to her room and closed the door. When they entered the house, Angela was waiting on them.

"If I were ten years younger, you coulda walked through that door to a switch to your behind! What in the world were you thinking!? You're lucky Mr. Luthor showed up when he did! You know how scared we were when your friends showed up here and told us you had almost drowned!"

She began to cry as she spoke.

"We've already lost your mother.... Now that we have you, I'll be damned if I lose you, too!"

Erik bent down and gave Angela a hug and said he was sorry.

Over the next few months, Erik's aunts made him do chores around the house and had a much more strict curfew. He would get out of school and only have about an hour and a half to play. On the weekends, his aunts had made an arrangement with Luthor for Erik to come help him around the house. Over the school year, Erik began to become very close with Luthor.

The following summer, Sam went to her grandparents' place and Christian went to camp. At first Erik thought it was going to be an awful summer, but he quickly realized that would be untrue. He decided to spend more time at Luthor's. He began to become like a grandpa to him. Over the summer, he taught Erik how to fish and ride horses. He would let him sit around and drink Coke and watch westerns all day. The crazy old man would even play pretend with Erik from time to time, running around the yard shooting pop guns.

On Erik's 12th birthday, Mr. Luthor bought him his very own horse. Erik couldn't believe it. It was clear Mr. Luthor cared as much for Erik as Erik did for him. He hugged the old man around the neck and thanked him.

A week later, Christian returned from camp and Sam from her grandparents' house. Christian looked the same, maybe a bit taller, but Sam... Sam came back different than she had left. She wasn't the rough and tough tomboy anymore. At least not on the outside. She had started to become a woman, and it caught both Erik's and Christian's attention.

Over the next year, the three of them would spend most of their time at Luthor's house. They fished, they rode horses, they swam. In the colder months Luthor even taught them how to shoot a gun and hunt. It was one of the best years of Erik's life.

On Erik's following birthday, Sam walked him outside. She had a giant smile on her face.

"I've been thinking a lot lately and I have something for you."

She reached her hands behind her as if she were getting something. As Erik leaned in to see what, she lunged forward and kissed him on the lips.

Erik's face lit up bright red.

"Wowza. That's one heck of a birthday present!" Erik said with a smile ear to ear.

When they came back, Erik was still beet red and they were holding each other's hand. It was pretty clear what had transpired. Angela and Brenda both made eye contact with Erik and smiled. It made him turn a whole shade of red darker. He was embarrassed, but on top of the world, nonetheless!

Turning of the Tides

The morning after Erik's birthday, Angela went to the doctor for a routine checkup. Only it turned out to not be so routine. Later that day, Angela had to break the news to Erik and Brenda that she had been diagnosed with breast cancer. It was pretty far along. The doctors had only given her a few months to live.

From then on there were many silent days. Erik and Angela would sit in the room and paint. No words were said, but sometimes no words needed to be said. It was the time spent together that mattered. Brenda tried her best to hold it together during it all, but Erik would see her crying often. She and her sister had always been together. They weren't just sisters, they were best friends.

Well, three months passed. Then six. Then a year. Then three years... three years full of memories and laughter, painting and playing cards. They went on with life and lived it to the fullest, the best they could.

Sam and Erik had officially been an item for a while now and were always together. Mr. Luthor was getting up there in age and couldn't take care of his things the way he used to. Sam and Erik had gotten in the habit of going down to his house and helping with his garden and animals. He had truly become a grandfather figure to Erik, and even Sam at this point.

Erik knew without a doubt in his mind that he wanted to marry Sam. He had it all planned out. As soon as they were done with high school he was going to propose.

Erik drove through traffic, making aircraft noises in his head as he went. He wasn't just driving through traffic, he was flying a fighter through enemy aircraft. To him there was no such thing as "getting too old" for something such as playing and pretending. To him, imagination was his sanity. The only time he ever seemed one hundred percent was when he was with Sam.

When it came time for Erik to ask the question, he didn't have a doubt or second thought. He had bought the ring and began to plan how he was going to pop the question. Everything was in motion when Sam told Erik they needed to talk. She sat him down and explained to him that she wanted to be free to do what she wanted when she went away for college. That she loved him and that maybe one day in the future they could pick back up, but that she wasn't ready to settle down just yet. It was like Erik could feel his heart strings snapping. This was not at all what he had planned. He didn't say anything back and simply walked away with tears running down his face.

When he got home and walked in the door, Brenda was there waiting for him. She had news to tell him. He paid her no attention and ignored all attempts of her trying to start a conversation. He simply pushed past her and went to his room. The next day Brenda learned of the breakup and decided it was best to wait to tell Erik what she had on her mind.

Erik had never been so lost. He began to drink a lot. Anything he could get his hands on to numb the pain, he did. He was on a self-destructive path and didn't care about anything around him except filling the void within.

One night Erik came home after being out drinking, and Angela was up waiting on him. Her face was red like she had been crying. She could see something wasn't right with him, everyone could. She knew he was in pain. She didn't yell, she didn't cuss. She simply asked Erik to come sit with her in the living room. He scoffed a bit but obliged.

"I'm worried about you," she said as they entered the room.

"I'm fine."

"No, you're not. I've seen this look. You need help, you need to talk."

"Really, I'm fine. I'll be okay."

Angela took a deep breath.

"It's time I told you the truth about your mother. Maybe then you'll understand where I'm coming from."

"What are you talking about?"

Angela lowered her head as she talked. She wasn't proud of keeping a secret from him for so long. Even if she thought it was for the better.

"Your mother didn't come to stay with us. She went to a special hospital for people with mental problems."

"Like an insane asylum!?"

"Your mother wasn't insane, she was lost! But yes. While your father was away in the war, she had taken up amphetamines. It only got worse after he returned home. It was her escape. Little by little, the drugs took her. They drove her mad. I thought she was getting better, she was getting clean. But she was sick. Not in a way our doctors could really fix. After only a month in the asylum, she hung herself."

Erik instantly sobered up.

"Why are you just now telling me this! My mom was crazy and no one thought they should tell me!?"

"She wasn't crazy! She was sick! Please sweetie, sit down and talk with me."

"Why? You think I'm crazy, too?"

"I'm not saying that! I'm saying you're lost! Please. Talk with me!"

But he didn't... though, he should have. The next morning, Angela finally lost her long battle with cancer.

One Thing after Another

Erik tried to be strong. Tried to be numb to it all. He felt so much regret, so much anger and hate for himself. He could've had one last conversation with her. Instead, he got angry with her and ignored her. The last memory he would have of Angela was her basically begging for him to sit and talk to her.

During the funeral, Erik couldn't take it. He had to get away. About halfway through the sermon he got up and walked out of the church. He didn't know where he was going, he just knew he couldn't be there. It hurt too much.

As he walked, he began to think about all the disappointments and regrets in his life as of lately. He realized during the last few months of his self-destructive behavior he had completely neglected Mr. Luthor. He had only seen him maybe once and had to leave almost immediately. It reminded him too much of Sam to be there. He soon found himself reaching Luthor's gate.

Everything looked different. All the dogs and horses were gone. The beautiful garden had been reduced to a third of what it was. Outside was a young black man, building what looked to be a new house. So much had changed in only six months. Erik instantly thought the worst. The young man noticed Erik and climbed down his ladder and headed towards him.

"Can I help you?" he asked

"Where's Mr. Luthor? What happened?"

"Luthor's my uncle. He moved out about four months ago now."

"What? Where'd he move to? What happened to all his animals?"

"You sure are full of questions. You must be Erik."

"Y...yeah... I'm Erik."

"Luthor wanted to say bye to you. You and that young lady meant the world to him. He was always saying you were like a grandson to him.

Sam came by from college to see him off. She said she tried to get ahold of you. Even went by your house."

"Uhh... yeah. I've been a little harder to get a hold of lately. So, what happened here?

"Well. Luthor had started sending my father letters about five years ago. I suppose about the time you showed up. Over the last year they got sadder and sadder. I came down to help him around here, but

Luthor just got to where between the house, him, and my job it was just too much. Eventually my father decided it'd be best for him if he went and lived with him. So Luthor left me his house. As much as I loved it, I don't have time to keep up with it the way he did when he was younger. I travel for my work now. So, we found new homes for all the animals. They all went to good places. We made sure of that. We knew how much he loved them."

"Oh. Well... I guess that's good you found them all homes. Do you know where Trigger ended up, by chance?"

"The pretty golden one? Luthor went out of his way to make sure it had a good home. Went to a wealthy family south of here. Little girl is just getting big enough to ride."

"That's good. I'm glad he went to a good home. He deserved it. He definitely deserved more than me."

"Don't beat yourself up about it. We all make mistakes. We all have our dark times. It's all in how you handle it. You can let it get to you or you can let it make you stronger."

Today was not the day Erik wanted to hear advice. He already hated himself for how things happened with Angela, now come to find out his selfishness made him turn away when Luthor needed him most.

All he could think about is that he didn't want to let Luthor go without saying goodbye. He was going to find a way to see him at least one last time.

"Where does your father live?"

"In Chicago. About a twelve-hour drive from here."

"Thank you. And thank you for taking care of Luthor and his things when I wasn't here too."

The two said their goodbyes and Erik headed to his house.

The Drive

When Erik got home, Brenda still hadn't returned from the funeral. He took the opportunity and packed his bag and pulled Angela's old car from the garage. Thankfully, it started right up and Erik was on his way.

For the whole drive there, regret ate away at him like vultures on a carcass. He had treated Angela and Luthor so poorly. He had never felt such a strong hate, and all that hate was for himself.

He drove well over the speed limit. During one of his stops he managed to score some uppers from a truck driver. Twelve hours may not seem like much, but having no sleep the night before and the never-ending drag of the road began to take its toll.

Between the lack of sleep and the pills quickly wearing off, he began to drift off. The road he was on was long and straight but had many ups and downs. After a while of this, he began to feel as if he were on a raft, subtly drifting over giant waves. His eyes began to close. Over the waves he went, up and down. The warm air blew in his hair. The open sea began to free his mind. Little did he know the long, straight road was coming to a turn. Over another wave he went....

CRASH!

Reality rushed back to him in a hurry. Luckily, he had not been driving very fast and only dented the guardrail. He got out of his car and looked around. The damage was minor, but could've been so much worse. He looked over the guardrail into the canyon below. If the railing hadn't stopped him he surely would've plummeted to his death. He noticed two crosses near where he was. He was beyond lucky not to be the third. He drove to the nearest place he could pull off the road and slept till morning. The next day he sobered up and made his way to Luthor's new home.

Home Away from Home

Luthor's brother's home was in a big city. Bigger than any city Erik had ever seen before. The roads were busy, and the buildings reached high into the air. It was quite the sight to behold.

Luthor's nephew had called ahead and told them Erik was coming. As Erik drove up to address, he was surprised to see several people standing on the stoop waiting for him. They welcomed him as if he were one of the family. He was greeted by nothing but smiles and hugs.

Clearly, Luthor had only told them the good things about him and left out how much of a shit person he had become. He welcomed the warm greetings, even if he felt as though they weren't earned.

Erik found it strange Luthor hadn't been standing out on the stoop to greet him with the others.

Upon entering the house, he quickly saw why. Mr. Luthor was no longer the burly man he once knew. He was skinny and shrunken. He had seen him age over the years, but this was different. Luthor laid on an unmoving bed placed in the living room. He looked so frail. His face looked nothing like Erik had remembered.

The TV was on (old westerns, of course), but Luthor wasn't watching it. Instead, he stared off at the ceiling with clouded, gray eyes. Tears began to swell up in Erik's eyes. He hated seeing him like this. He felt even more anger towards himself at that moment. Luthor's brother Jim tried his best to comfort him.

"It started to get bad about three months ago. It's going downhill quickly. I'm glad you were able to come see him. He talked about you all the time, you know. I think you're the reason he started writing letters to me. We hadn't spoken in many years. You seemed to spark something in him. Gave him a new breath of life. A reason to keep pushing forward. In his letters he would call you his adopted grandson. When he first started to get really sick he would talk to people about you and say you were his son. That man loves you so much."

Erik couldn't help but let his emotions show. Tears ran down his cheeks despite him trying so hard to hold them back. He stared at Luthor for a moment. He knew Jim had tried to lift his spirits, but instead it only made him feel worse about himself.

Erik finally mustered up enough courage to go try to talk to Luthor. He stood next to him with his hands upon the old man's. He didn't know what to say.

"Hey, Mr. Luthor. It's me, Erik. I'm so sorry for everything. I'm so sorry for not being there when you needed me most. I love you so much. Please forgive me. I know I'll never forgive myself."

The far-off look in Luthor's face began to fade for just a moment, and he lifted his head up ever so slightly. His clouded eyes began to move wildly around the room as if he were trying to see something. Finally, he stopped at Erik. He wasn't looking directly at him, but in his direction, as if he could sense where he was.

"E.... Erik?...," Luthor said with a weak and trembling voice.

"Yeah, it's me, Mr. Luthor! I'm here!" Erik replied.

Luthor slowly laid his head back down into the pillow. He didn't say anything else, but had a smile on his face from ear to ear.

Erik stayed in the living room by Luthor's side all night. They just sat and watched old westerns in silence. Luthor never tried to say anything else, but even after he fell asleep, he still had a giant smile on his face.

Erik stepped outside for a smoke. He wasn't out there long before the door opened up behind him. He tried frantically to put out the joint he had in hand and blow away the smoke.

The person opening the door was Luthor's great niece, Amelia. She was a striking young woman. Beautiful and unique in every way. She didn't dress like anyone else Erik had ever seen. She was quite intriguing, to say the least.

She began to laugh as she walked outside and saw Erik trying to blow away the smoke.

"I can still smell it, silly!" she laughed as she reached out her hand to take a hit.

Her smile was enchanting. It stunned Erik for a moment. He was taken aback by her beauty.

She thought it was because he was still trying to hide the weed from her. She began to laugh out loud.

"Chill! I'm not going to tell you. I was on my way out here to do the same," she said with a big smile. She then reached into her hair above her ear and pulled out a joint of her own.

"See, goofball, you ain't busted or nothin'.'"

Erik laughed and handed her his already lit joint that had singed his hand a bit from trying to hide it. The two talked for hours. Everything from her uncle to music. The whole time, Erik couldn't look away. He was hypnotized.

As the sun started to come up, Amelia decided to go inside and cook breakfast for her family. The smell began to slowly pull everyone out of bed and into the kitchen. While she cooked, Erik sat and watched Luthor. He still had a giant smile across his face. The smell of breakfast seemed to be reaching Luthor's nose now, as well, as he woke and started sniffing the air around him. Amelia walked through the door with a plate in hand. Erik thought for a moment Luthor was going to sit right up, the way he showed attentiveness when the food entered the room. His vision may have dimmed, but his smell seemed to still be quite keen.

Everyone else began to come into the living room with plates full of delicious looking food. Jim brought in an extra plate for Erik.

They all took turns helping feed Luthor in between talking, laughing, and stuffing their own faces. The whole room was full of smiling faces. Erik could feel the love that filled the room. The entire house.

After breakfast, Erik said his goodbyes to the family. As he leaned in to say goodbye to Luthor he felt Luthor's hand lay on top of his own. He began to tear up again as he looked at the old man. He couldn't even begin to explain how thankful he was for everything he had done for him over the years. The man had helped raise him, basically. Taught him how to be a man. The only words he managed were "thank you."

Luthor's hand patted twice on top of Erik's. As if him saying, "you're welcome," or maybe even a thank you back.

As the city began to disappear into the rearview mirror, Erik thought of Luthor's smile, and Amelia's, the family's. All engraved in his head forever.

The Long Drive Home

Erik drove slowly down the road. He was awake and alert, only this time it wasn't because of drugs. His mind was simply racing. Many great memories began to play in his head. Memories of Angela and Luthor. The good and the bad. Unfortunately, the bad began to overshadow the good. Every thought that emerged grew darker. He fell deeper into his own head.

The road began to turn to dirt. An eerie blue light began to fill the air. Then, the all-too-familiar smell and taste began to fill his mouth. He began to lift his foot off of the gas and down onto the brake.

Ahead of him, standing in the road, was a hooded figure with an antler crown.

The ogre was standing directly behind him, as if waiting for the order to pounce. They both stood unmoving as the car grew closer. The brakes screeched as they dug into the calipers as hard as they could. The car stopped only inches from the hooded figure. Smoke poured out from the back tires. Erik sat, staring at the faceless, hooded figure that still stood motionless in front of him. Though the man seemed to not have a face, Erik couldn't help but shake the feeling he was being watched by the figure. His heart raced.

A strange light began to fly around outside of his window. At first he thought it must be a firefly. As it grew closer, Erik could see it was a fairy.

He worried it was one of the two fairies that had plagued him, along with the evil men, his whole life. Upon further examination, he noticed this fairy was different. It wasn't gnarled and mangled like those two. The features on her were much more elegant than the others. In fact, she looked much more like the fairies that were drawn in his mother's green book. As he stared at all of this, the fairy light began to grow around him. He had forgotten all about the evil beings waiting for him.

Somehow, he knew the beautiful creature was there to help him. She reached out her hand.

Erik's windows were suddenly open and he was moving again. The face of the fairy began to become more clear. Suddenly, a familiar voice brought Erik to open his eyes. It was his Aunt Brenda's voice!

"You know how scared I was when I got a call from Sheriff Brown!? Taking the car! Driving halfway across the country! Leaving in the middle of your aunt's funeral! What's gotten into you!"

Erik looked around at the scenery out the open window. He was almost home. He was in utter confusion as to what had happened and how he got there. He didn't know what to say to his aunt. He could tell by looking at her she was not only angry, she was scared. All he could force himself to say was "I'm sorry..."

This seemed to ignite an even hotter fuse in Brenda.

"You're sorry! Yeah! I hope so! You take off without a word! Wreck the car! How about instead of saying sorry you tell me what the hell is going on with you!"

Erik didn't remember anything about wrecking the car. Last he had remembered, he was on a dirt road.

"Did I black out?" he thought to himself.

Erik wondered what was wrong with him. He sat speechless as he watched the trees pass by. After driving in silence for a while Brenda had cooled off a bit.

"You're not the only one hurting, you know," she calmly said before returning to the silence.

Those words resonated with him for the rest of the ride. The two rode the rest of the way home in silence. No radio playing. Only them and their thoughts.

When they pulled into the driveway, Brenda cut the car off but sat for a moment. She clearly had heavy thoughts on her mind. She took a deep breath. She then proceeded to tell him the news she had learned the day he and Sam had broken up. She had tried to find time to tell him.

For almost a year now, Brenda had been fighting cancer. She told him she hadn't taken any medicine or treatments. Nor did she plan to. She said she didn't want to be sick. Angela had always put on her best face in front of Erik. Brenda had been there with her during the worst of it. The nights she would be too sick to go to sleep, laying in Brenda's arms, crying.

Erik wrapped his arms around Brenda and squeezed as hard as he could. They sat and held each other. Tears ran down both of their cheeks. There were so many things that needed to be said, but at that moment, none of it mattered.

The Call

The next morning the quiet house was blasted awake by the phone ringing. Brenda angrily wrapped her nightgown around her body and made her way to the phone.

"Who in the world is calling this early!? The sun isn't even up yet!" she fussed as she walked.

She hastily brought the phone to her ear.

"Hello?"

Her tone quickly changed when she heard the other voice on the line. Erik stood above in the hallway and listened.

"My goodness.... Okay... Okay... We will be there... thank you... and I'm so sorry for your loss."

Erik couldn't hear the voice on the other end of the phone, but he had a pretty good idea as to who it was.

The Service

They packed their nicest Sunday clothes and started the long drive back to the big city. Luthor had passed in his sleep the night after Erik left.

During the drive, Brenda tried her best to entertain Erik. She told him all sorts of stories and jokes along the way. Some even involved when she and her sisters were a bit older and got into trouble with the law. Until now, he had never heard any stories like that! As terrible as everything seemed to be, just for a moment, it didn't feel quite so bad.

The funeral was small. It was in a big church but only the first three rows were filled. Mostly with Luthor's close family. Erik and Brenda seemed to be the only ones there as friends. Erik nodded to Luthor's nephew and thanked him for telling him about Luthor so he was able to see him one last time. He then proceeded to Luthor's brother and his family and greeted them all with hugs. He had only met them just three days before, but he felt as if he had known them for years. As they sat down for the service, Erik saw a man in the back of the room whose face he had seen before, sitting by himself. He couldn't quite place it at the time, but he knew he had seen him somewhere.

What the funeral lacked in numbers it made up for in heart. Almost everyone went up there to talk or share a story about Luthor. After the family spoke, the familiar-looking man made his way from the back of the room. As he got closer, Erik was able to get a better look at him. He was someone Erik knew. His name was Henry Orwell. He was the owner of the feed shop back in their hometown. It was strange to see someone else from home, this far from it.

Erik didn't even know they had much of a friendship other than their biweekly feed buy.

"That's being close to your customers," Erik thought to himself.

It wasn't long into Henry's speech he realized it was much more than that. Henry spoke with a heavy Southern drawl.

"When I was a dumb, young kid I was riding in the truck with my brother and some of his dumb friends. We had been harassing a beautiful young lady about her mixed children at a stop light. My brother said some pretty horrible things. The woman tried to speed up to get away from us, but my brother and his friends hadn't had enough yet. They sped after them."

Henry paused for a moment to dry his eyes and refocus.

"I'm sure many of you have already heard this story. About the night Luthor lost his family... but what many of you don't know is his forgiveness that followed. Over the years following the accident, my brother and his friends all ended up in jail for various things. I started working for my father's feed store to keep from going down the same path. Luthor would come in at least once a month and load up his truck with feed for all sorts of animals. He was my dad's best customer, probably. Which is why it scared me so much to talk to him. I knew who he was. I knew how much pain me and my brother brought to him. Mostly I kept my head down and loaded his truck without a peep. After about two years I decided to tell him I was in the truck the night of his wife's accident. That I was there when it all happened. That I was part of the cause of it. You know what he said to me after I confessed to him?

"I know you were."

He had been coming to our store for years and never mentioned a word to my dad. Never even shot me a mean look. He could see the look of confusion on my face when he told me he knew. "You were a young boy following around some dumb people. You weren't driving the truck," he said to me. I started to cry like a baby. Even if I hadn't been the one driving, I still felt bad. I was part of it. I felt horrible that it had happened at all. I told him over and over how sorry I was. As I babbled on, Luthor pulled me in close for a hug. As he held me tight, he looked me in the eyes and said to me, *"Son, I forgive you. They forgive you, too."* A wave of relief washed over me. A man who should have so much hate for me forgave me without a second thought. Later

I would ask him how he could forgive me so easily. You know what he told me? "Hate and anger don't change a thing. You can't change what happened, no matter how hard you try. You can carry that weight on your back or in your heart. You can hold onto it all, have it weigh you down, or you can hold the good things dear, let go of the bad, and have faith things will work out the way they're supposed to. Even if it ain't our plan." From that day on, I never looked at life the same. He not only lifted a weight off of me for saying they forgave me. He gave me the strength to forgive myself. Just a few simple words and the power to forgive changed me forever. Though it may seem small to some of you, this man, this moment, transformed my life. I couldn't be more thankful for this man and what he did."

Erik was stunned by the man's speech. Luthor had never mentioned anything about Henry, yet had such an impact on him. Parts of Henry's speech repeated themselves in Erik's head. Luthor forgave Henry, maybe he would forgive Erik, too.

Erik wanted to go up and make his own speech. It was almost as if everyone expected him to. He couldn't seem to find the nerve to do so. Brenda saw the worry on his face, she patted him on his leg and walked to the front of the room.

Her words were short and sweet. She spoke of how she and her sister wouldn't have known what to do without Luthor. That he had such a big hand in raising Erik. He was always there when Erik needed him. That the love he had for Erik was like no other. That he was part of the family.

This small speech was all Erik needed to be reassured. He walked to the front of the room slowly. He could feel everyone's eyes upon him. He looked around the room at all the faces. There were tears running down faces, but for the most part everyone was still wearing a smile.

He had written part of a speech when they first arrived. It spoke of how sorry he was for everything and how Luthor deserved so much more. As he walked to the podium he thought about Henry's words. One part stuck out among the rest. The part about where he talked about being able to forgive himself.

Erik looked out at all the smiling faces. They didn't want to hear sad sob stories and anger filled apologies. They wanted to hear about how great of a person Luthor was. Stories about his life. Erik crumbled up the depressing speech and shoved it into his pocket. A giant smile crept up on his face.

"First time I met Luthor the grumpy old man was waving a gun at me! Who would've thought years later he'd be my best friend."

Everyone began to laugh.

"This is what Luthor would've wanted" Erik thought to himself.

He spent the next fifteen minutes talking about all the adventures he had been through with Luthor. All the things he had been taught. He could've gone on for hours.

As he stepped down he looked around the room at the tears of joy and laughter and the smiles that lit up the room. One in particular caught his eye. Luthor's niece Amelia.

Fields of Green

After the sermon was over Erik and Amelia spoke for a while. The two connected on so many levels. There was never an awkward moment between them. (Except for maybe when she would catch him getting lost in her eyes) which she would simply reply.

"Uh, hello? Earth to Erik."

They walked around and talked to all the family members. At one point she and Brenda went off talking amongst themselves. Erik wasn't sure how he felt about that. As everyone conversed with each other Erik walked outside.

It wasn't a gloomy day. In fact, it was quite a beautiful day. Erik closed his eyes and focused on the warmth of the sun as it beat down on him. All the hustle and bustle around began to fade. All he could hear was the wind calmly blowing through the trees.

He opened his eyes and saw green pastures as far as the eye could see. Far off in the distance he could see a small herd of horses galloping across. There were two adult horses and two foals. The largest horse stopped running and looked towards Erik. It was like he could feel Erik's eyes upon him. Though it was quite a distance the two seemed to lock eyes.

The horse reared up on his hind legs and kicked his front legs wildly. As he came back down it looked as if he nodded his head at Erik. He then proceeded to join back with his family and the group of them ran over the planes. Erik watched as they disappeared over the horizon. The sun began to set, covering the fields with a beautiful golden hue.

A tap on his shoulder and the sound of his aunt's voice brought Erik back to the present. He was sitting in the front row of the chapel. Almost everyone had left. The tears in his eyes had dried and a smile ran across his face.

"Let's go sweetie," said his aunt in a soft voice as she laid her hand on his shoulder.

They said their goodbyes to the remaining family and headed to the cars. As they walked to the door Amelia came running over. Before he could say anything she grabbed his face and kissed him passionately.

"Thank you for everything. He loved you and I see why. You're an easy person to love. I hope our paths cross again one day!" she said as she backed away from him.

Erik and Brenda walked to the car. Erik was as red as an apple and Brenda couldn't help but giggle at him.

The Simple Life

Erik began to not carry so much blame. Over the next year he tried to live his best life. From time to time he would get sad thinking about Angela or Luthor. Then he would think about that horse. He knew it was a sign. He knew that somewhere Angela was flying high in the sky as a bird or something in those same fields.

He had gotten a job at the feed store with Henry to help pay his way and help his aunt out as much as he could. It also kept him busy. Brenda grew sicker with each passing day. Erik would work all day at the feed store and then come home and cook and clean for her. His friends had all moved on. Gotten jobs out of town or went off to college. He didn't mind though. It gave him the time he needed to spend with his aunt. He wasn't going to regret missing time with a loved one again.

From time to time he would walk down to Luthor's old property. His nephew had built a new house and had a little family of his own. Everything was changing around him. The town grew larger yet his world seemed to grow smaller. He didn't really day dream or imagine things very much anymore. He felt like he didn't have the time to. He was happy yet he couldn't help but feel an emptiness.

One evening when Erik got home from work, before he began to cook, his aunt called him into her room. Much like Angela and Luthor, Brenda looked nothing like herself. She had withered away before Erik's eyes. She reached up and pulled him towards her. She held his hand tight with hers.

"It's time my sweet boy.... I can't hold on any longer," she spoke to him in her weak voice.

"No! no! Please, I can't lose you too! Not yet! You're all I have! Please, no!" he pleaded with her as if she had a choice in the matter.

Brenda smiled a soft smile.

"I'm so sorry. I've fought as hard as I can.... You'll be okay. In fact, you'll be better than okay! You're a smart, loving, creative young man. You can do anything you put your mind to! Sick ol' me is just holding you and all that potential back from the world!"

"No! How dare you say that! I'm who I am because of you! I don't know what I'll do without you! I know I'm being selfish, but I don't want to let go! I don't want to say goodbye!"

"You'll be okay.... You'll figure it out I promise... it's a big beautiful world out there! Go out there and live in it!"

Erik leaned in and held her fragile body in his arms. As he did she whispered in his ear.

"There she is.... My big sister is waiting for me... it's so beautiful!"

With that she closed her eyes forever. Erik held her tight and cried. She was gone. Everyone was gone.

Quicksand

After the coroner left Erik stood alone in the big empty house. All his energy seemed to leave him as soon as the door was closed. He laid down in the middle of the front corridor on the cool ground. There he stayed. Night and into the next day. He didn't eat or drink. He barely moved at all. He got up to use the bathroom but returned to the spot on the floor right after.

The phone rang and rang. It could've been his work, it could've been the funeral home. He didn't care. He didn't feel like talking to anyone.

He sat and stared off into space. He wasn't angry, he didn't cry. He was empty. It wasn't the same empty he had felt before when his grandmother passed. Then he didn't know what to feel. Now, he knew what he was feeling. He just didn't want to feel any of it. There were too many emotions swirling around his head. He just wanted them all to go away.

The ringing of the phone began to fade into the background. He laid his head back down on the cold floor. It was like the floor was pulling him down to it like quicksand. Strangely, he welcomed it. He fell asleep there on the floor as the world kept turning around him.

The town, though growing, was still a small town. Word traveled quickly about Brenda's passing. Knock after knock pounded away at the front door, but much like the phone, the sound faded into obscurity. Erik would watch as several silhouettes took turns standing in front of the frosted glass door. As the sun began to lower and another day was spent on the floor Erik decided to make his way towards the door. He opened it and saw the porch full of casserole dishes and gift baskets. So many people had already reached out. The outpouring of emotion should've filled Erik's heart. Instead it did nothing. He locked the door back and went back to his spot on the floor and laid back down. Almost as soon as his head hit the ground there was a loud knock. It seemed much more aggressive than the other knocks. It was going to be much harder to ignore. Erik turned away from the door and tried his best to zone out the knocks. Only the knocks grew louder and the pace even quickened. It was clear whoever this person was they weren't leaving. Erik rolled back over and to his surprise saw a familiar face squished against the door trying to look in!

His heart skipped a few beats before he jumped to his feet and ran to the door to open it.

"About damn time!" Amelia said as she greeted him with an enormous hug.

A Much-Needed Friend

Amelia's father had told her what had happened and she got on the first flight and headed down right away.

She still had the same beautiful grin, but she seemed different to Erik. Not in a bad way, if anything it made Erik even more intrigued by her. Her hair was long and wild and her clothes were loose fitting and colorful. She wore a headband made of flowers. Erik had never seen anything like it, but he loved it.

Just like the first time he had met her, they stayed up and talked most of the night. They talked about the last year of their lives. They had gone on very different paths following Luthor's funeral. While Erik had settled into the small town life Amelia had traveled out into the world and explored its greatness. She talked about all the cities she had seen and the wild adventures she had had.

After a while catching up and telling stories Amelia put her hand on Erik's leg and gave him a serious look.

"You can't ignore that this happened Erik. I know she was your whole world. But life keeps going even after the bad stuff happens. I came here to help you any way I can, and from the looks of the porch the town will help too. We have some arrangements to make. Let's get to it babe!"

Erik couldn't understand why she was being so nice or why she had gone so far out of her way to help him. Regardless he was happy she was. Over the next few days she helped him get everything arranged and in order for the funeral. Just like Amelia had. Having suspected the town was hands on, several people did what they could to help. The local nursery provided beautiful flower arrangements free of charge. The diner brought free food to the repast for everyone. It all seemed to come together quite nicely.

Erik tried to write several different little speeches, but couldn't think of the right words to say. It all hurt so bad. He was functioning now, but that didn't mean he was okay. A few people came up and talked and shared stories. When it came time for Erik to talk he got to the front of the chapel and froze. He would try to read some of the words he wrote but he couldn't seem to talk. Every other word he would start to choke up. Amelia walked up to his side and held his hand while she began to read some of his notes out loud.

After the funeral, Amelia went back home with Erik. He didn't say much of anything on the way home or when they got there. All he could muster up was a very heartfelt "thank you". He walked upstairs and began to take a scalding hot shower.

He hadn't cried in front of anyone all day. In the shower he let it all out. He fell to his knees and sobbed. After his tears had run out and the water had begun to grow cold he got out and collected himself. He walked into his room to find Amelia fast asleep in his bed. She had worked so hard over the last few days helping Erik and helping push him to do what needed to be done. He began to cut off the light and walk out when her half asleep voice called out to him.

"No, don't go. Lay with me."

He laid next to her and she snuggled in tight into the bends of his body. He held her tight in his arms and fell into a deep sleep. It was the best sleep he had had in a long time.

When he awoke she was gone from his bed. He thought to himself it seemed too good to be true. That it must've been another one of his daydreams.

To his delight when he got downstairs he heard music playing in the kitchen and the smell of bacon filled his nose. There she was, as real as can be, dancing around the kitchen in her underwear and one of Erik's button up shirts. The music she was listening to was nothing like he had ever heard before, but he loved it! Seeing Amelia dance to it made him love it that much more. She greeted him with a kiss on the cheek and a "good morning". Erik almost felt guilty for how happy he was feeling.

After breakfast she led him back upstairs to his bedroom. The whole way up he couldn't help but stare as her cheeks hung out of her underwear ever so slightly. He wasn't sure what they were going up there for, but he knew what he had hoped for. It had been over a year and a half since he had been with someone intimately. His wish was granted. When they entered his room she turned to him and began to unbutton her shirt.

Peace, Love, and Adventure

Over the next two weeks Amelia helped Erik get things in order at the house. A lawyer had come by and revealed his aunt had a life insurance policy she had been paying into for a very long time. It was all left to Erik in her will.

Erik couldn't find it in him to sell his aunt's house. There were just too many memories in it. Instead he took a good amount of the insurance money and finished paying off the house. Planning to return to it one day.

After that, when all settled, he decided to listen to his aunt Brenda and finally go see the world. He and Amelia bought a van and said goodbye to the small town.

Life on the road was unlike anything Erik had ever experienced. They met all sorts of people on their travels. Including a man claiming to be a doctor that drove a bus with wild drawings on it. The next five years of his life were a bit of a blur. It was full of weed, acid, music and sex. Not always with Amelia. Either. Sometimes in a group. It was all about the love and the connections with others.

Erik was lucky with his acid and never seemed to have a bad trip. He began to see life in a new light. He began to look at things that once brought him pain and learn to pull the good from what had happened. He felt as though he finally had control. Even if the world around him seemed to be in chaos.

The Turning Point

Amelia's brother had been sent off to war and killed. She began to protest with hundreds of others to bring an end to the war. The drug use continued but the feelings behind everything began to change. Amelia began to go down a dark path. Erik tried everything in his power to pull her up like she had done him. It was no use though. She had gone from wanting to explore life and her mind to just chasing the next high. She began hanging out with new people Erik didn't really care for. They always spoke down on everyone else and simply showed no regard to anyone around them. It was the complete opposite of what he had grown used to being around. She and her new group of friends would do a newer drug called heroin together. Erik tried it once with them, but hated the way it made him feel. He couldn't draw, he couldn't write, he couldn't do anything.

Erik and Amelia had gotten an apartment together in a big city. Though, since meeting her new friends she hadn't been there too often.

One night Erik sat on his balcony smoking a joint, looking out over the city. He held an entire sheet of acid in his hand. He thought he was where he wanted to be. Where he was supposed to be. It seemed like every time he began to be happy the rug was pulled out from under him. He grew tired of this world. This reality. He took the sheet and laid it across his tongue.

It didn't take very long for it to start to take hold. He looked way down below where an ambulance sped by. It's lights trailing behind it. Everything began to breathe. The wallpaper designs on his apartment walls began to twist and intertwine. Though it was night, everything seemed so bright. For the first few hours everything seemed fine. Erik was even enjoying himself... Then came the peak. It was almost as if every light in the city began to dim. He sat back in his chair and began to take it all in. His eyes were wide open, but everything began to go dark as if he were closing them.

As he sat there his nose began to fill with a foul stench. He knew he had smelt it before, but he couldn't quite place it. It sent a strange sensation through his body. He began to feel very uncomfortable. Two lights lifted up from the streets below and began circling around in front of his balcony.

He began to feel something slowly coming over his shoulders onto his chest. The weight was heavy and began to sting. He couldn't move his neck or body. Only his eyes.

He watched as two decrepit hands eased over him. He began to feel a cold breath on his ear. Then it spoke.

"I've been waiting for you for a long time.... Wasn't sure if I would ever see you again...."

The voice sounded so familiar to Erik. Something he had buried away a long time ago.

Erik still couldn't move or speak. He watched as the hooded figure began to walk around. As Erik followed him with his eyes he began to notice that all of his surroundings had changed.
He was no longer on his balcony, or even the city for that matter. He was in a room that looked very old from what he could see. Everything was dark except an eerie green glow coming from high above.

All of the bad memories and feelings that had been shoved down came rushing back. He tried to get up and run with everything in him, but he couldn't. It was almost as (.) if he were being held down by invisible chains.

The hooded horned figure began to lean down towards Erik. Even though he was so close Erik still couldn't make out a face under the hood, or if there even was one! All he could see was darkness and two glowing yellow eyes.

As he looked upon the eyes they began to draw him in. He couldn't look away. Soon, the glow is all that Erik could see. He began to feel cold. Colder than he had ever been before. The glow began to fade and Erik stood on the edge of what looked to be a well.

The fat ogress man and the hooded figure stood behind Erik. He could now move, but didn't seem to have control over what he was doing. The fat man laughed as Erik inched closer to the edge. Fairies flew around madly in every direction. The hooded figure stood, motionless, watching Erik's every move. Maybe even controlling them! The figure spoke to Erik but not out loud. Erik could hear him in his head.

"Below holds all the answers you seek. All the truths you yearn for. Drink from the waters and know. Know any... *COME HOME*..."

The yellowed eyed figure's voice faded to the background as it spoke. Another voice began to drown it out within Erik's head. A woman's voice repeated the phrase "come home."

She spoke over and over "come home."

"Come home."

Erik began to feel a prick on his hand at every syllable the woman spoke. It was in perfect sync. Though every time Erik looked down to his hand nothing was there.

Meanwhile, his feet still moved forward as the hooded man spoke of the water's magic in the well below.

"The only way to know the truth is to know these waters."

Erik's foot reached out over the top of the well. "COME HOME!"

The second voice in his head now screamed, and the pain in hand doubled.

Erik brought back his foot and looked at his hand. Blood dripped down his palm and onto his forearm running all the way to his elbow.

The surrounding fairies began to grow larger and brighter. Erik began to feel wind on his face. He looked down and the well was gone. Instead there was a busy street several stories down. Erik quickly realized where he was and jumped down from the railing back onto his balcony. He looked around. In complete shock and disbelief.

As he went to wipe the sweat from his forehead he noticed his hand was covered in blood. As he washed it he could see several tiny holes in his hand. It looked as though a bird rapidly pecked away at it. How could his hurt hand be real but nothing else. He seemed to have lost a grip on what he thought was reality and what wasn't. He walked inside and sat on the edge of the bed and stared at his hand.

"Come home," he thought to himself.

He laid back on the bed and managed to fall asleep even with the ceiling swirling.

The Letter

The next day Erik packed his things and left a note for Amelia.

Dear Amelia,

I'm finding myself in very dark places within my own head. I'm scared of what may come of them. I know we have grown apart. I'm so very sorry. I'm sorry I couldn't help you in the way you helped me. Sorry I didn't know what to do. Sorry I didn't find new ways to fight for us. I want nothing but the best for you. I know I'm not that. You are everything that is great in this world and you deserve everything you ever desire.. I hope you find someone able to do so.... I hope you're able to find someone to help you out of the hole I helped dig. I'm going back home to try and clear my head. I wish you the best of luck.. know that I will always love you. Maybe our paths will cross again one day.

Always,

Erik

Erik wouldn't find out until several years later that Amelia would never read the letter. In fact she would never make it back to the apartment at all. She died from an overdose the very night Erik had come so close to death himself. He would never forget her or the love they had shared.

Coming Home

Erik barely recognized his aunt's house as he pulled in. Weeds had grown all around it. Windows were busted out and the front door stood wide open. He knew his aunt had wanted him to explore, but he still could not help but regret what had happened to the house in his absence.

He walked around the house. Every corner of it was filled with memories. Though much of the house had now been vandalized and looted. As he began to walk up stairs he heard a noise come from his old room. His pace quickened. He swung open the door to his room scaring a poor mama bird trying to work on her nest.

It flew out the broken window and sat on a nearby tree branch. She watched as Erik entered the room. Like much of the old house his room had been ransacked. Nothing he had left behind seemed to remain. Nothing except some old books on the shelf that were now damaged and molded beyond repair. He skimmed over them. Some of them were very hard to make out. They were all classics such as Moby Dick and Treasure island. It was a waste of good books Erik thought to himself. That's when he remembered the most important books of his childhood. He quickly scanned over the old moldy books looking for a sign of the green book, or Alice, or Oz,... but there was nothing. Not even one of them. As usual his glimmer of hope was doused.

Erik turned to walk back out of the room, but before he could reach the door the bird that had been watching him flew past his head and blocked him from leaving. It was one of the strangest things Erik had ever seen. It was as if the bird was trying to shoe Erik back into his room. Erik swatted lightly at the bird and tried to pass by. It maneuvered around his swats and flew back into the room.

Erik stood and watched the strange bird. It flew to the back of his old desk chair and pointed its head towards the ground.

"What is it, mama bird? I see your nest! Don't worry, I won't bother your babies!"

The bird began to fly in small circles at the foot of Erik's bed before returning to the back of the chair. It was clearly trying to point its beak towards the ground but Erik wasn't seeing it. The bird began to get frustrated. Finally, the bird jumped to the floor and started pecking at a rug that sat at the foot of his bed. At this point Erik began to think maybe, as crazy as it sounded, the bird was trying to show him something. So, he walked over to the bird and lifted up the rug. The bird watched in relief. There, below the rug was a handle!

"What the?...." Erik spat out loud.

All his years living there he had never noticed this little door beneath his bed! So he carefully lifted it up. The space beneath was small. No larger than maybe three feet. There, laying between two studs sat a chest. Erik pulled it out and dusted it off.

There was no lock on the chest, but it did have Erik's name written on a tag that hung from the handle.

It really was a treasure chest. Not one of gold or silver, but to Erik, something much better. There, on top laid an old friend that had been through many adventures with him.

He squeezed Teddy tight in his arms. He was a grown man hugging a teddy bear and he didn't care in the least bit. Lying under Teddy were all the books he had thought he had lost forever! The lore book, the Alice books! Even all of the Oz books! He wasn't sure how they all ended up here, but he was ecstatic that they did!

Like a small child he sat with Teddy in his lap and began to read his old books. The mother bird flew to her nest and watched him as he read.

Page after page, soon book after book. He read until the sun had gone down. What should've been creepy (being in an old rundown house) was surprisingly comforting. He used his lighter and managed to find an old oil lamp in the kitchen. He returned to his room and continued to read by the lantern light.

His eyes eventually grew heavy and he fell asleep right there on the moss-covered floor.

The Adventure Begins

Erik could hear a rooster crowing off in the distance. The sound was what began to wake him. He was surprisingly warm considering he slept on the damp floor with no blanket. He looked around. The room seemed different. He couldn't quite place it, but everything seemed just a bit different. For one Teddy and all of his books from the night before were missing!

He began to frantically look around for them. As he shuffled about on the floor he began to hear voices.

"Mommy, mommy. I'm sooo hungry!"

"Yeah mommy! More!"

"Goodness you're hungry little ones! I suppose a second breakfast is in order!"

The voices sounded as if they were coming from in the room with him! Erik looked around in confusion. The bird noticed him looking very confused.

"What are you looking for dear?" asked the mother bird.

Erik's eyes grew big. He had truly lost his mind. For he thought for certain the bird was talking to him. He talked back to the bird in hopes he had just imagined it.

"D.....did you just talk!?" he asked

"Well.... Ummm. Yes?" she answered with her head tilted. The question seemed to confuse her.

"But.... You're a bird, you can't talk!"

The bird's head shot back. She was clearly offended at this comment.

"What's that supposed to mean!? We can talk just as well as any other animal! or boys for that matter!!"

Erik got up and began to walk out of the room holding his head. All the while the mama bird was still fussing at him for his insult. He had had some strange mornings and dreams, but this one took the cake.

"Did I fall and hit my head?" Erik thought to himself.

As he walked out of the room he passed a broken mirror in the hallway. As if talking animals weren't crazy enough, what Erik saw in the mirror was beyond crazy. When he had gone to sleep he was a bearded young man that stood much higher than where the mirror stood. Now, his head barely reached the bottom of it! He had short hair and a clean baby soft face! He was a young boy!

He ran to the bathroom to get a second glance in another mirror. It was the same! He stood and looked down at his childlike hands in disbelief.

"Am I still tripping!?" he said out loud.

A loud crash of pots and pans came echoing out of the downstairs kitchen.

"Now what!?" he thought

He held the railing as he went down as his center of gravity felt way off. Being a few inches shorter all of a sudden can do that to a person.

Erik stood at the doorway of the kitchen bewildered at the sight before him. There, standing in the kitchen surrounded by pots and pans on the ground stood a massive bear! He seemed to be trying to cook something by the looks of it.

"Oh, hey! sorry if I woke you! Trying to get this ol' thing to work. Had a bit of a mishap."

Erik didn't know what to think at this point. The bear did however seem strangely familiar. Erik remained quiet and the bear kept talking.

"Anyways, I was going to make a pie... guess it's just berries now! We have a long few days ahead of us. They'll make for good snacking."

"Uhh... long day? Where are we going exactly?" Erik asked the bear.

"What do you mean where are we going? To see king Oberon, of course! It was your idea!" he replied.

"Oh... uh, right, of course..."

Erik had no idea what the bear was talking about. Although the name Oberon did seem to ring a bell.

Erik sat at the kitchen table and the bear served him a big bowl of berries. As they sat and ate their breakfast Erik and the bear talked. Though the bear did most of the talking. The bear spoke as if the two had been lifelong friends. He spoke of Erik's aunt's house like he had visited it several times before.

"This place sure has changed over the years, hasn't it?" the bear asked as he looked around the room.

Erik glanced around the old house. Vines grew everywhere. Nature was retaking the home. In a way it was actually quite beautiful. Right there on the kitchen wall hung wild lavender, one of Angela's favorites. Erik smiled at the thought.

"Maybe the shell, but the heart seems the same."

After breakfast Erik took a stroll through the house before setting off on the adventure he seemingly planned.

He walked to the back of the house to the sunroom where he and Angela had spent so many evenings painting. Like much of the house the walls were covered in greenery. Wild flowers hung down on vines. There in the middle of the vines Erik could see an easel with a painting on it. At first glance he thought the vines had grown over it too. Yet as he grew closer he could see it was indeed a painting. The background perfectly aligned with the painting! It was as if Angela had come back to the old house and painted it in its new beauty. That, or nature liked her painting so much it

108

decided to copy it. Either way the sight was truly amazing to him. He sat for some time and gazed at the picture.

Eventually, he returned upstairs to see if there was anything useful to bring on his supposed ventures. There on his bed laid a little brown satchel with a blanket rolled up on top of it. The little mama bird stood on top of it. She spoke as Erik entered the room.

"You seem a little better now, dear. Glad to see it!"

"Uh, yeah,, I guess so?" he wasn't exactly confident in his answer.

He didn't exactly "accept" that he was talking to animals as if they were people. The little mama bird continued on.

"Well, I packed a bag for you sweetie, and a blanket to sleep on. There's some things to help you along your travels and some to pass the time. Also, some bread to eat.. if it were up to Teddy you'd probably end up eating berries the whole trip!"

Erik's ears perked up at the name she mentioned. "Teddy!?" he thought to himself. "It can't be!"

He was referring of course to his childhood teddy bear!

The boy thanked the bird and equipped his satchel. He was ready for whatever journey he was about to begin. Or so he thought at least. Thinking deep down it was a dream or trip he would awake from at any moment. Funny thing was, he didn't really want it to be. Wherever he was he was happy. Confused, but happy.

He was in his childhood body and with it seemed to come his lost bewilderment of the world and his sense of adventure. He only cared about that very moment and the journey he was about to take!

He and Teddy headed out the front gate. The mama bird sat in the window and waved them goodbye.

Their adventure had officially begun!

The Bridge

Erik had walked out that front gate and down the road a million times. Only this time was very different. There was no road at all. Only a large dirt path. There were no other houses on either side of the path, only forest as far as he could see. They walked for quite some time before finally coming to a tiny rope bridge suspended over a raging river below.

Teddy stepped out first. The board instantly snapped from beneath his foot and fell to the river below. He was clearly too heavy for this little bridge.

Three massive, filth covered trolls emerged from the far side of the bridge. They were all laughing and poking fun at the bear. Each uniquely ugly themselves. Though the strangest thing was the shoes they wore. Not so much shoes as boards tied to the bottom of their feet.

The largest of the trolls approached our travelers first. He was almost as big as Teddy in height and twice as large in the waist. He clearly weighed more than

Teddy, yet here he was walking across the bridge with ease.

"Ain't no bears allowed in these parts! Too dangerous!" shouted the big troll across to Teddy.

"We're just passing through. He's the most well mannered bear you've ever met I promise! A teddy bear in fact!" replied Erik.

The troll scoffed at the boy's retort.

"Ain't no such thing. Wild animals, every one of them!" the troll rudely shot back.

The other two trolls started to chime in from the end of the bridge.

"Yeah! Good for nothin' bears"!

"We don't want 'em near our homes"!

"Go back to where you came from"!

Erik could see the frustration in Teddys eyes and watched as the bear's fists began to clinch. He leaned over to the bear's ear.

"Don't... they're trying to get a reaction out of you. Don't let them win"!

Still, the trolls kept slandering Teddy. From his species to his size. Erik could tell his blood was now just about boiled.

Teddy took another step forward towards the troll. Another piece of wood snapped off and fell below. The biggest troll began to laugh hysterically and taunt Teddy further.

"See! You're too fat to get across the bridge anyways"!

Erik could see it in Teddy's eyes he was ready to lunge towards the rude troll and risk the fall afterwards.

"What will it take to let us pass?" Erik asked in haste.

The fat troll thought for a moment. As he did he ran his hands down his greasy mangled beard.

"Doesn't matter. He's too fat to cross!" he finally spoke.

Erik looked over the troll and then Teddy. "How?" He thought. Then he looked down at the troll's feet. That's when it hit him. The strange shoes!

"What would it take for him to borrow your shoes just long enough to cross?" the witty boy asked.

The troll made a stunned face and looked down at his feet.

"My shoes!?"

"Yes, let him wear your shoes to walk across the bridge!"

The troll began to laugh uncontrollably. He then threw his head back and shouted.

"HA! Let that bear wear my shoes! Never! No self worthy troll would be caught dead doing such a thing!"

The other two trolls now roared with laughter, as well.

Teddy had had enough. He let out a great roar that scared the troll. The troll hastily stepped backwards. When he did the board beneath one of his feet cracked apart. He was too shocked by the roar of the bear to notice. Still the troll poked.

"Told ya! Ain't no such thing as a good bear! Look at 'em! You heard that roar! A clear killer here!"

Teddy began to jump towards the ignorant troll. Only when he did, the bridge below him and Erik began to collapse. All of the boards below their feet began to fall. Teddy moved fast and put a foot on each rope that held the bridge. Erik did the same. They stood there balancing high above the water.

The troll was now laughing so hard he could barely breathe. He stood and pointed at the two ogre elders as they carefully balanced on the ropes. Teddy growled and the troll stepped back quickly.

CRAVAACK.   POP.

The troll's shoe had broken in half and his foot ran straight through one of the boards below. He surely would've fallen to his death if his giant belly hadn't gotten stuck between the other foot boards. His legs dangled below the bridge. His eyes began to grow wide as he heard the remaining floor boards begin to give way. He pleaded for help. The two other trolls cowered on the far end of the bridge too scared to get on it themselves. Even to help their friend. He pleaded out-loud.

"PLEASE! Someone! HELP ME!"

It would've been easy for Teddy to turn and go back the short distance they had come. It would've been easy to let this rude insulting creature fall to his death. Teddy had hate in his heart for the bigots, but nonetheless didn't wish to see them die.

The bear shifted all four of his feet as securely as possible onto the ropes. He grabbed Erik's shirt and lifted him to his back. He then darted across the bridge!

Just as the boards under the troll snapped, Teddy reached down and caught the troll by his long mangy beard with his mouth. All three managed to make it to the end of the bridge thanks to Teddy. The troll complained about his chin hurting and Teddy griped about his mouth having a horrible taste in it, but after all was said and done the troll was able to muster up a "thank you."

After their praises and thanks the trolls warned the adventurers not to proceed down the road they were currently on.

"We are forever in your debt. For this we warn you! Troll city is no place for a bear, or a child for that matter. Trolls care for trolls and that's it. You won't be welcome. Some residents may even treat you worse than us."

Teddy looked towards the horizon towards the troll city then to either side of the path they stood. There was nothing but thick forest in every direction except towards the city.

"There's no trails or paths. The city is surely the quickest way to King Oberon."

The troll Teddy had saved, clearly the oldest of the three made a strange face at the mention of Oberon.

"Oberon? What business do you have with that old fairy king!? Nobody's traveled from the south to see him in some time. So long in fact the king's highway has grown over."

"Our business is our own. But yes, we are going to see him, which is why we must pass through," Teddy insisted.

"What about disguises? We can put on cloaks or something and sneak in!" Erik suggested.

"No, that won't work. Troll's have a strong sense of smell. They would get a whiff of the two of you as soon as you went through the gate. Especially him!" the older troll said as he pointed to Teddy.

"We could pee on em' to cover up their stench," the second biggest troll blurted.

Teddy and Erik both shook their heads in disapproval.

"There may still be some of the king's road left to see." Finally, he spoke to the youngest of the trolls.

"Where would that be?" Erik asked.

"Over that way. Maybe an hour's walk through the woods."

Teddy snorted at the young troll's remark.

"Or we can go straight there! Through this city!" he said in frustration.

Erik thought for a moment. Weighing his options and trying to think of the best solution.

"I say we cut through the woods. Try to find the king's road. If all trolls act anything like these. I don't think we should pass through a whole city of them!"

Teddy didn't like the idea of going out of the way, but agreed with Erik and the two headed to the thick forest in search of the king's road. If it was still there to be found.

The Other Fairy King

The trees in the forest were so close together barely any sun made it through the tops of them. Strange noises surrounded our heroes. Normally a situation like this would scare a young boy. Yet, something about this place made Erik fearless. He had a sense that whatever came at him he could handle. Maybe the fact that a giant grizzly bear traveled with him helped a bit too.

After walking a bit they began to see the sun again through the bottom of the trees. It was almost level with the ground. They needed to make camp sooner than later.

They came to an opening in the thick woods. The top was still covered by branches and leaves but the trees were spaced enough for them to make a cozy camp between them. They cleared a spot and began to look for firewood.

By the time camp was made, the moon was high in the sky. Though, the travelers couldn't see it. As hard as it tried, the moonlight couldn't quite pierce the thick canopy of the trees. The only light the two had was that surrounding the fire.

Erik laid out the blanket the mother bird had packed him and quickly fell asleep upon it.

A cold breeze woke Erik from his sleep. He could feel goosebumps running up his arm to his neck. The fire had burned down to just embers. The forest was no longer producing strange noises. Just an eerie silence filled the air.

The cold breeze or whatever it was that had woken him from his sleep kickstarted his heart and he knew he wasn't going back to sleep anytime soon. He sat and watched as the last few ambers began to go out. The darkness slowly crept in. He could feel the goosebumps running up his arms again. Only this time there was no breeze. He was sure of it. Erik couldn't see or hear anything but he couldn't help but feel that someone was right behind him.

He began to feel an icy breath upon his neck. The untouchable feeling he had carried with him all day quickly fled. An all too familiar smell began to fill his nose and mouth. Erik clenched his eyes tight. He didn't dare open them. Though he couldn't see anything he knew for a fact something was there in front of him now inches from his face! He could sense its presence lurking over him.

Suddenly the feeling stopped and the blackness in his eyelids began to turn red! There was clearly an amended light coming from somewhere. Erik opened his eyes to see what had lit up the camp. At first it was too blinding to see anything. As the light dimmed a voice began to emit from it.

"Aye boy, what ye doin' in these parts?"

The light was now dim enough to see who spoke. There before him stood a tall burly man with reddish colored skin. The light came from him yet he held no lantern or torch.

Teddy had awoken and began to realize what was going on. The bear was shocked and soon relieved as he knew the glowing man standing in their camp. The bear shouted in excitement!

"Ailill ! Old friend!"

The two embraced in a powerful hug. The glowing man was almost as big as the bear! Erik had heard the name Ailill many times in Irish lore. Many kings over the years had held the same name. So naturally that was the first thing Erik thought to ask the glowing man.

"Are you a king?" asked the boy.

"Am I a king?! Why boy o' I'm THE king! King of the fairies!" the man boasted.

The smile faded a bit when he saw the look on the boy's face. It was as if he knew the next question that was going to be asked. A question he had annoyingly heard several times before.

"I thought the king of the fairies was Oberon? Are there two of you?"

The glowing king scoffed and rolled his eyes at Erik.

"One stinkin' writer tells a story with' em in it and' everyone thinks he's the one true king! Himself included!"

He let out a few choice words beneath his breath before speaking out loud again.

"No, Oberon ain't the king of da fairies, nor I to be fair. In fact der be six of us all together."

"Six!?" the young boy exclaimed.

"I knew of MAYBE two before, you made three. But six!!"

The king gave Erik a strange look at this comment.

"Tree ya say? Who be the third if ya don mind me askin'"?

"Well, I knew of the good fairy king ... and of the bad fairy king," Erik answered.

The King looked Erik up and down and put his hand on his shoulder. He could tell the mention of the evil king brought up something in the boy.

"So you know of tha Erlking do ya?"

Erik shook his head and proceeded to look at the ground. The king could see the fear in the boy just at the mention of the Erlking's name.

"Aye, ya done more dan 'eard of em ain't ya lad?"

121

The king paused for a moment. He tried to think of what to say to the boy for comfort.

"Well... ye be safe wit me lad!... let's go to me kingdom an av us a drink... ur um... bite to eat."

Within a blink of an eye, Erik, Teddy, and the king were all standing in a beautiful grotto. Fairies flew about lighting the area up splendidly.

The king filled a tankard for himself and Teddy of fine mead and sent for juice and fine foods for the boy.

A grand meal was soon presented before Erik. He instantly began to dig in. Teddy had just pulled the leg from a giant roasted turkey when Ailill called him to the side.

"Let the boy eat. I need to speak with you, alone," the king said where only the two of them could hear.

As Erik stuffed his face, the two slipped away into the king's private quarters to speak without curious ears.

"What is it Ailill? What troubles you friend?" Teddy asked.

"The boy... where did 'e come from?" asked the King with a stern, serious look on his face.

"Uhh,... here, same as us."

The fairy king shook his head.

"No, dis boy ain't from our world. 'Es somethin' else. Somethin powerful. More powerful den anyting I've seen!"

Teddy was more than taken back by this remark.

"Powerful!? What in the world are you talking about? He's just a human boy!!"

The king shook his head in disagreement.

"You wanna know why I was in those there woods? Cuz I felt somethin' callin to me. Draggin' me to it. I was drawn to that power like fly on shite. To the boy!.... I can see why the Erlking wants him so bad. He wants whatever power it is that lad holds!"

"The Erlking has been after him since he was just a baby! He's upset he couldn't lure him away, as hard as he tried!"

"An why da ya tink dat is! He wouldn't give a shite bout some child who slipped through his fingers all dem ears ago,.... Not less der was somethin special!"

Teddy took a large gulp of his mead and let out a sigh.

"I always knew he was special. Never occurred to me just how much... so... is he... Fae?" the bear asked hesitantly,

"No, not like any Fae I ever saw! Like I said. E's not from dis world. Dat magic in em is somethin much more than mere fairy magic."

The two were interrupted by a knock on the door. They opened it to see Erik there holding his belly with a grin on his face.

"I'm stuffed! Thank you so much for dinner... eh breakfast?.... You wouldn't happen to have a place I could lay my head for a bit. I'm still quite tired and after a meal like that I believe it would do me some good to get some shut eye before we hit the road again."

Before Erik could even finish his sentence another door appeared within the grotto next to him.

123

Erik opened it. Inside was a beautiful room with a massive bed in the middle of it. The boy walked over and jumped into it. He sank down into the cloud-like cushions and almost instantly fell asleep.

Teddy and the king finished their ale and sat in silence. Before Teddy retired to his own bed the king spoke up one last time.

"When tha lad wakes you need to make haste. Every moment he's ere you further endanger em an each an every one of us. I've put a spell over him. It should keep the Erlking at bay for now.... He was there with you ya know, by the fire... at least part of him was. I was able to run em off, but he'll be back. I promise you that. He grows more powerful every day already. He can't have whatever power it is the boy holds. If he does den we are all doomed."

"Come with us then! Help me keep the boy safe!"

"I feel da boy's power callin ta me. Like a ringin' in my head I can't stop. I crave his powers, maybe almost as much as the Erlking himself."

"You're nothing like the Erlking!"

"We fairy kings each hold ill intent. Some more than others. We all lust for power. Craving, wanting for more.... Any of tha kings that tell ya different be lyin' to ya... Oberon included!.... I've done all I can do. I dunno how long the spell will last. So best be on your way before the sun gets tooo high into the sky."

"Can Oberon help the boy?"

The king let out a sigh.

"I dunno ... to be honest, I'm surprised the boy has made it this far. The Erlking is not like the rest of us. His magic is older, darker. Your best bet may be to take the boy back to where he came from."

The Rolling Fields

After a few hours the sun was high in the sky. Erik emerged from the bedroom relaxed and refreshed.

"That was the best sleep I think I've ever had!" he exclaimed as he stretched.

All the fairies had disappeared. Around them the entire grotto was empty as if nothing had ever been there. Erik was ready to take on the new day and rushed to get back on the go. Teddy on the other hand moved a bit slower. He couldn't help but think about the conversation he and Ailill had the night before.

The two walked through the thick forest for another few hours before finally coming to an opening.

The sun was high in the sky and incredibly bright after being in the cover of trees for so long.

There was no sign of a road or even some sort of path to follow anywhere. Only hills of wild flowers that stretched as far as the eye could see.

The wildflowers and surrounding grass were tall. It came all the way to Teddy's waist which was about shoulder height on Erik. Teddy paved the way out in front of Erik and Erik was sure to step close behind where the grass and flowers had been laid down by the bear's feet.

The wind blew across the tops of the flowers making it look like a grand colorful ocean. Erik ran his open hand across the top of them. They were soft and silky, cool from the morning dew yet warm from the sun at the same time.

He watched as the colorful ocean of flowers flowed perfectly with the wind. It really looked like waves rolling across a purple sea. It all flowed perfectly... All but one spot it seemed. Erik watched in curiosity as the perfectly synchronized field seemed to have a crack begin to break in it. Something moved through the field, breaking and folding the grass and flowers beneath it. The crack in the field began to move faster and straight towards them!

Erik grabbed Teddy's attention and pointed towards the anomaly coming towards them. Teddy was much taller and much more likely to be able to see whatever it was moving towards them. Though he could see the rift he still wasn't able to see whatever was the source of it. Whatever it was didn't move in a straight line. It seemed to sway back and forth in an "s" motion.

Teddy snatched Erik up and dropped to all fours. He threw the young boy onto his back like a back pack and began to sprint. The bear couldn't see too well as to where he was going, but it didn't matter as long as he widened the gap between him and whatever was in pursuit. Teddy never saw whatever it was, but everything in him told him to run. So he listened.

He ran as fast as his paws could take him. Unfortunately, bears aren't made to sprint for very long distances. He began to slow. Erik could tell Teddy was losing his momentum. He carefully balanced himself and stood upon the back of the bear and looked back behind them.

At first he didn't see anything. Maybe they had outran whatever it was. Just before he began to say the coast was clear something made its way onto the path Teddy had just made. There quickly slithering towards him was the biggest snake Erik had ever seen! It was a vile and evil looking creature. It had blood red eyes and four horns on top of its head. Once its target was in sight its pace quickened even more.

"Teddy." Erik screamed as he pointed at the horned snake close behind them.

Teddy turned his head and saw the space between them and the serpent shrinking. He knew if he tried to push himself to run any further that he would have no energy left to protect the boy if the snake caught them. He had to stand and fight.

He screeched to a halt and told Erik to get off. The snake was almost immediately on them. Before Erik even realized what was happening Teddy and the horned snake stood nose to nose.

"Mooove assssside beeeaar!" hissed the serpent.

Teddy didn't budge. The snake reared its head up high into strike position. Teddy stood up on his hind legs to level the playing field. Though the bear was tall the snake still stood a bit higher. The snake seemed to stare straight though the bear. His target was clearly the boy! Every move Erik tried to make the snake seemed to follow. He swayed his head back and forth as if waiting for the right time to slide around the bear. As he did he noticed though the bear was powerful he was not as agile as the snake was. He knew if he chose just the right moment he would easily be able to get to the boy. He slowly inched his way to the left of the bear acting as if he were about to make his strike. Then just before he did and the bear hastily stepped towards him he jolted back to the right of Teddy. His prediction was right! The bear was too slow! The horned serpent lunged towards Erik, venom dripping from its fangs!

Erik didn't have enough time to react. Before he knew it the snake was inches from his face. He closed his eyes tight.

He could feel the breath from the snake on his face. It grew heavier and more frantic as it spewed onto his cheeks... then, it stopped.

Erik opened his eyes and saw the snake lifted high into the air. The snake slithered frantically as it gasped for air. The great grizzly held tight to the snake's throat, choking the life from it. Finally the serpent stopped moving.

Just as it did one single drop of venom dripped from his fang. It fell straight down into the onlooking boy's eye.

At first the burn was slow, Erik almost didn't feel it, but the pain quickly grew. Within seconds the pain was excruciating. Erik dropped to his knees and began to scream.

Teddy threw the lifeless snake to the side and dropped to his knees next to Erik.
Erik held his face tightly in his sleeve trying to ease the pain. He felt as if his eye was melting away in its socket!

Teddy cradled the boy and looked around for signs of anything that may help. He couldn't make out a body of water or sign of civilization in any direction.

The bear knew he had to get the boy some help one way or another. His second wind began to fill his lungs as panic and adrenaline coursed through his body. He ran as fast as a bear on two legs had ever ran before. He continued in the direction they were heading hoping he would eventually cross paths with something of use soon.

Teddy ran until the bottoms of his paws were raw, then he kept running. The determined bear ran until the mats on his paws had been torn from his feet. He now had a trail of bloody paw prints behind him. He was trying as hard as one could possibly try, but the fields seemed to never end.

The pain tried to slow Teddy. All the sensors in his body screamed at him to stop! But he wouldn't stop. He couldn't stop.

Somewhere along the way Erik had passed out from the pain. Teddy looked at the boy's limp body laid over his arms.

"Please..... please be okay..."

Still though, hill after hill, field after field. It never ended.

The bear stumbled as he ran. His legs were giving out. Rather he wanted to keep going or not, his body had given out. Finally, his legs buckled beneath him and he fell to the ground.

He and Erik laid there in the middle of the beautiful flower ocean.

Teddy watched helplessly with a tear in his eye as the sun began to set on the horizon behind Erik. The pain and exhaustion had finally caught up to him. He shamefully accepted defeat and laid his head down into the dirt next to the boy.

The Dark Room

Miles away, a familiar glowing king had been lowered to his knees in a dark, cold room full of strange instruments. He pleaded no begged for his life.

"Stop! I swear I know nothing'! I didn't do or see nothin' I tell ya!" he screamed as blood ran down his face.

The glowing king was beaten and bruised. His face had swelled to almost double in size. One eye had swollen completely shut!

The giant Ellerkonge towered over the beaten king. He held a bloody hammer in one hand and a pair of pliers in the other. Several other tools and instruments were in the ogress man's belt and scattered about the room. All of them covered in the king's blood.

The door behind the Ellerkonge opened and the giant man stepped to the side. The horned king emerged from the shadows behind him.

He stooped down to the bloody king's level and looked him in his eyes. The evil king's glowing yellow eyes looked deep into the eyes of Ailill.

"I know you crossed paths with the boy! What spell did you put on him? What magic have you used?" the horned demon questioned.

"I swear! Yes I saw da boy! But I dint put no curse or spell on em!!" pleaded Ailill.

The yellow-eyed Erlking grabbed the man's face with his skinny, long cold fingers.

"These games grow old quickly brother. I had the boy in my hands!! I know you feel his power! You are a fool for not taking them for yourself! Instead you somehow shield him from us. Why! Why protect this boy! Why betray your own kind!"

"You are not my kind. We are not the same. Your lust for power, your dedication to the dark magic! You are no longer Fae! I don't know what you've become! Other than a monster! You know why I let him go! Why I hid him from all of us! So none of us would become you! And that you couldn't become something even worse!"

"So then.... You aren't going to tell me what spell you've used on the boy are you?"

The bloody king stared boldly at the Erlking. It was clear he had said all there was to say.

"Very well then..."

The horned king stepped to the side and the giant Ellerkonge stepped forward again with his bloody tools in hand. He raised the hammer high in the air before coming down onto the king's head with incredible force. Blood sprayed over the walls and floor. The glowing king slouched down low. Blood poured from his head. The Ellerkonge lifted his hammer high again, and again he came down with ungodly force. The sound of something like that of a melon or coconut busting open filled the room and Ailill fell to the ground.

He had remained strong and silent in the end. He would pass with a sense of pride for he was the only one who knew how to break the protection spell he had put on Erik. Even in death, Ailill had still won.

The Little Mice

    Teddy jolted up from his deep sleep. He was in a heavy panic. He looked around him, but couldn't see Erik anywhere! He jumped to his feet and quickly noticed something different. His feet no longer hurt! He looked down and saw they were all bandaged up.

    Curiosity of his feet plagued him, but such things didn't matter at the time. All he cared about was finding Erik!

    Before he began to take off he felt a small tug at his ankle. He looked down to see a small mouse trying to get his attention!

    "Unless you know where my friend is I have no time for you little mouse!" bellowed the bear.

    "I do indeed. Sir! I will take you to him!" replied the tiny mouse.

    The mouse signaled for the bear to follow. So he did. He followed him over a few more hills until they came to an old tree that looked to be half uprooted. The part that stuck up from the ground was full of holes.

There looked to be an entire tunnel system worked into the bottom of this tree. An entire city, if you will.

The tiny mouse ordered the bear to wait and entered one of the tunnels.

"The boy couldn't be here," Teddy thought to himself. "It's much too small for him to fit!"

As the bear puzzled over the mouse city the tiny mouse emerged with another mouse with her. This mouse looked to be much older. He had the beard of an old man or a wizard that hung down to his feet.

"Thank you o' great bear for killing the vile Cerastes! That serpent has plagued these beautiful fields for a very long time."

"You're welcome!... Not to be rude but I'm not here to play hero. The young mouse there said she knew where to find my friend. It's very important that I do so," replied the bear as politely as he could.

"Ah, the young boy! No, he isn't here. He's much too big to fit inside of here! I will take you to him though. If only you would be so kind as to carry an old mouse. These brittle old bones don't let me move as swiftly as I once did."

Teddy carefully picked up the elder mouse and put him on his shoulder. From here the mouse would direct Teddy in the direction of the boy. After what seemed to be a few miles from the mouse's tree Teddy had begun to get weary of the old mouse and grew impatient.

"How did the boy end up so far away?" asked the suspicious bear.

"We are as strong as many. We knew we had to get the boy help as quickly as possible. My people all worked together to carry him.... It took almost my whole kingdom to carry the small child. I'm sure you could imagine why we would have no chance at moving you or we would have! A grizzly is a bit much, even for us! We did what we could to help you where you lay."

"Where did your people take him?"

"Don't worry. The boy is in good hands. There is a healer on the edge of our fields. She knows much about healing herbs and medicine!"

Finally, the end of the seemingly never ending flower field ran into the edge of the tree line. There, in the middle, right along the forest's edge sat a small little cottage with smoke billowing out of the chimney.

News Travels Fast

An ugly fairy with a tainted glow weaved its way through the bone corridor towards the horned king who sat upon his throne awaiting the messenger.

"What news do you bring me? Has the boy been found?" inquired the Erlking.

"Not yet my lord. The serpent Cerastes was slain by the bear in the flower fields just South of The Walking Woods! We have many spies not far from there! We will have the boy in no time!" assured the messenger.

"Don't forget, the trees are not the only thing that walks among that forest. A creature forgotten by time. A creature once feared by so many men.... We must find the boy before SHE does!"

The Cottage by the Woods

Inside the cottage it was simply put together, but very comforting and inviting. It was all one large room. There on the other side of the room laid Erik fast asleep with a bandage across his face. A strange smelling liquid sat next to him on the nightstand. The same strange smell seemed to be coming from the pot on the fire as well.

Teddy had to squeeze in the corner of the cottage to be sure not to knock over anything. The giant grizzly had barely made it through the door!

The owner of the house was a woman of middle age with stringy hair and tattered clothes. She spoke with a soft voice.

"He's healing incredibly fast. It's amazing really. I thought for sure the boy would go blind. Yet, he's shown no signs of having lost any sight at all! In fact, even the burns that were around his eyes when he arrived have almost completely disappeared!"

"Well, thank you for saving his life!"

"I would love to take the credit for such things but I had a very small role in all of this! Sure I put herbs on his wounds and a hot meal in his belly, but the boy was already well on his way to being healed... which leads me to my next question....what is he?"

"Uhhh, human. Same as you?"

The healer shook her head.

"No, I've healed many humans over the years. Also been around the Fae many times. Whatever the boy is, he's like nothing I have seen."

Teddy sat like a stone. He didn't know what to say. It seemed as if everyone around him saw or felt something he couldn't. He always knew Erik was special, yet to Teddy he was still just a boy.

The Visitor

They all quietly ate dinner as Erik slept. Just as they finished dinner there was a knock on the door. The door opened and in walked the most beautiful woman. Head to toe perfect in every way! Teddy and the old rat were in a trance like state as they gazed upon her. She spoke with a sweet, yet authoritative tone.

"I've come for the boy," she spoke very matter-of-factly.

This comment instantly dropped Teddy from his trance.

"What! the hell you are!!" roared the bear.

She let out a small smile and reached out and put her hand upon the bear's chest.

"Dear Teddy, you've done such a good job at protecting the boy all these years! I know you mean the world to each other, but the time for your paths to diverge has come!"

The bear now stood up from his chair.

"Look lady, I don't know how you know me, or him, or anything about us, but you're crazy if you think you're taking him from me!"

At this comment the healer burst out in anger at Teddy.

"How dare you speak to your queen in such a way!" she shouted.

The queen looked at the healer and motioned her hand for her to calm herself. The queen then looked back up at Teddy. Her soft smile and glowing radiance staring right at him. She again put her hand on his chest.

"Erik knows you're worried about him. He says you can let go though. That he will be okay.... I promise you that he will be in good hands with me."

"How can he say anything to you!? He's sleeping! When have you talked to him!?" Teddy inquired.

The queen smiled.

"I've been talking to him. Why in fact, I'm talking to him right now!"

"What the hell are you talking about?" Teddy demanded.

"Right now, as he sleeps. I'm talking to him in his dreams," the queen rebutted.

While the two argued the old mouse stood quietly and watched the beautiful queen closely. Her body language, every move her mouth made as she spoke. Though, it was no longer infatuation, but suspicion.

You see, when the mouse was still young and spritely he had met king Oberon and his breathtaking queen. He remembered how she was beautiful inside and out. She gave off this radiance almost that instantly calmed you. Though this queen acted quite similar there was no calming feeling. Something felt... different.

As the two continued to argue the old mouse began to grow more suspicious. The healer now seemed mildly frantic and had moved closer to the boy. The mouse had lived for a very long time. He knew many things. He knew the healer had lived by herself for many years and had always used her powers and knowledge for good. He had always trusted her. Though on this visit she seemed different. Dark circles surrounded her eyes. Her teeth had rotted away and her skin had grown pale.

The mouse knew the dark practices and what physical toll it took on humans. He began to grow worried.

"Then let's wake him and let him tell us for himself!" the bear roared.

The healer chimed into the conversation.

"We cannot wake the boy. The medicine I've given him put him into a deep sleep. It will be hours before he wakes."

The queen began to pet the bear's chest to try and calm him.

"Everything will be fine. I will take good care of him, I swear. I must take him now though. As we sit here arguing a great evil makes its way towards us! The horned king will stop at nothing to get his hands on this special young boy! I can keep him safe! I can protect him! Can you say the same Teddy!?"

The bear's posture slumped down and he thought to himself for a moment. He had always protected Erik. Yet, they had both just come so close to death because he wasn't able to protect him. Maybe it was time to let the boy move on to someone with powers such as hers to actually keep him safe.

"Fine, if you swear to me that you can keep the boy safe... then take him."

The queen smiled wide and turned towards the sleeping boy. She spoke as she did.

"Don't worry, the Erlking won't lay a finger on him!"

She began to reach out towards the boy. Just as she was about to reach him the old mouse jumped onto the boy's chest with a small dagger drawn.

"No demon! You will not lay a finger on this boy!" the little old mouse shouted.

Teddy instantly shot back to attention.

"What's going on here!?" asked the bear in a worried tone.
The mouse spoke to Teddy but kept his eyes locked on those of the imposters.

"This is no fairy queen. This is a demon! A succubus! She wants the boy for herself!"

Almost as soon as the mouse spoke the creature before him started to take on its true form. Torn wings sprouted from her back and horns began to grow from her head. Her beauty quickly turned to ugliness.

The old mouse stood his ground in front of the demon. Teddy couldn't believe what he was seeing.

Before he could react the demon swatted the elder mouse off of the boy's chest and across the room.

As she reached for Erik again, Teddy lunged forward at her. Grabbing her by the wings and flipping her around towards him. He instantly swung his massive paw down across her chest splitting her open like a log of firewood! The succubus flung her wings wide open. The force of them sent Teddy stumbling backward before falling through the dinner table. As Teddy began to pick himself off the ground he watched in terror as the demon's wounds began to heal themselves. The demon then knocked the table out of the way with her powerful wings. She tried to come down onto Teddy with her sharp claws, but the bear was able to grab her wrists just in time!

The two stood pushing on each other with all their might, trying their best to get the upper hand. Back and forth they went. Teddy tried to bite the demon, but she was too fast and dodged every attempt.

Finally, he had his moment! He was able to get one foot forward and push her enough to knock her off her guard. When she stepped back, the grizzly lunged forward and took a massive bite from the demon's chest, just beneath her collar bone. Black blood began to pour down her body.

Teddy turned to check on Erik, but he was nowhere in sight! He was gone and so was the healer! Out of the corner of his eye, through the window, Teddy got a glimpse of what looked to be a lion or large cat with something laid across its back. That something was Erik! He quickly turned back to head out the door.

Only, once again he was met face to face with succubus. The demon seemed to be completely healed again!

Teddy knew he had to get to Erik but he didn't know how to defeat the foe that stood between them. He had thrown everything he had at her.

The succubus stood straight and spread her massive wings wide open. The span of them almost takes up the entire length of the cottage. The grizzly braced himself for another attack from the winged nightmare when suddenly the demon let out a blood curdling scream and grabbed her leg. Smoke poured from four small holes in her calf!!

She looked around but couldn't see anything.

"AHHH!" The succubus let out another scream!

Four more tiny holes that began to smoke appeared on her other calf. A small voice called out with a firm tone.

"Go after the boy! I will take care of this foul beast!"

As the demon bent over to grab its newly wounded leg she was struck again. This time in the neck! Steam poured from the holes like a kettle on the stove. She screamed in agony. As this unraveled Teddy finally saw what was causing the succubus so much pain. The tiny old mouse made his way up the monster's dark greasy hair. He held a silver fork tightly in his hand. As he ran onto the demon's head he shouted to Teddy again.

"Go! Hurry!"

Teddy dropped to all fours and began pursuit into the woods. As he ran from the shack he could hear the screams of the demon coming from behind him!

It was getting dark and Teddy's vision was depleting, but he had locked onto the lion's scent and was close behind. He chased the lion deep into the woods. The scent grew stronger and stronger. He was close now.

Finally, he was on it! Or so he thought. He could smell the lion as if he were on top of it, but couldn't see anything. As he searched he began to hear rustling in the trees above! He looked up and saw the lion twisted in the branches of the trees. It was fiercely struggling to break free, but it seemed to be too tangled.

Suddenly, the lion transformed into a bird, then a mouse. Though valiant in the attempt the trees were able to grab it and hold it through the transformations. Through every change it only seems to tangle itself more among the branches.

Teddy stood and watched in the moonlight as the creature tried to escape the clutches of the trees to no avail. Finally, the struggling stopped and a lifeless woman fell from the trees! It was the healer! Clearly there was much more to her than what was thought.

"Teddy!?" a tired voice sounded from the surrounding trees.

147

Erik came running out of the trees and grabbed tightly around Teddy's waist. Teddy lifted Erik into the air and squeezed him tight.

The trees began to move apart and open a pathway to a valley straight ahead. The two thanked the trees and walked into the valley. It was dark but the moon was full and high in the air so it made it very easy to see.

They gathered some dead wood and built a fire for camp.

A Well-packed Bag

Erik, having slept for almost two days, wasn't very tired. Teddy on the other hand was exhausted and was asleep in no time at all. The bear slept soundly while Erik entertained himself. As he poked at the fire he began to grow very hungry. He then remembered that the mama bird had packed him some bread in his bag! He dug into his bag and pulled out the wrapped up bread. As he did he noticed something underneath.

It was an old green book! His mother's book of Irish folklore! Erik sat up the next few hours eating bread and reading several splendid stories! All sorts of stories of the Fae!

Even though so far the journey had been nothing but peril Erik couldn't help but feel relaxed and even happy as he read the stories. As the fire died down Erik did as well. His eyes began to close as he read until he was eventually asleep.

The next morning Teddy woke up early and hunted, and then had some wild rabbits for breakfast. They were almost fully cooked before Erik had woken up.

"Figured we could use a good hearty meal to start the day. Especially after the last couple of days we've had!" Teddy proudly exclaimed as Erik woke to the smell.

The bear was very pleased with his culinary skills. Not only had he managed to catch and cook the rabbits, but he had also found some wild carrots and potatoes! He had turned it all into a splendid stew! He of course had also picked some berries to go along as with every meal.

The two enjoyed their mid-morning hearty breakfast and prepared for the day. The morning had revealed a great mountain range on the far end of the valley. They still had a long journey ahead. Truth be told, Teddy wasn't sure they were even still heading in the right direction.

The two agreed they needed to find a path or road to some sort of civilization. That way they could figure out exactly where they were and how far they had traveled away from Oberon's kingdom. There was no point to face the perils of a mountain if it wasn't needed.

The Mountain Town

Thankfully, it didn't take much longer to happen upon a road. It seemed to run parallel with the mountain range. It wasn't long down the road that they began to see a town emerging in the distance. It was a quaint little town. No more than twenty houses or so in all. They were all nice houses, very well kept. Almost every house had a little garden outside of it.

As the boy and the bear approached the town they noticed people start to go inside their homes. Windows and shutters closed all around them as they entered the town. Everyone seemed to be afraid of the two. When they had reached about the midway point of the town two men in funny looking hats made their way towards them.

"Welcome! Welcome!" one shouted excitedly as they approached.

"Not much of a welcome if you ask me. Everyone seems afraid of us!" Erik replied as he looked around at the closed off houses.

"No, well sort of. Not you though. More so him," one of the men stated as he nodded towards the bear.

"People round here just aren't used to such a well mannered bear. That's all," the other defended.

Teddy rolled his eyes at the comment.

The two men hastily led the adventurers to the back of the town to a strange building. While most of the houses were made of wood, this one was made of stone and had bars in the windows. It seemed to be a prison of some sort.

Erik gathered that the hats on their heads seemed to represent some sort of authority.

Once inside the men with the funny hats pulled out chairs for their visitors. Though it was quite clear Teddy wouldn't. be able to sit in said offered chair.

"Coffee? Tea? Ale?" offered one of the lawmen.

The adventurers politely declined and got to the point. Erik wasn't sure why he was in a hurry. Or why he was on his way to Oberon's in the first place. It was like he had entered a dream that had already started. Only this dream he didn't seem to wake up from. He had no idea where he was or how he got there. It all seemed so fuzzy. Yet, somehow, none of this bothered Erik. He had lost his mind and was completely okay with that. The only thing that seemed right to do was push forward.

"We are on our way to see king Oberon. We got off course and were trying to find somewhere to get some sense of direction," Erik was very to the point with his comment.

The two men looked at each other quickly. One of them smirked just a bit, but too fast for anyone else to catch.

"O, but of course! You'll be happy to know you haven't strayed far at all!" spoke one of the officers.

"We just didn't want to go through the mountains if we didn't have to," added Teddy.

"Well, I hate to break it to you, but you for sure will still have to cross through the mountains." Informed one of the officers. The other quickly spoke up.

"Luckily for you, we know a shortcut through them! So you don't have to track through the snow."

"Not to mention the mountain trolls and wild animals!" they continued.

"You can go right through all of that nonsense with ease," they assured him.

It didn't take much convincing for our adventurers to opt to take the short safer route. The two officers gave them clear direction. There was a pass not far from the town that they would take straight through the mountain. As they left the town, still not one person made eye contact with them.

"Strange town," Teddy said to Erik as they left.

"Strange indeed," Erik said as he looked back at the town.

The Pass

It wasn't far down the road that they came across the dirt path they were told would lead to the pass. The dirt trail wound through the foothills for quite some time before they found the entrance of the pass.

Though the sight of the "pass" made them both quite uncomfortable. The entrance of the pass looked more like the entrance to a cave! The two stopped and examined the entrance before entering.

Not far off, high in the trees, a small set of eyes watched them.

As the two examined the projected path they began to suspect maybe it wasn't the safer path after all. They began to debate amongst themselves.

"This doesn't look like a pass at all! That's a cave! I know a cave when I see one!" exclaimed Teddy.

"So what if it is? You're a bear! What kind of bear is afraid of caves!?" Erik shot back.

They went back and forth until the sun was almost even with the trees. A small voice cut into their arguing from above them in the trees.

"Well, you've surely waited too long to go in there now! He's awake now!"

Erik and Teddy looked around for the source of the voice.

"Who are you? Who's awake now?" Erik called out into the tree tops.

Just then a vine unraveled between him and Teddy and a squirrel came sliding down it. The squirrel had wild matted fur and seemed to be missing part of his tail. Despite his appearance he seemed very well mannered.

"Hello there, travelers! Name's Ratatoskr!" As he spoke he held out a tiny hand to shake the companions. They obliged.

"So, you said someone was awake now... who were you talking about?" asked the boy.

"Why, Typhon the great serpent of course! Everyone around here knows him! That's HIS tunnel you're about to foolishly enter!" replied the squirrel.

"Snake tunnel!? The men in the town down the road assured us it was a pass through the mountains. The easiest way through!" exclaimed Erik in a confused and disappointed tone.

"Well... technically they're kind of right. It's the *quickest* way through to the other side of the mountains. Wouldn't say it's the easiest though. Don't know of many if any who make it through..." Ratatoskr shrugged his shoulders as he spoke.

The squirrel reached into his little satchel he wore on his side and pulled out a plump berry. He took a bite out of it as he continued to speak.

"He's usually up and about at night. If you all are sleeping here tonight I suggest you don't make a fire! He can't see too well sometimes but he surely could see a fire!"

After talking to the squirrel the two decided that not only would they wait to pass through the "pass," but they would also not light a fire for camp. As the night grew darker Ratatoskr invited Erik into the trees with him assuring it was safer. Erik accepted the invite and climbed high into the trees with him.

As Erik climbed into the tall trees, Teddy went away from the trail a bit and made himself a spot to lay next to a large rock, but still close enough to keep an eye on Erik if the squirrel ended up not being trustworthy.

When Erik's head popped out of the tops of the trees, his eyes lit up with amazement. The view was amazing! The sky was riddled with stars. He had never seen so many altogether at once before.

While Erik was in awe at the sight Ratataskr began to gather branches and vines from below. Before Erik had even realized what was going on the squirrel had made him a bed there in the tops of the trees. Erik snuggled into the nest-like bed and gazed at the stars as he feel asleep.

Just before Erik fell into a deep sleep he began to feel the trees sway heavily. The squirrel quickly jumped to his chest and held his tiny hand over Erik's mouth. He then motioned for the boy to look down below them. It was too dark to see exactly what was at the bottom of the trees. Yet the way they moved it was clear it was something very large! The trees seemed to part like blades of grass as the creature made its way by.

Clearly Ratatoskr's eyesight was better than that of Erik's because he seemed to follow the monster as it made its way through the woods. Finally, when it emerged from the tree line, Erik could also see it. It was a massive serpent. It made the one in the fields look like an infant! It took up the entire road as it slithered towards the nearby town.

"Hmm. That's odd," said the squirrel as he watched.

"What's odd?" asked the boy.

"Haven't ever seen him travel that far before!" Ratatoskr said with his thumb and index finger under his chin.

He seemed to be thinking hard about what was happening. He and the boy watched as the massive serpent grew closer to the tiny town.

"We have to help them!" exclaimed Erik as he began to climb down the tree.

Ratatoskr seemed more than hesitant, but followed the boy down the tree regardless.

"Teddy!.... Teddy!" the boy called out.

The great bear rose from the pile of rocks he had been sleeping by with his eyes wide.

"Did you see that thing!?" the bear exclaimed.

Being at ground level he was able to get a good look at the size of the monster serpent. He was in shock to say the least.

"We have to go help the townsfolk!" Erik shouted behind as he already made his way down the path.

"Are you mad!?" Teddy screamed as he ran after the boy.

Though Teddy knew what they were about to face and Ratatoskr had no business in their affairs they both proceeded to follow Erik back to the town.

The All-Powerful Typhon

The snake had surrounded the entire town! Any light the town tried to give off was blocked by the massive body of the serpent. The closer they got the more Erik started to have second thoughts. He wanted more than anything to help the townspeople, but he had not the slightest clue how to even begin to combat a creature of this stature and size. Even the mighty grizzly was but the size of a mere rat to the snake. As they approached they heard a booming voice echoing through the town.

"I've come to collect my dinner!" the voice spoke.

Before they foolishly rushed in, Erik climbed a nearby tree to get a better look at what was going on. The entire population of the town seemed to be gathered in the center of the town just below the serpent's head.

The serpent seemed to be talking directly to the two officers who had given Erik and Teddy directions. They were begging the beast.

"Please NO! We sent travelers your way as always! A good meal at that! A boy and a bear!" pleaded one of them.

"There was no boy and certainly no bear in my tunnels! You lie through your teeth! It does NOT serve you well to lie to me!"

The second officer fell to his knees.

"Please 'o great one! I beg of you! You know we serve you! We sent the travelers right to you I swear it! They must've taken a different path," he cried.

The serpent let out a great HISSS.

"FOOLS! Cattle do not walk themselves to the slaughter. They are led! You fail me yet again and I tire of it! You claim to serve me, but don't sacrifice in my name!"

The knelt officer continued to plead.

"Please! We've sacrificed so much! Loved ones! Children! All in your name! We can't give anymore of our own! We won't have a town left!"

The serpent seemed unfazed by the outpour of emotions displayed before him. Unamused at the officer he quickly struck down. With the bat of an eyelash the officer was gone - gobbled up like he was nothing.

"Am I not worth the trouble? Am I not a worthy god!? I could end all of you in one swoop! I don't kill you and ask for so little in return.... And this is how you repay me... lies.... Groveling..."

The other officer stood shivering. Trying to choose the next words he spoke very wisely.

"Great Typhon, I beg for your forgiveness! We all do! We are but simple minded servants my lord! Please, take what you must. Eat until your heart's content o' great one!"

The massive serpent smiled a giant pointed smile.

"Good!"

He swept his great head down and scooped up a mouthful of villagers in just a moment. Many cowered, but none dared to try to run.

He raised his head high before swooping down again. It looked like a pelican scooping out a mouthful of fish from the ocean. Only the sea was a sea of people!

Erik couldn't take any more. He wasn't sure what he was going to do but he knew if they didn't do something soon there wouldn't be a village left. He would try his damnedest to help the townspeople, even if it meant his own demise.

He slid down the tree and ran towards the town. His companions quickly fell in behind. The little nimble squirrel quickly gained the lead. Before Erik and Teddy had reached the serpent Ratatoskr had already run up the length of the snake and was at his head!

As Tyhpon raised his head for another pass at the sea of frightened villagers, he felt a sharp jab in his right eye. His vision from that eye instantly went black and pain seared through his body.

Typhon shook his head madly, but the squirrel held tight. With one hand Ratatoskr gripped a giant scale on the snake's head and with the other hand he held a small saber. The monster tried to use his tail to slap off the rodent but to no avail. Teddy had grabbed onto the serpent's tail and held tight.

The snake writhed around trying to free himself from his attackers. He grew more angry by the second. He was a powerful ancient being. He would not be thwarted by a couple of wild animals!

In desperation the snake slammed his head into the ground. Leaving Ratatoskr crushed into the ground with the serpent's scale still tightly gripped in his hand.

Typhon quickly turned and struck at Teddy. The bear was able to move just in time, causing the serpent to sink his teeth into his own tail. When it did Teddy wildly began to slash at the snake's head. Scales tore from the top of Thyphon's crown and blood poured, yet still it seemed to leave the massive beast unfazed.

The snake whipped its tail at Teddy. This time he wasn't as fast. The massive tail struck Teddy and sent him flying into a nearby tree!

While the battle had raged on, Erik had tried to corral the villagers out of the square and back into their homes. At first no one moved. Erik wasn't sure if they were in some sort of trance or just too scared to move. The longer the battle raged the more the townsfolk seemed to come to. One by one, then two by two, the villagers finally began to leave the square and get to safety.

As they did, the remaining officer tried his best to prevent them from doing so. At first pleading with them before finally turning to violence. He began shoving the townsfolk back towards the square. Screaming profanities at them. As more began to shove past him he eventually pulled his saber from his belt. He began waving it wildly at the fleeing villagers. He wounded several in his fit. Still though, despite his efforts the square had almost completely emptied. Erik saw this man as just as much of a villain as the snake himself. Something had to be done. Erik grabbed a pitchfork that laid close by.

The enraged officer stood over a cowering woman with his sword in the air. His eyes were mad looking and unhinged. He swung down at the helpless villager, but his blow was caught by the handle of Erik's pitchfork. The sword busted the pitchfork in two. Luckily, it had bought the woman the second she needed to roll safely out of the way.

The officer stood with his sword in hand seething at the boy. He had such hatred for the young boy. The way he saw it, everything that was happening was all the boy's fault.

"Look what you've done here! You've gone and ruined everything! All of this death! It's your fault! Why didn't you just take the damn path you were told to take!" the officer screamed.

"We were lucky to have crossed paths with a knowledgeable traveler who warned us what your "pass" really was! How many lives have been lost because of you!? How many travelers were sent to their deaths because they trusted you!"

"Better strangers than our own! If we kept him fed he would leave us alone!"

"You coward! One life is not worth more than that of another!"

"Tell me that after one day you have children of your own! I would kill every traveler that passed with my bare hands if it meant keeping him safe!... they have to die.... You have to die for him to stay safe!"

The officer swung at Erik with all his might. Erik jumped back and the sword grazed across his shirt.

At this very moment the serpent had tried to strike at Teddy, missing and biting its own tail! As that battle continued blood began to pour over the dirt roads Erik and the officer stood upon.

Again the officer struck at the boy. This time. Erik was able to block the attack with the handle of the pitch fork. Unfortunately the force of the officer's strike knocked the handle from Erik's hands! He now stood defenseless!

The officer, now covered in blood and mud, stood with a smile on his face. His eyes almost red with rage. He looked truly deranged!

"Now you die!"

He rushed at the boy. Hate and madness in his eyes!...

Only, in his frenzy he neglected to notice the serpent's tail wildly flailing behind him. Erik ducked down just in time to have the snake's tail hit the man, knocking him just past where he was. Erik turned and saw somehow the man hadn't fallen to the ground. He stood with his back facing Erik.

Erik picked back up the handle of the pitchfork and prepared to defend himself at another attack. Though the deranged officer didn't turn to attack, he didn't even turn his head. He stood staring off the opposite way. His sword slowly began to slip from his hand and fell onto the ground next to him.

Erik slowly approached him with caution. As he reached the officer he began to see why the man hadn't moved. The other half of Erik's pitchfork stuck out from the muddy ground. The broken jagged tip now plunged into the chest of the officer. Erik watched as the man's eyes went from rage, to fear, to nothing.

Suddenly, a loud crash drew Erik's attention. Teddy had been thrown into a tree by the massive serpent.

Teddy laid motionless at the foot of the tree. Typhon hovered above the bear waiting for him to move. The predator wasn't done playing with its prey yet. His one good eye fixed upon the bear.

His concentration was quickly broken when a rock was hurled at that very eye. His vision instantly began to blur.

Erik tried to move slowly so the snake might not hear him. Unfortunately the snake still had a very keen sense of smell. Thyphon instantly turned his head directly where Erik was standing!

"You cannot hide from me boy! Soon you and this whole town will be my very filling dinner!"

Erik stood frozen in fear. He had to think quickly. As he tried to hatch a plan on the fly, he noticed Teddy had gotten up and was climbing up the side of a nearby house. Clearly, Teddy had a plan. So, Erik's plan was now simple. Keep the serpent busy and try not to get eaten.

"Why would you eat the whole town in one sitting? What would you do for dinner tomorrow or the next? Without their help travelers will never go down the path towards your tunnels! You'd be ridding yourself of dinner for the foreseeable future!" asked the boy.

"It would be their punishment for failing me. We made an agreement many years ago. They didn't hold up their end of the deal. So why should I? I am a god. I do not NEED anyone to provide me with food! I could take whatever I please. Kill whatever I want!"

"Yes! I'm sure! But as a god hasn't it been nice to have people worship and fear you?! To fill your every need! Not NEEDING to hunt. Having your food served to you?"

As Erik tried to finesse the snake, Teddy had made it to the top of a nearby house. When he reached the top he saw a familiar face. Clearly, their squirrel friend had a similar plan in mind! They each took an end of a clothesline hanging from a window and waited for the right moment.

"I have lived on this Earth longer than you could imagine, boy. I've had entire civilizations worship me!

This town and these followers are simply a blip in my life. I will consume it as I have so many others. Then I will move on. I will have new followers, and this town will be forgotten. As will you."

The massive snake rose up to striking position! Just before it had the chance to come down on Erik Ratatoskr and Teddy jumped from the roof, clothesline in hand! Teddy fixed himself above the snake's head as the squirrel swiftly ran under the snake's neck and returned with the other end of the line. Teddy held both ends of the line and planted his feet and pulled back as hard as he could. The clothes line sank into the serpent's neck. The snake began to flail wildly, knocking over anything around it. It even tried to curl on the ground, but it was no use. Teddy was not letting go of that line!

Tyhpon's head began to swell and his eyes and nose began to fill with blood. Teddy knew the creature didn't have much longer, but the monster was resilient. The clothesline had broken down to its very last strand of string. It was so tight it cut into the snake's neck. Yet still he refused to fall.

Ratatoskr watched as the final string began to give way. He knew if something wasn't done soon they would lose the upper hand.

As the serpent opened his mouth to let out a scream of pain and anger the hero squirrel did the unthinkable. Without a second thought Ratatoskr jumped into the mouth of the beast!

SNAP! The final string broke and Teddy flew backwards falling hard to the ground far below. The snake reared up in glorious stature. He knew he had now regained the upper hand. He stared down the bear with wickedness in his eyes.

Erik picked up the fallen officer's blade and started to slash and stab at the beast. The attack merely felt like a toothpick in the side of the great snake. He flicked his tail and sent the small boy flying.

The snake then set his sights back on Teddy. Tyhpon decided to give the bear a taste of his own medicine, and so, he began to curl around the grizzly. Squeezing the life out of him just as he had tried to do to him. He laughed as he did so.

"You are a fool to think you could kill me. I was here before man and even bear. I will be here long after they've died from this world as well. I have lived eons and shall live several more. The likes of you could never kill a god like myself!"

He began to squeeze. Teddy could feel his bones begin to crack and break beneath the might of the serpent. It wouldn't be long until they snapped. Just as Teddy began to accept his fate at the hands of the mighty serpent the snake's grip began to loosen. Typhon quickly unraveled from the bear and wrapped its tail around its own neck. He began to make a choking noise as blood began to dribble out of the corner of his mouth.

"No..... nooo!"

The snake screamed. His voice began to gurgle. Soon blood began to run down his chin.

"This.... This can't be...."

Before he could finish his sentence, his foul tongue began to slide from his mouth. He watched in terror as it fell to the ground.

The snake turned to try and flee. It began to twist and turn in pain as it tried to make its way back to its home. Not far down the road the snake stopped and began to roll violently. The ground shook as the beast turned about on the ground in misery. As it rolled blood spewed from its mouth like a fountain. Body parts began to fall from the monster's mouth. First his lungs, then his heart. Little by little, the great serpent spit up his insides. Finally, the mighty Typhon laid still on the ground.

Ratatoskr the Brave!

Erik and Teddy ran to the snake to see what had happened. As they got closer they began to see the mouth move. Teddy readied for attack, but to their surprise a small creature began to climb from the bloody mess and out of the snake's mouth. It was Ratatoskr! His tiny sharp sword was still tightly gripped in his hand! He moved slowly and looked to be in great pain. After only two steps, the little squirrel fell to the ground. Teddy rushed over and scooped him out of the snake's remains.

The fight had lasted all night and into the morning. As the sun came up the remaining villagers came to see the mighty fallen serpent. They all gathered around the great beast. They couldn't believe their eyes. For all of their lives they lived in fear of this thing. Now it was finally gone. They began to cheer for their heroes, but Teddy and Erik remained quiet as they stared at the bloody beaten squirrel in Teddy's hands. The snake's venom had burnt off most of his fur and caused severe damage to his skin. He still took breaths, but they began to slow and become further apart.

As the townsfolk cheered and celebrated their freedom, our two travelers quietly walked away from the crowd - the little wounded hero still in tow. Teddy had now passed Ratatoskr to Erik and walked with his head lowered.

Erik watched as the squirrel's breath grew fewer and fewer. until finally there were no more. Tears poured from Erik's eyes onto Ratatoskr. He stopped walking and fell to his knees. He hadn't known the squirrel for very long, but he felt so much love for him. If it weren't for that little hero, no one would still be alive.

As they walked away, a little boy no older than six came running up behind them. When he reached them he saw the little squirrel in Erik's hands. He looked at the little creature. At first, he began to tear up at the sight. Then he began to smile.

"So, he's the one who killed Typhon?"

Erik nodded his head.

"May I?" asked the little boy as he reached out his hands.

Erik placed Ratatoksr in the small child's hands. The boy looked down and began to talk to the little hero as he pet him gently.

"Thank you! Thank you so much for everything. You are the bravest little warrior I've ever seen. You will be remembered as our hero for years to come I promise! You will never be forgotten!"

The boy proved to be true to his word in the years to come. He was no mere boy, but the son of the main officer and rightful leader of the town. When he became of age he led the town to great prosperity and led with love rather than fear. He would erect a statue of the brave little squirrel in the middle of the town and the story of Ratatoskr the brave would go on for many years to come.

That night the town celebrated and cooked part of the snake. A small section would feed the whole town for the entire night and then some. Though their houses were destroyed and several people perished, their deaths were not in vain. The town was free and would never have to worry about the treacherous snake again. They toasted in honor of the fallen ones and the future that was now possible.

The Tunnels

The next day Teddy and Erik said their goodbyes. On the way out of town they stopped where Ratatoskr had been buried the night before. Flowers, candles and notes already littered the little grave. They thanked their hero and continued on their journey.

They walked past the remains of the giant serpent and back down the dirt path to the tunnels. With Tyhpon gone it would now be safe to pass through, or so they hoped.

The tunnels were dark and seemed to go every which way. A labyrinth that overlapped on itself. They tried their best to go on a straight path, but the many turns and intersecting paths made it near impossible. The further into the maze they got the darker it grew. Soon Erik could no longer even see his hand outstretched in front of his face. He and Teddy both ran their hands along the walls to try and stay on some sort of path.

In the dark depths of the cave a freezing chill rushed over the two. The hair on Erik's arms stood to attention. The chill was soon followed by a haunting voice. A voice neither of which they ever thought they would hear again.

"You may have managed to kill me, but I live on regardless. You may think it ended with me, but it will never end. My many children will avenge me and wreak havoc onto this world. Mark my words. This world will be ruled by my kind once again. Your children or even grandchildren will never be safe from me and my kind. You will be the one responsible for it all!"

And just like that the voice and chill in the air was gone as fast as it had come. An uneasy feeling settled over the two adventurers. They slowly inched their way through the pitch black tunnels. Erik's heart was racing. He had already had a bad feeling before the voice, now that feeling was only intensified. He couldn't shake the feeling that someone was right over his shoulder. Waiting to grab him at any moment. From time to time he would look back, but behind him was just as inky as in front of him. The feeling continued to grow. The darkness even began to play tricks on him. Every now and then he would think he saw an outline of a person or even hear something.

CRUNCH. CRUNCH.

Teddy stopped in his tracks. He had begun to step in something. There were no rocks or twigs. They were solid but fragile. They broke beneath his heavy feet with ease. Teddy had a good idea as to what they might

174

be, but didn't want to frighten Erik any more than what he already was.

"Be careful not to trip. Lift your legs high," suggested Teddy.

So Erik, trying to be careful, began to drag his feet so as not to get too tripped up. Whatever was on the ground began to become higher and more dense as he walked. What started around his ankles now rubbed along his knees. Parts of whatever it was were jagged and felt broken. The sharp edges began to cut at Erik's legs. He tried his best to stay right behind Teddy and take the same path through the debris because it seemed to be crushed down more and easier to pass through.

Teddy ran his paw along the wall until suddenly there was no more wall! He stepped out in front of him slowly with one foot. There was also no more floor!

"Wait a second!" He called behind him to Erik.

They had come too far to turn back now. They didn't dare try to navigate back through the maze of tunnels. As Teddy stood and pondered their next move Erik's bad feeling grew. His heart pounded and his stomach churned. Every hair on his body was standing up. The feeling someone was behind him was overwhelming.

As he stared behind him into the darkness a crunch echoed through the corridor. Erik's heart began to feel as if it were going to pop out of his chest. He slowly raised his hand in the direction the sound had come from. He began to walk forward with his arm outstretched. As he walked forward his hand trembled

175

wildly. He could feel that someone or something was there. To his dismay... he was right in his thinking! His hand flattened against something that was not a wall. It felt cold and damp. It moved in and out as seemingly taking heavy breaths as Erik's hand laid upon what he assumed was the things chest.

Erik's heart stopped. He quickly pulled back his hand. The objects around their feet began to shuffle. Whatever it was, it was moving even closer! Erik turned, forgetting why they had stopped in the first place, and ran into Teddy. The force knocked the unsuspecting bear off balance, and soon they were both plummeting into the vast hole in the ground!

Everything remained too dark to see. They had no idea how long their fall might be. Down into the possible abyss they fell. Erik waited for the worst to happen. He imagined hitting the ground or a row of stalagmites at any moment. The best he could hope for was a body of water, although the distance it had felt like they had fallen would do no good. It would be just as solid as the ground at this point. As all these thoughts rushed through his head, the pit came to an abrupt end.

It was none of the things he had conjured up in his head. It was possibly quite worse. His body hung suspended in air - his arms caught above his head in a strange stringy sticky substance. He was covered in whatever it was. From the sound of it, Teddy was too.

The two struggled and fought to break free. Teddy was able to break several strands, but the further he fell down the more he became entangled.

The two struggled for what felt like forever. They both hung in the air, both too worn out to try and free themselves anymore. As they lay suspended they began to talk and came to the very unsettling agreement that what they were in was none other than a spiderweb. So they waited.

The web began to shake wildly.

"Teddy, is that you?" Erik asked with a trembling voice.

"Wish it was," the bear answered back in a nervous tone.

The web began to shake more and more. It was clear something else was on the web with them! The web began to sink down next to Erik. Something was right next to him! Suddenly the slack returned to the tight lines next to Erik. Whatever it was had gotten back off of the web.

Teddy stared hard in Erik's direction hoping his eyes would adjust just enough to at least see an outline of something, anything. As he stared into the black nothingness eight bright red eyes began to open and stare back. The eyes were right above Erik's head! Erik turned and looked up just in time to see them descending down towards him!

The Orders

Not so far away, the repugnant fat man and his two fairies sat. He reached his hand into a bowl pooled full of a red liquid and pulled out a young fairy-like creature. Its wings had been clipped and its feet and hands bound. It hung limp and looked too worn out to fight as the fat man took an enormous bite from the helpless sprite. He tore away the head, arms and upper body all with one bite. The bottom half with another. He reached down into the pool and pulled out another de-winged victim.

His snack was abruptly interrupted as the door to the throne room swung open. He watched as a messenger made his way to the king.

The seemingly annoyed king looked up from his palm as his spy hurried towards him.

"Tell me you have news of the boy!" he bellowed out before his spy could reach him.

The spy's eyes widened. He had news, but it wasn't the news he knew the king had hoped for. He stuttered at first and then paused. He was afraid to be the one to tell the king the news he had.

"Well?" insisted the Erlking.

"Umm... well sir.... The boy was seen, yes..."

"Excellent. Where is he now? Has anyone captured him yet?"

"Well, sir... he was last seen near the mountains. Entering Typhon's tunnels."

"That's not the outcome I had hoped for... Typhon will surely kill them....I wanted the boy alive... Regardless, the boy will be taken care of. Go to the tunnels and fetch me his body while it's still fresh! This will finally be over!"

The spy's face turned pale.

"Umm.... Actually sir.... The great Typhon has fallen.... He was slain by the boy and his companions in the mountain town...."

"WHHAAATT!!!" roared the evil king.

The dim fires that lit the room erupted. The room was now lit brightly and the Erlking could see the frightened look on the man's face. The explosion had also caused the Ellerkonge to spill his bowl of clipped sprites. Everyone was afraid of what would come next.

Unexpectedly, the king sat back down into his throne and the fires began to dim back down. He sat quietly in deep thought for a moment.

"This boy continues to exceed my expectations... to kill a creature of the old world... This is no small task..... Regardless, despite the luck this boy seems to carry with him he will never make it out of that labyrinth the snake has made in the mountains.... And even if he manages that somehow... When he emerges he will be in the desert. My desert. There will be no more hiding. Spell or no spell!"

He began to laugh maniacally.

"The fools are walking right up to our front door!"

The horn king looked over to his henchman. The fat slob still had blood running down his multiple chins.

"Ellerkonge..... I have a job for you."

"Anything, my lord."

"Be sure that if the boy does emerge from the tunnels he is met with a warm welcome."

"Yes, master."

"O, and Ellerkonge..."

"Yes?"

"Do NOT let him get away again! he's managed to slip through your grubby fingers one too many times!"

The ogress man nodded his head, and he and his fairies exited the throne room.

The Depths

Erik wasn't sure what had happened. Last he remembered, eight red eyes shot down towards him while he was helplessly caught in the web.

"I must've passed out," Erik thought to himself.

Regardless he and Teddy now sat on the floor of an empty cavern surrounded by strange glowing mushrooms. There seemed to be only one tunnel attached to the cave and it had heavy curtains of webs hung over the entrance. Above they could see the intersection of webs they must've been trapped in. They went up for as far as they could see.

"Where are we?" Erik asked Teddy, hoping he remembered more than him.

"Not sure. Right after the eyes came down on you I began to fall slowly through the webs. After I broke through the bottom I seemed to be lowered into this cavern." He too seemed almost as confused.

The more they looked around, the more curious the cavern became. All sorts of odds and ends were scattered about. Some were even set up on janky shelves

181

carved out in the walls. There was even a stack of books perched in the corner. It looked as though maybe someone lived in the cave!

Out of nowhere, music began to play. An old phonograph on the opposite end of the room had begun to turn. The web curtain in front of them swung open to reveal a bright room full of glowing mushrooms. There in the center of the small room was a skeleton in a top hat and coat.

"Welcome, travelers!" spoke the well-dressed skeleton.

Erik and Teddy both jumped a bit when it began to talk. Things only grew more strange from there. The skeleton began to tap his foot to the beat of the music. The next thing they knew the skeleton had broken into full song and dance, singing every word to his song in perfect step while doing so.

The two adventurers starred in total bewilderment. Neither one of them had ever seen a skeleton talk... much less sing... and dance! How had they gone from falling down a hole and getting stuck in a spider web to watching a skeleton perform _Dardanella_!

"I think I hit my head on the fall...,." Teddy stated as he stared at the performance.

"Did we die?" Erik asked half seriously.

When the skeleton was done with his performance, he made a proper bow. As he did Erik noticed several strings tied to his back that ran to the top of the room. It was a puppet! After the bow the curtains closed back.

"Well, what did you think of our show?" the voice seemed to be coming from all around them.

Erik and Teddy weren't sure how to answer. It was like nothing else they had ever seen. That was for sure.

"Splendid," Erik finally answered back.

"O, good. We've practiced for years. Never had an audience to perform for!" the voice excitedly replied.

"Come out where we can see you," Erik requested.

There was silence for a moment before the voice replied.

"Okay... but if I do you have to promise to not be afraid!"

"We promise!" They both said in unison. Their curiosity was maddening at this point.

At their answer an enormous hairy spider began to emerge from a hole in the wall. Erik and(.) Teddy both jumped back in horror. The spider recoiled a bit at the sight of this.

"You said you wouldn't be afraid!" he said timidly as he began to recoil back into the hole in the wall.

"I'm sorry. We don't mean to be!! You're just not what we were expecting. Your looks don't quite match your personality! You're quite menacing in looks!" replied Erik.

"Not to worry! I love humans.... Or at least I think I do! All the ones I've read about anyways! The Joad family, Thomas Sutpen, Addie Bundren, George Milton and Lennie Small! Your species is so fascinating!

183

I would never hurt you! Or any of your kind for that matter!""

Erik looked out of the corner of his eye at the stage.

"What about him?" he said, pointing towards the stage, referring of course to the skeleton that had been on stage.

The spider looked at the boy very confused. Well, as confused as a spider could look.

"What about 'em?"

"Well, he's not alive. Something had to have happened to him!"

At this remark the skeleton popped his head out from behind the curtain.

"Not alive!!!" the skeleton remarked with an offended tone.

The skeleton's mouth dropped open, and he turned to look at the spider.

"Can you believe this kid!? Just because he's got a little more meat on his bones he thinks he can talk down to me! Just saw me perform an entire routine and still has the nerve to say I'm not alive!....."

At first Erik was taken aback. "Was the skeleton alive?" he thought to himself. It wouldn't be the strangest thing he's seen. He soon noticed one of the spider's arms moving ever so slowly. He was still puppeteering the skeleton!

The spider and skeleton began to converse with each other or with themselves. As they did so, it was clear to Erik and Teddy that maybe this spider wasn't all present in this world. Not only that, but he had clearly been alone and very lonely to say the least.

The spider noticed the strange looks he was receiving from his guests and decided it was best for him to talk to them directly.

"I'm sorry, it's very rude of me not to introduce myself. My name is Anansi. My friend here is Norm... if you can't tell we've been down here a very long time. As long as I can remember actually. I live in these tunnels. Collecting treasures from them. All sorts of knicknacks from your kind. I must admit, you're the first human I've met besides Norm. Much more talkative too. It took Norm years to start talking to me! No one. Ever makes it this far into the tunnels. You're quite the surprise!"

"Well, it may have something to do with the giant snake being dead. Made passing through much easier," Teddy said with a tiny smirk.

The spider's demeanor instantly changed. The skeleton head fell back behind the curtain and the spider began pacing about on the walls.

"It can't be! The mighty Typhon can't be slain!"
Erik shook his head.

"He can be, and he was!"

The spider's pace quickened. He practically ran back and forth on the wall. He was muttering to his left as he did so.

"No, no, no, no... they lie... he can not die... and yet... they've made it this far into the tunnels... maybe.... Could it be so? ....."

185

Anansi crawled over to the curtain and stuck his head behind it to talk with Norm. The two of them began to have a conversation.

"Do you believe them, Norm?"

"They did make it through his tunnels...."

"Now what! How will we get our treasures... how will we eat!"

"No meat, no bugs! Not any worth eating anyways!"

"We'll starve to death! Well, I will, anyway!"

"They've ruined everything!"

Erik thought now would be a good time to cut in and talk to the spider before he dove too far into his own head. Which clearly could be very deep.

"Excuse me, I know you are dealing with quite the dilemma... but we are in a dilemma ourselves. You say you would never hurt a human... if we don't get out of these tunnels we'll die. You say you collect treasures from them. Does that mean you know the way out?"

The spider seemed to focus back into reality for a moment.

"Out??.... Sure, we know a way. Never really needed *out* though. Everything we needed was *in*. The tunnels provided for Anansi and Norm... maybe it's time we go to the "out"!...."

Anansi stared off into space seemingly trying to figure out what to do. Finally, he made a decision.

"We will lead you out."

"Thank you, Anansi! If there's anything we can do to repay you please, let us know!"

"Well.... We were wondering if maybe you would let us join you in the out. We've known nothing except these tunnels and those books. Maybe an adventure would be fitting for us! See the world we've grown to love so much! Meet more humans such as yourself!"

Erik didn't want to tell him the harsh reality that a giant spider would probably have a difficult time integrating with the outside world. He hated to give the spider false hope, but he knew that was the only way he'd ever get out of the tunnels. Besides, maybe there was a small chance the giant arachnid would be welcomed somewhere. Erik gave the spider his answer.

"Of course you can come with us! Maybe Oberon will need a mighty spider in his army! Or even a grand puppet master to entertain his kingdom!"

And so it was in motion. The excited spider grabbed two large bags and began to pack. With one, he carefully folded up Norm. With the other he packed some of his favorite treasures. Soon they were off.

Erik and Teddy each picked some of the glowing fungus that grew on the walls to take. Even with the spider leading the way it would be much easier if they could see where they were going. Erik even grabbed some and stuffed them into his bag just in case.

They wound every which way through the tunnels. One not familiar with the caverns would surely be lost. A light began to shine into their current path. They were reaching the end!

At first Erik began to run towards the light. He was beyond excited to be out of the caves. As he reached the opening a wind brought in a whiff of a familiar pungent smell. He slowed and eventually stopped as the smell grew the closer they came to the exit. Teddy became instantly alert. He too knew the smell of the Ellerkonge all too well. Anansi seemed quite confused as to why they stopped.

"Why have you stopped? That's it right there, that's the out!" the spider exclaimed.

The boy lowered his voice to a whisper.

"Are there other ways out?" he asked.

"No, only the way you came in. Why do we not go out here though? What's the matter?"

"I believe there's a very bad man waiting for us outside."

"Does he mean you harm?"

"Yes... he does."

"Then I will go see this bad man. You are my friend, and if he means you harm then he is my enemy."

Anansi dropped his two bags and walked past Teddy and Erik towards the exit. The spider emerged from the tunnel throwing the Ellerkonge off for a moment. Being that most of the Arachne served the dark lord he knew most of them and where they lived.

"Who are you? What brings you to these caves?" the Ellerkonge asked in a demanding tone.

"I am Anansi, and these caves are my home for as long as I can remember!"

"So you aren't an Arachne of the king's army? A feral creature?" the fat man scoffed.

The decently well self-educated spider was appalled at the grotesque man's statement. He immediately shot back.

"Feral!?...Sir, I assume you do not know the meaning of the word. For one, I am not wild. More so, I have never been in captivity. If anything you are more feral than I... you are for sure in the least, a malodorous ignoramus!"

The Ellerkonge didn't understand what the spider had said, but he could gather that it was offensive. His face became bright red with anger.

"If you're not part of the king's army then you are trespassing!"

"Trespassing!? How could I have lived somewhere my whole life and be trespassing in it now!?"

"By law, I could kill you.... But today I have an offer for you! One where you get away with your life. To be free to do as you please. A small simple task is all I ask."

"And what would this simple task entail?"

"There's two people roaming around in those tunnels. A bear and a small boy. Bring them to me and not only will you be free to go but will be rewarded for your efforts as well. The king is a generous king."

Anansi looked back towards the tunnel where Erik and Teddy stood. The easier and probably smarter thing to do would be turn them over and reap the many rewards. For just a brief moment the spider even thought of it.

"I have seen these trespassers among the tunnels! I passed them on my way here, in fact!" exclaimed the spider.

"How far back are they? Would you be able to find them again?"

"Of course! As I said, I've lived here my entire life. It will be quite easy to find them!"

"Then go! Bring them to me, here! Then you will be vastly rewarded!"

The spider looked back towards the tunnel again.

"Okay... very well.... But I will need your help.... As you said the boy travels with an enormous bear!"

"Fine! Then lead the way!" The Ellerkonge said as he struggled to get up off of the stump he had sat himself upon.

"Just this way. It shouldn't take long at all."

During this conversation, Erik and Teddy could hear every word as it echoed into the cave. They slowly backed up as the spider and the Ellerkonge entered the cave. Erik took he and Teddy's glowing mushrooms and put them in his bag so they were completely shrouded in dark. Erik hoped that the spider had some sort of plan and wasn't leading him straight to them as it somewhat sounded.

The spider had made a small lead out of a web that the Ellerkonge had tied around his fist to not get lost in the tunnels. As the two turned from the exiting tunnel it instantly went dark. Erik couldn't see them but he could hear the cumbersome footsteps of the

Ellerkonge moving closer. He then made out Anansi's eyes. They were heading right towards them!

Teddy and Erik dare not make a move at this point. Even the slightest shuffle and they ran the risk of being heard. At this point Erik had put all of his trust into Anansi, and he hoped he hadn't made a mistake in doing so. The tunnel they stood in was wide and so Erik and Teddy squeezed to the side the best they could. It was especially challenging for Teddy as his gut hung out a bit.

To Erik's relief the spider led the ogress man down the opposite side of their tunnel. Anansi and the Ellerkonge walked past them and further into the caves. The smell almost burnt Erik's nostrils as he passed by. His first instinct was to gag, but he knew it would be heard so he held it in the best he could as the bodily function fought hard.

As the Ellerkonge was led further into the caverns, our heroes slowly began to make their way back towards the exit tunnel. As they did, Teddy accidentally kicked over a small pile of rocks that were on the ground. They listened in horror as they heard the rocks roll towards the Ellerkonge. The giant man stopped in his tracks and looked back. He couldn't see anything but he knew something was afoot. As he tried to head back towards the exiting tunnel the string around his hand tightened.

"You play games with me! Release me now!" demanded the Ellerkonge.

Anansi tried his best to hold the man, but the angrier he became the stronger he grew. The web eventually snapped, and the Ellerkonge headed back the way they had come. There at the end of the exiting tunnel the Ellerkonge could see the out lines of the bear and small boy. They had almost escaped!

For the Ellerkonge to be the size he was he was surprisingly fast. He began to gain on them quickly. As Erik and Teddy exited the tunnels, the Ellerkonge was right at their heels. Just as he was about to reach the opening, the light at the end was suddenly blocked. The giant spider stood before him and the heroes!

"Go, my friends! I will deal with this bad man! If I don't ever see you again, know that I'm thankful for the small time that I knew you!" Anansi shouted out as he guarded the exit.

The two ran as fast as they could into the open desert.

They were just passing over the horizon in the distance when the Ellerkonge emerged from the cave wiping blue blood from his hands.

In the White Room

An old man filled with self-hate and a bag full of regrets walked down the white hallway with his head staring at the ground. He had been scared many times before, but it was nothing compared to this. He felt as though he was sinking into the floor as he walked. There were so many things he felt inside. So many things he had to say. Things he may never get the chance to. Everything he had tried in life he seemed to fail at. Constantly making the wrong choices. Just as he had begun to love himself finally the rug was pulled out from under him. The call was unexpected. A shot in the dark really. On the other line awaited the news no person wishes to hear... he came to the end of the white hallway and opened the heavy door. Machines kept that which he loved most alive. He was helpless. He was angry. He was ready to wake up from the nightmare at any moment.

Making Camp

As the sun set the temperature quickly began to drop. The bear and the boy had traveled quite far into the desert now. The caves were far behind. With them they hoped for the Ellerkonge.

"I'm getting cold," shivered the boy.

"We can't risk making a fire. The desert is too flat. We could be seen for miles," Teddy replied.

The two found a large rock that blocked some of the night winds and huddled together. Teddy did his best to keep the boy warm in his arms through the night. The night grew colder and colder and into the early morning Teddy had even grown frigid. Even with his thick coat. Frost had begun to gather at the tips of his fur.

He looked down at Erik bundled tightly in his arms. The boy was sleeping but shivering violently as he slept. His mouth had begun to turn blue.

Teddy knew if he didn't do something soon Erik may not make it through the night. With one arm Teddy cradled Erik closely. With the other he began to gather brush and dead wood that was close by. Luckily, the open white sands and bright moon made it very easy to see. It didn't take long for Teddy to gather enough for a bundle to start a fire. The only thing he needed now was a way to start a fire.

He began to rummage through Erik's bag, eventually finding a pack of matches that the mama bird had packed. Now, striking a match isn't necessarily a hard task to most, but when you are a bear and have paws as opposed to fingers it makes it a great deal more complicated. First, he struggled to open the box. Once he got it open, he couldn't pull a match from said box. After much struggle and serious concentration, Teddy managed to grab one with the tips of two of his claws. After one pass of the back of the box, the match he had struggled with fell to the ground. This happened two more times. Teddy began to get frustrated. He sat Erik on the ground next to him and tried again.

All of the moving around and struggling had woken Erik. He was curious as to what was going on. So he quietly laid with his eyes open and watched as the bear tried to pull another match from the box. Teddy concentrated hard. He moved incredibly slowly and even had his tongue sticking slightly out of the corner of his mouth. After a few passes he was able to pick one out. Then, lo' and behold, he dropped it at the first strike.

Erik looked at the ground and saw the several matches that had fallen. He couldn't help but laugh out loud. Teddy quickly turned to the boy.

"You think it's funny!? I'm over here trying to keep your scrawny ass alive! How long have you been watching!?" he roared

"La... Long enough." Erik giggled as he struck a match for the bear.

"I th-th-thought you sss-said it was ttt-too risky to light a fff-fire," he continued. The poor boy shivered as he spoke.

"We shouldn't, but I don't see many choices. It hasn't even reached the coldest part of the morning yet. I can only do so much to keep you warm," replied Teddy as he blew on the fire to get it to catch.

So they lit a small fire behind the big rock and huddled close to it. It wasn't much, but it was enough to make it through the night.

The Ellerkonge knew his master would not be happy that he had failed him again. Even though now they were on the edge of the Erlking's domain, there would be many spies and soldiers among them. HE had to be the one to bring the boy in. No one else. He was tasked with the job. He wasn't going to return to the king empty handed. He stood on high ground and scanned the desert all night. He could see for miles in every direction. He waited patiently for any sign as to which way the boy could have gone.

Around two in the morning, the tiring Ellerkonge saw a flicker in the distance. It looked like a lightning bug hovering. It was so small and far off. If it was the boy he had made it quite a ways from the caves. He watched as the light remained. It was a fire! It had to be them!

Even though it was quite the distance, he knew he could still make it to them before daybreak. He began to head towards the distant glow.

The Red Morning

The top of the sun barely peeked out over the desert. A reddish hue filled the air. The Ellerkonge had reached the unsuspecting duo. Their fire had burnt down to embers and they slept soundly under a massive rock. Erik was almost completely covered by the massive bear. This made things more difficult for the Ellerkonge, but nonetheless, he would finally complete his task.

He pulled a knife from his side and inched towards the bear quietly. As he did so the bear's nostrils began to flare. They had started to fill with the rank stench of the man. Just as the Ellerkonge was about to jab the knife into Teddy his eyes shot open. The great bear jumped to his feet and in one swoop batted the knife from the Ellerkonge's hand.

Erik awoke to the two locked in hand to hand just above him. He quickly rolled out of their way and watched as the two went blow to blow. The Ellerkonge, though bulbous, was incredibly strong. He fought toe to toe with the grizzly . Neither seemingly having the upper hand. They threw each other back and forth and landed heavy blows upon each other. The white sand surrounding them had begun to turn red.

As the fight raged on, the Ellerkonge began to grow desperate for an upper hand. Teddy thrashed his massive paw down on the Ellerkonge's head, knocking him to his knees. When he did so the putrid man grabbed a handful of the hot coals from the dying fire and threw them into Teddy's face. The coals burnt the fur on Teddy's face and the soot filled his eyes; temporarily blinding him!

The bear stepped back holding his face in pain. When he did so the Ellerkonge picked up the knife from the ground nearby. As Teddy's vision returned, though blurry, he could make out the fat man thrusting his knife towards him! He tried to move but it was too late. The blade pierced deep into his ribs. As he drew back his paw to retaliate he was stabbed again in the pit of his arm, then the stomach. The Ellerkonge wildly stabbed at the bear. Piercing him several times.

"Die! Die damn you!" he shouted as he repetitively jabbed the giant animal.

Teddy was determined to keep fighting. His purpose was to keep Erik safe and he would gladly die doing so. Blood began to mat in his fur, but still he kept fighting. He fought hard, but began to wear down. He wobbled back and forth until finally falling to his knees before the Ellerkonge.

He looked over to see if maybe Erik had been able to escape during the fight. That maybe he would be safe... to his dismay he hadn't. Erik had been tied up by the Ellerkonge's two fairies. The boy screamed in horror as he watched his best friend fading from this world. The Ellerkonge laughed as he wiped the blood from his knife.

He had won! He had conquered the mighty bear and captured the boy. After all these years... he had finally won. As he laughed and celebrated his victory Teddy managed to lunge forward for one final blow. He came down on the Ellerkonge's head with as much force as his body would allow. Splitting the foul man's head almost in half!

As he did so the Ellerkonge plunged the final blow of his knife into his gut. Teddy fell face first into a pool of his own blood. The Ellerkonge screamed in pain and held what was left of his face up with his hand. His eye swung below his hand. It held on by one thin string of tendon. Blood poured down the side of his body.

The two fairies that had captured Erik were now in a complete frenzy. They flew frantically around their master's head not knowing what to do. He stumbled a bit before falling to his knees. During all of this Erik managed to break the tiny strands that held him. He didn't know what to do. He stared in horror at Teddy's lifeless body, covered in blood. The overwhelming sense to run over took him and without even realizing he was doing so he was high tailing it across the desert. Leaving the Ellerkonge and the fairies far behind.

Only a Matter of Time

The Ellerkonge entered the throne room. A cloth wrapped around his head and eye. Fresh blood still seeping through it. The horned king was less than amused at the sight.

"I see no boy Ellerkonge! Failed me yet again!!" he bellowed.

"Yes, my lord. The body escaped. But he won't make it far! He travels alone now!" the Ellerkonge pleaded.

"I may have failed you in retrieving him, but I did manage to kill his bear!"

The king's temperament began to calm.

"So, the bear is dead?"

"Yes, my lord!"

"So... the boy wanders my desert alone? Maybe I won't kill you today for your continuing failure. You've been by my side for eons. For that and the killing of the bear I will only consider this a partial failure. I warn you though. Partial or not, it WILL be your last! Now go... get your head put back together. You have a search party to lead!"

After the Ellerkonge left the room, the horned king called upon one of his servants and advised him to send word to all of his spies and generals.

"The boy is here. Find him and be rewarded beyond your wildest dreams!"

It wouldn't be long before every scoundrel in the desert and close by was on high alert and on the lookout for the boy. It would now be only a matter of time before the boy was in the clutches of the Erlking!

The Old Town

Erik's lips cracked and his body ached. He had been running all day. The heat had taken its toll on him. His legs shook with every step he took. As the sun went down he welcomed the initial cold front. Though soon he would remember the harsh night of the desert. He began to worry.

As he passed over a dune, he could make out a group of lights in the distance. It looked to be a town there in the middle of nowhere!

He was almost crawling by the time he reached the town. Every few steps his knees would buckle, but he did it! He made it to the town. To his delight there on the edge of town sat a water pump! He drank until he almost made himself throw up. He had never been so parched before in his life. After he rehydrated himself he began to look around.

The early morning cold had begun to settle in. The rest of his body began to tremble like his legs. A close by barn seemed more than inviting at the time. It was well insulated inside and a good place to hide and get some sleep. He grabbed an extra horse blanket that hung from the wall and made him a space in a pile of hay.

The next morning, Erik was awoken by the sound of a rooster right at daybreak. Though it was still early and Erik was still quite tired, he figured it best to get up and out of the barn before the owner came along and he was discovered.

As he snuck out of the barn and onto the streets, he noticed many of the town's folk were already up and about. Everyone seemed to have a task or destination in mind and paid the boy no attention. He made his way down the Main Street. If you would still call it a street. It was not paved or even had gravel or stone. It was all dirt! Minus a few spots that had wood laid across. Erik assumed it was for some of the many holes that were abundant.

The more Erik looked around the more the town seemed familiar. The stores and buildings were all made of wood. They all stood side by side and faced towards the road he walked on. Then it hit him! The town looked like the towns in the old westerns he would watch with Luthor!

"Luthor...," Erik thought to himself.

It all seemed like another life. Maybe it was another life. A whole childhood, even into adulthood. His memories seemed so clouded, so distant. They all seemed jumbled up and unclear. He could remember so many things from his life in a world so different. One with loving aunts and adopted grandfathers. Yet he remembered so many things from this world so clearly. Even memories seemed familiar to this place. It was a mess. As what seemed like two life's worth of memories began rushing through his head he sat on a nearby set of stairs.

There were so many memories and feelings all speeding through his brain at once. Then, they caught up to the present. Erik had grown so used to having Teddy by his side that he had taken it for granted. The morning before had been so surreal. It was like his head had just ignored what had happened and Teddy was still right there beside him.

The morning began to replay in his head. Every bloody detail. The look in Teddy's eyes just before they closed. Erik burst out into tears.

As he sat and cried a strangely familiar sounding voice came from over his shoulder. One he had not heard in a very long time.

"What's the matter boy?" asked someone with a Southern American accent.

Erik wasn't sure if it was because Luthor was on his mind, but the voice sounded just like him! He quickly turned his head to see. Unfortunately, it wasn't Luthor. Although Erik wasn't sure why he thought it might be.

Erik had seen some strange creatures while in this world, but what stood before him was definitely one of the most unique. He had heard of centaurs before. Half man, half horse, but they usually had the top half of a human. This thing speaking to him seemed to be a horse walking on his hind legs like a human! He even had hands like a human! As Erik stared, the horseman spoke again.

"Is everything okay?" he asked.

The boy looked up at the horse with his eyes full of tears. He wasn't okay, not at all. He couldn't think of what to say though. He had too many things in his head to gather even just one thought. Erik simply turned and buried his head in his arms. Trying his best not to cry out loud again. It was clear to the horse that something was wrong.

"Why don't you come on over to my house. It's not far. My wife can cook you up a good meal. A good warm meal can ease a little bit of any pain." The horse extended his hand to help Erik up.

Erik accepted the invitation and the two began to walk down the street. Erik noticed as they walked that the horse man wore a badge on his vest.

"Are you the sheriff?" he asked in a mildly excited tone.

"That I am," the horse smiled.

"Then you're one of the good guys right?" Erik timidly asked.

"Well, I try to be, yes. I have an example to set for my children and a town to keep safe. I do my best to do what's right.... What about you? You one of the good guys?"

Erik nodded his head reassuringly.

"Well, since we're both good guys, maybe we should be more acquainted. My name is Enbarr. What's yours?"

"My name is Erik."

"Erik, good name. Strong name. Well Erik, what brings you to Pronghorn? This place ain't exactly on the way to nowhere. Nowhere good anyways."

"Well, to be honest, I got a little lost."

Erik wasn't sure how much trust he could put into his new acquaintance. He was careful as to what he said.

"Got lost? Well, where were you trying to get to?" Enbarr asked.

Erik thought for a moment. "What harm would it do in telling him where I was trying to get to... maybe he could point me in the right direction," He thought to himself. He decided it best to answer truthfully.

"I was on my way to see King Oberon," Erik answered.

Enbarr stopped walking and turned to the boy.

"Oberon? What does a boy like you want with the Fae?" he asked.

Not exactly liking the response he had gotten, Erik decided to not say anything more about his journey for the time being.

"My business is my own!" Erik said with an annoyed tone.

"Indeed it is, my friend. No need to be offended. I only ask because those pesky fairy creatures aren't nothin' but trouble!"

Enbarr could see he had made the boy uncomfortable and he wasn't going to elaborate any more on his journey. He tried to ease the tension.

"You're on the wrong side of the mountains if you're looking for Oberon. He's quite a ways from here. I'd say you're more than a little lost friend. Where did you travel from? It had to be from the West! Where are you from?"

Erik lowered his head as he spoke.

"I... I'm not entirely sure anymore...," answered the boy.

"You don't remember where you're from?"

"No, not exactly. I once did. Everything is such a mess now... I'm not sure I even know what's real and what isn't anymore"

"Well...," the horse proceeded to poke Erik.

"You seem real to me!... as far as I know, I'm real too. So.. seems like this is all real, right?" continued the horse.

Erik shrugged his shoulders.

"That's the problem. It all feels real. It's like I've lived in two worlds at once," he sighed.

"Some of us live in our dreams. To some they even feel more real than real life."

The two had now walked a little ways out of town and were approaching a humble little farm. Enbarr was greeted joyfully by two little foals.

"Daddy! Daddy!" they shouted as they jumped into his arms.

Enbarr introduced Erik to his children and took him to meet his wife. She was a very sweet and inviting person. She had a beautiful white mane that was braided and wore a pretty blue dress. Enbarr introduced Erik as his new friend. She greeted him as a new friend with welcome arms.

"Well, hello there sweetie! I was just finishing up lunch. Come, sit, have some!"

Erik sat and ate. Enbarr's wife had made a vegetable stew that was amazing to say the least! As he ate he watched Enbarr through the window playing with his children in the yard. Something about the sight made Erik feel at peace for a moment. A smile ran across his face. He finished his plate and took it to the sink and thanked Enbarr's wife for lunch.

"Thank you so much for lunch mam! It was delicious!"

"My pleasure. You're welcome to join us any time!"

Erik stood on the front porch and continued to watch Enbarr and his little ones play.

The Little Old Groundhog

Far on the other side of the desert, a little groundhog had journeyed from her burrow and was gathering some herbs. Normally she wouldn't travel all the way out to the desert, but she was in need of a certain flower that only grew on the cacti. As she gathered her flowers she noticed something strange. Many wild vultures had gathered around something quite large on the ground. She decided to go see what it was. As she got closer she could make out what the vultures had gathered around. It was a bear!

She shooed away the birds and began to look over the bear. Blood covered the bear and the ground surrounding it. The groundhog opened the grizzly's eye. They were badly glazed over and seemed to have no sensitivity to light. Next, she checked his mouth. She pried open the giant bear's mouth with her tiny hand

and looked in. His tongue had turned white. It was clear he had lost a lot of blood. Surely the poor thing was dead.

She held her little head onto the bear's chest. She listened closely. Though incredibly faint she could hear a heartbeat! The bear was alive!

The Gila Gang

Erik had joined in on the fun and the four of them were in the midst of a game of hide and seek when a woman came running towards Enbarr's house. She looked quite frightened. Enbarr met her at the gate.

"What's wrong Agatha?" he asked the panicked woman.

"The Gilas are in town tearing apart everything! They're looking for..."

She paused for a moment and stared right at Erik.

"A boy," she finished.

Enbarr ordered his children and Erik back into the house and headed into town. Erik watched as Enbarr walked down the road.

"This isn't right... they're looking for me! I have to go with him!" He pleaded to the wife.

"No dear, you're safe here. My husband will take care of everything," she replied.

"NO! they'll just keep coming. I can't lose anyone else. I can't have anyone else die because of me!" he pleaded.

Erik began to charge out the door but was caught by the tail of his shirt. He begged to be let go.

"PLEASE! Let me go! I HAVE to go!"

"It's Enbarr's job to keep the town safe, he's fought the Gila monsters before. He will be fine, I promise! Stay sweet boy, where you're safe."

"NO! You don't understand! As long as I'm here you're all in danger! You, your beautiful children! Anyone who tries to help me! Please, I beg of you. Let me go. Let me save your husband... let me save your family!"

"But you're just a child..."

She could see the desperation in the boy's eyes. There was much more going on than she could ever understand. Her motherly instinct wanted so badly to simply lock the door and block the way, but something else inside her assured her that the right thing to do was let the boy pass.

"Please, be careful," she said as she opened the door for him.

Erik could already hear gunshots in the distance. He began to run as fast as he could towards town.

When he arrived he could see Enbarr ducked down behind a stack of barrels. Two lizards lay dead in the street, but several more looked to be set up around town. Every time Enbarr tried to move they shot at him.

He was pinned down! Erik looked around trying to devise a plan as quickly as possible.

"Argh"

His concentration was quickly broken. Enbarr held his arm. He had been shot! Erik no longer had time to make a plan! He just knew he had to save his friend. He couldn't let someone else get hurt for his sake. Without hesitation he ran out into the street in front of Enbarr!

"STOP!" he shouted.

The leader nodded his head and all of his men lowered their weapons. He walked up to the boy and looked him up and down. An enormous grin began to stretch across his face.

"This is him! I'm sure of it! We got 'em boys!"

His gang began to hoot and holler in celebration. He turned Erik around and tied his hands together. Before he could take the first step Enbarr stood up from behind the barrels with his gun drawn. Pointed right at the gang leader's head.

"Leave the boy be!" he ordered.

Every gang member lifted their gun back up and pointed it right at Enbarr. The gang leader stepped close to the horse.

"Tell me sheriff. Is this boy worth dyin' for?" he hissed into his ear.

BANG

Enbarr shot the Gila monster under his chin. A fountain of blood began spraying into the air. He quickly grabbed the lifeless lizard and began to use him as a

215

shield to oncoming fire. Erik ducked behind some cover and began to untie his bonds. It was clear Enbarr wasn't going to let Erik be taken. Even if it was by choice.

The gunfire continued to erupt throughout the town. Erik couldn't even tell where Enbarr was. He was only seeing the Gila monsters falling from the rooftops one by one. Even though he was thoroughly outnumbered it was beginning to look like maybe he could win this fight!

Suddenly, the sky to the west began to turn black. Something was coming towards them! Whatever it was blocked out the sun!

The Oldest of Friends

Teddy slowly opened his eyes. Standing looking over him was a little old groundhog with one green eye and one blue. She had an enormous smile on her face.

"Glad to see you finally awake!" she spoke.

Teddy sat up and looked around. His sides ached as he did so. He was covered in bandages and smelled very strange. He had somehow ended up in a little house. A house that seemed to be underground given the walls made of dirt.

"How could this little groundhog have gotten me in her home?" Teddy wondered.

As he looked around he couldn't help but feel an overwhelming sense of *deja vu*. Everything about the little burrow seemed familiar.

"How did I get here? And where exactly is it?" Teddy asked.

"Don't tell me you've forgotten all about me Teddy!" replied the sweet little groundhog.

Teddy's eyes grew big. It took a moment for him to recognize her. He hadn't seen her in such a long time. She had grown so old. So had he. Soon as it hit him he grabbed her up and held her tight in his arms.

The Old Woods

Erik looked towards the dark cloud that quickly descended upon them from the West. Only it wasn't a cloud. It moved way too fast to be such. As it grew closer Erik could see it was a giant murder of crows! He began to panic. Enbarr was holding his own against the Gilas but he wouldn't stand a chance against what headed towards them!

He had to keep Enbarr and his family safe. He ran out of town as fast as he could towards the crows. He stood out in the open and wildly flailed his arms about to get their attention. Like an ocean wave they crashed down onto the boy. When the cloud of birds lifted from the ground Erik was gone!

As Enbarr killed the last Gila monster he looked to the west just in time to see the boy disappear into the swarm of birds. He let out a deep sigh.

"Damnit kid!" he muttered as he watched them fly away.

The crows carried the boy over the vast desert. The golden and white sands began to turn red then turned to dirt. Soon they flew over dark red mud and a ground riddled with twisted old roots and deadwood. Past the mud they began to enter a tangled forest filled with mossy trees. The trees themselves all bent over and curving and twisting every which way.

The crows flew down into the trees and dropped Erik into a ring made of rocks. Erik jumped to his feet. The old forest seemed familiar but in no way good. His stomach curled and heart began to pound heavily. As he tried to step out of the circle of rocks he was stopped in his tracks by some sort of invisible wall. He tried to escape for quite some time, but it was no use. No matter what he tried, the invisible shield stayed. He was trapped!

As night approached the Ellerkonge's distinct repugnant smell began to fill the surrounding woods. Erik hoped he had died from the blow to the head he received from Teddy, but he wouldn't be so lucky. He knew that smell all too well! He was close!

Erik tried even harder to break the barrier. Still to no avail. He began to hear a laugh coming from behind him. Erik slowly turned to see the Ellerkonge standing there holding his belly cackling. The ugly man was even more scared now. He sported an eye patch and a metal plate that looked to be nailed down on half of the top of his head.

"Like to see you wiggle your way out of this one!" the Ellerkonge boasted.

"I'm sure you would! Sure it's hard to see anything nowadays! Eye patch and all," replied Erik with a snide tone.

The Ellerkonge did not find it amusing at all. He growled like a wild animal and proceeded to walk into the circle with Erik.

"Glad you're amused boy!" snarled the ogres man.

As he spoke, his two fairies began to circle around his lower half, lighting up his filthy pants. The Ellerkonge continued to chuckle as Erik looked in horror at the blood stains that covered him.

"See this smear here, the blue one?... that's your spider friend... and all this here... the blood that's still a little fresh?... That's your pain in the ass bear friend. This may be all that's left of him. The vultures have probably picked him clean by now." The Ellerkonge now had a giant smile on his face as he spoke.

Erik clenched his fists. He had never wished to harm someone so bad in his life.

"You bastard," he muttered.

The Ellerkonge was amused at the boy's anger and began to laugh even harder at the apparent rage. He knew the boy couldn't do him any harm. With the bear gone he was helpless. This was his world now. He wouldn't burn from the touch of the boy. There was nothing in his way of victory! He leaned in to grab the boy. Erik didn't know what to do but he could feel his anger boiling in him.

AHHHHHHHH!

Erik screamed in rage at the Ellerkonge. As he did the ground shook violently and the sound of breaking glass surrounded them. Erik took a step back. His foot stepped over the rocks. He was out of the circle! The barrier had broken! He turned and ran as fast as he could into the old woods. The Ellerkonge screamed after him as he ran.

"Go ahead! These are HIS woods! You'll never make it out!"

The woods were thick and before long Erik was covered in cuts and bruises. He began to slow his pace and gather his thoughts. He took in his surroundings as he did. He hadn't realized how dark it had gotten while he was running. He sat on a fallen log and began to catch his breath. As he sat there in the cold dark forest, out of breath and all alone, he wondered if it was even worth it anymore. Just give up. Let the horned king take him.

Then, as if the king had been listening to his thoughts, the evil fairy king emerged from the darkness before the boy.

"You've finally made it home," spoke the Erlking.

He reached out his hand to the boy. Erik, tired, broken, lost... reached out and took the king's hand.

In the White Room (Part 2)

The machines began to make wild noises. Suddenly everything had taken a turn for the worst! The man in the white room screamed down the empty hallway for help. There was no one. The noises grew louder. He began to pray to whatever God may listen.

"Please, please no."

Many Years Past

The groundhog walked to the table with a teapot in hand. She and Teddy had been talking for hours. Teddy didn't recognize her at first but it didn't take long to realize she was the very person who helped raise him as a cub. She was the reason for his calmer nature and mostly proper etiquette. She played a huge part in who he was. He felt bad he hadn't recognized her right away. It just seemed so long ago. So many things had happened since then. Things that overshadowed his cub hood.

As she poured the tea her burrow began to shake wildly. Teddy jumped to his feet.

"Earthquake?" he asked.

The groundhog only smiled as she picked up a picture that had fallen to the ground.

"No my dear. He's just finally remembering who he is!" she smirked.

"Who?"

The groundhog turned the picture around towards Teddy. It was a picture of a much younger him and a very small boy. That boy was Erik!

As You Do Onto Others

When Erik opened his eyes he was inside of a dark room. Vines ran over the top of it. One wall was made completely out of bars and didn't even seem to have a door on it. Outside stood a small troll. Erik's first instincts were to stoop down into the dingy hay pile and await whatever fate the Erlking had in store for him. He had been caught. It was finally over. Or so he thought. Like a scratching in his head he heard a voice. It urged him not to give up. That he couldn't give up. The voice grew louder and louder.

"Now is NOT your time!" screamed the voice in his head.

"Okay, okay!" Erik said out loud as he sat up.

The troll looked into the cell with a curious look on his face.

"What was that?" asked the guard.

"Uhh.. nothing... talking to myself."

"Already losing it eh? That's not a good sign, "joked the troll.

When the troll turned back around Erik began to look around the cell for any sign of a way out. There were no hinges or cuts in anything. Either the way into the cell was very well hidden or like the circle, there was some sort of magic involved.

"You won't find a way out," remarked the troll with his back still turned.

Erik thought about the circle and how he had broken out. He screamed as loud as he could to see if it would break something like it had before. Only this time there was no ground shaking or anything giving way. The goblin held his ears tight and yelled at the boy.

"What on Earth are you doing!? Quiet boy! What good will yelling do? Other than making us both go deaf!"

Erik slouched down and mumbled to himself.

"It worked before..."

The troll, having exceptional hearing, heard the mumble.

"What worked before?" he asked.

"Nothing," scoffed the boy.

The troll poked his head closer to the bars and began to look Erik up and down.

"You're him!.... You're the boy they've been after!"

"I suppose so, yes."

"How did they finally capture you?"

"I let the Erlking capture me. I was tired of running. Tired of getting people hurt."

"The Erlking you say? He's tethered to his castle that can't be right. The wolves are the ones who brought you here. Maybe you remember it wrong?"

"No, I took the Erlking's hand I'm sure of it."

"Hmmm...... interesting... Maybe it was him. Or part of him at least."

"What do you mean, part of him? And what do you mean he's tethered to his castle?"

"Many years ago the kings and queens all put a spell on the Erlking. He was to rule the entire underworld, just as he wanted, but they tricked him. They made it where he was unable to leave his castle. That's why he uses the Ellerkonge for all of his work on the surface world."

"But that's impossible. I've met the Erlking several times. Many times outside of the castle. I've felt his cold touch. His icy breath!

"There's something about you. Where maybe part of his spirit can leave, but not his physical form, not yet. You're his way out. That's why he's been after you for so long!"

"What's so special about me?"

"I'm not sure. But clearly something."

There was silence for a moment. The troll looked as if he were debating something amongst himself. Erik could see the troll was clearly torn about something.

"Why are you telling me these things? Why are you being so kind?"

"You traveled with a bear not that long ago. What happened to him?"

Erik lowered his head. Tears almost instantly began to well up. The response answered the troll's question instantly. The guard began to press on random spots on the wall with bars. A door suddenly began to appear. The troll reached into his pocket and pulled out his keys and unlocked the door.

"The Ellerkonge is on his way to take you to his king. We don't have long." Said the troll as he swung open the door.

Erik was stunned. He didn't understand what was happening.

"Why... Why are you helping me?" he asked.

"Not that long ago a young boy and his bear companion came across a bridge. At this bridge my brother harassed and teased these travelers. He told me that despite his sour behavior there soon after that the same bear he had poked fun at saved his life... you are a good person. Your bear friend was good as well. You choose to be good even towards bad people. Now I believe it's time for someone bad to do something good. Thank you for saving my brother."

The two crouched down and quickly made their way down the corridor. The troll slipped into one of the rooms for a second and returned with Erik's bag in hand.

"You may need this," he said as he handed it to him.

The guard took Erik's hand and led him through a labyrinth of hallways. As they did so a view from one of the windows caused Erik to stop in his tracks for a moment. Through the window he could see a cliff that hung over the ocean. He had been there before!

"Come, come, hurry," urged the troll.

"WHERE'S THE BOY!!" The Ellerkonge's voice roared through the corridors.

The Ellerkonge's smell quickly grew closer. Or so Erik thought. The troll pulled Erik into a tiny room and lifted a piece of wood. The stench was awful.

"Go, hurry!" panicked the guard.

"In there?" Erik said as he held his nose and looked down into the latrine.

"YES! It's the only safe way out! It will open out into the sea below. You will be fine, just a bit smelly, but you have to go NOW!"

Erik held his breath and stepped down into the cesspool. As soon as he did the troll pulled a lever and Erik and a whole lot of shit fell into an even larger cesspool below. It took everything in Erik not to puke. The river of fesses slowly flowed out to an opening. Erik was soon spit out into the ocean just as the troll had told him he would.

He had made it out of the castle. Now what? He thought to himself. He looked up at the massive castle. It looked to be falling apart. Moss covered it. It looked to be almost as old as the surrounding forest.

He began to ride the surf to the shore. From there he walked close to the water so that the tide would wash away his footprints. He moved quickly because he didn't know how soon he would be pursued. The castle began to disappear in the distance. Erik kept looking back and so far no one had followed him. All the time the old decrepit forest ran parallel to the beach. Something told him to keep his distance from it. So he stayed on the beach.

As the sun set over the ocean Erik debated going into the woods for shelter. He would surely be seen if he stayed out on the beach in the open. Then, as if by magic, a cave appeared in the distance.

The cave was wet and cold, but it provided the needed cover. The caverns sprawled deep into the earth. Erik didn't want to lay too close to the entrance for fear someone may see him. Yet he also didn't want to journey too far into the caves and get lost. After some minor exploration he found a place fitting to sleep. It was a notch in the wall just big enough for him to fit. It was also one of the few surfaces that didn't have a puddle on it. So, he took out his blanket and curled into a ball and went to sleep.

The Hunt Begins

Not that far down the beach a pack of mangy flea ridden bloodhounds led by the Ellerkonge sniffed their way along the beach. They would only get a whiff of the boy from time to time being that he was smart and walked in the water mostly. Along the forest tree line traveled a pack of malicious wolves.

The horned king sat staring into his chalice. The body of the traitorous troll strewn across the floor in several pieces at his feet. He could feel that the boy wasn't far. Yet he was nowhere to be seen. His spies scattered every which way. Scouring the beaches and forests around. He himself continuously looked into his seeing stone. He was so close. The power he craved so long was finally within reach.

The tide rose higher and higher until finally it had come all the way in and the beach was almost completely under water. The Ellerkonge and his hounds had walked up to the tree-line. As the Ellerkonge prepared a camp the eldest of the hounds and the leader of the wolves spoke amongst themselves.

"I keep getting a hit on him, then it's gone," complained the old hound.

"Every time I get a whiff of him it's blown up from the beach. Clearly he's used the water to his advantage," replied the wolf.

"Clearly, the boy is smart."

"Clearly, he has managed to evade and escape our king and his closest men on several occasions." As the wolf said this he nodded his eyes toward the Ellerkonge.

"Where do you think he's gone to?" asked the hound.

"My guess is we will find his body washed ashore come morning. The tides come quickly, and the undertow is powerful... smart he may be, but he's still young and naïve. His plan to stay in the water may backfire on him."

The Ellerkonge finished the camp and he and the hounds rested on the edge of the beach to wait out the tide and see what it revealed. Meanwhile, the pack of wolves continued their hunt into the dead of night.

The Makings of a Fellowship

A healed Teddy and the groundhog made their way across the desert. They were headed to a small town in the middle of nowhere. The groundhog had mentioned she had business to attend to. All Teddy had talked about since he was able to fully function was finding Erik. She assured him they would meet again soon.

Teddy was curious as to the earth shaking that had occurred several days before that the groundhog had claimed to be from the boy. He had never seen anything like that from Erik before. Then again so many people of late had talked about Erik like he wasn't just a boy. Maybe he really was something else. Something more.

As they approached the little town they could see a pile of dead lizards piled up just outside of it. The town looked like it had seen quite a battle. Almost every building was riddled with bullet holes.

Teddy stopped to observe the damage, but the groundhog kept walking past all of it, paying it no mind. She continued to walk clear out of the other end of town until they happened upon a small farm.

Enbarr's wife was making tea when she heard a small knock on the door. She was quite shocked to see a feeble little groundhog and massive bear on the other side!

"O my!" she exclaimed as she looked up at the bear.

"Don't worry. He's a big teddy bear," giggled the little groundhog.

"How can we help you?" asked the wife.

"Is your husband home, dear?"

Enbarr's wife stepped to the side to reveal her husband. He was slumped over the table with his arm in a sling and empty liquor bottles surrounding him. He looked up at the visitors with blurred vision. He wore a sad and defeated look among his face.

The little groundhog walked past the wife and over to the defeated horse.

"Get up!" she said as she poked at Enbarr.

He looked at the groundhog in great confusion.

"Who are you?" he asked.

"It doesn't matter who I am. Who are YOU? Some hero you are. The famous Enbarr chasing his problems to the bottom of a bottle. You should be ashamed."

The horse lowered his head.

"You wouldn't understand little groundhog."

"Understand what!? That the boy risked his life to save yours?"

Enbarr's head quickly shot back up.

"What do you know of the boy?"

"I know he's more important than any of us know. And that soon he will need your help. He will need all of our help!"

The horse instantly stood up. He stumbled a bit as he did so. His wife quickly intervened.

"I know you want to help the boy Enbarr. But you're in no condition to go anywhere!" she exclaimed.

The groundhog looked him over then looked at his wife.

"Easy peasy," she said with confidence.

She then proceeded to take several herbs from her satchel and tasked Enbarr's wife with starting a fire. Within the hour the groundhog had made a paste of some sort for his arm and a drink for his inebriation. In no time at all he was sober and his arm had done weeks worth of healing.

"Ready to go now?" asked the groundhog with a bit of sass in her voice.

So he was. Enbarr said his goodbyes to his wife and children and the three of them headed towards the vile forest. Towards Erik.

The Rising Tide

    Erik was sleeping soundly bundled in his blanket tucked into the cubby in the wall. That is until his feet began to get soaked. The cold water instantly woke him. The cave was much darker than when he had fallen asleep. It was as if the opening had closed up. Erik thought fast and reached into his bag and pulled out some of the mushrooms from the spider's cave.

    He held them up and instantly began to panic. The cave he was in had almost completely filled with water! It came all the way up to the edge of his cubby and was rising quickly. He had to think quickly. He was too far from the entrance to try and swim to it. He knew it would be dangerous to swim further into the caves as well. As the water filled his cubby he knew he had to move. The ceiling wasn't far above him. He took a deep breath and dove further into the depths. Hoping that maybe it would open up into a new cavern or at least have an air pocket. It was a dumb plan to say the least, but he trusted his sense of hope as opposed to his skills of swimming.

He swam further into the cave system where he thought he had seen some bigger caves when he was exploring briefly earlier. Or at least he was hoping he was swimming in that direction. The shrooms only lit up a small area around them under the water. Between the darkness and the confusion that already comes with swimming under water he couldn't really tell which way he was going.

His chest began to hurt. He had never held his breath so long in his life. He wanted badly to take a breath in. He began to focus on his lack of breath and his pace began to slow. He started to become fatigued beyond his body's limits. His movement became wild and frantic as he swam. He couldn't hold his breath any longer!

Erik opened his mouth and inhaled a deep breath. Only. It wasn't air that entered his lungs. They opened wide and filled with water. His lungs instantly felt heavy. His body began to instinctively go into survival mode and he began holding his breath again. Only this time it was much more painful. It felt like his body was crushing itself from the inside. He swam until he couldn't swim anymore. Then everything went black.

On the Edge of the Vile Forest

The desert seemed to go on forever. The little groundhog now rode on Teddy's shoulder. Really her old body wasn't cut out for a journey of this proportion, but her determination drove her forward. She seemed to know something that the others didn't. Know more. There was a special connection to the boy. It was like she could feel him. Or see him even. Teddy wasn't sure how she knew where the boy was, but he and Enbarr trusted her and followed her lead.

In the distance, they could see the vile forest come into view. It was old and damaged looking. Many dead plants and trees bordered it. It looked like the life of the forest itself had been drained somehow.

"Finally," exclaimed Teddy upon seeing the forest.

"We have reached the forest, but we have much to overcome before we reach Erik... this forest is very old, very evil. There are things that dwell here that we couldn't even imagine. Dark magic runs through the very roots that cover the ground. The horned king will be able to see our every move if he wishes. It will not be an easy task. We will rest for a moment now and travel through the night. We dare not sleep beneath those trees. Too likely our nightmares will become reality." The groundhog's posture changed as she spoke. It was clear she was now on high alert!

Alpha

Erik came to with his body forcing him to puke. What seemed like pints of water emptied from him. He coughed for some time after. His insides all hurt as if he had been punched several times. Yet, somehow, he survived. He laid out on a wet rock and tried to get his breathing back to normal.

He had dropped his glowing mushrooms at some point but luckily he could see pretty well in his current cavern. Once he started to breathe normally and not hurt so much he began to look around. He could see where the little bit of light was coming from. Far overhead, though faint, Erik could see the light peeking through what looked to be a crack.

Erik thought about waiting until the tide rolled back out but even then he wasn't sure how to get back. He wasn't sure just how far down into the cave system he had come. He decided the crack above may be his best chance to get out. So, he began to climb the slippery walls.

Close by, the leader of the wolves came to an abrupt stop as the boy's scent ran across his nose. Though faint, it was enough for the alpha to follow. It seemed the rest of his pack had yet to pick up on it. He began to hatch a selfish plan.

"You all go ahead. Stay near the roads. He's bound to show up," commanded the alpha.

"What about you sir?" asked the second in charge.

"I'm going back to get the Ellerkonge off of his ass!" he lied.

So the pack continued on into the forest, and the alpha began to follow his nose towards Erik.

After several times slipping and a few times falling (luckily not too far) Erik finally made it to the crack. The moon shined bright and provided him with light. He was just small enough to fit through the crack onto the surface. He crawled out and began to squeeze out his clothes. As he did, a voice spoke out from behind him.

"So.... You're the famous boy.... The one who my master has chased for years on end... What's so special about you then?... What's his obsession?" the alpha wolf asked as he looked the boy up and down. He then stepped closer to get a good smell.

"You're not Fae! Seems to be merely a human," he continued in a slightly disappointed tone.

"I am! I am a human! I don't know why the Erlking wants me! He's plagued me as far back as I can remember!"

"You denied him as a youngling. He didn't take well to that... yet you are not the first to refuse the king's hand. Nor will you be the last... the master barely bats an eye and moves to the next child... So then why has he been so caught up on you?..."

"I wish I could tell you! Nothing in this world makes sense to me!"

The wolf's ears perked up.

"This world? ... Are you not from this world, boy?"

"I....I don't know.. or rather, I don't remember."

"Hmm... could it be? I've never heard such a thing... but perhaps..."

"Perhaps what!?" asked the boy intently.

"You're from the other world. The mid- world as we call it... the world between the fairy world and the underworld. The Erlking not only takes humans from this world, but yours as well... though I've never heard of someone from your world making it to ours... unless it was in the arms of the Erlking. He is the bridge between all the worlds..... perhaps you ARE special.... After all you've managed to slip through his fingers all these years..."

In the distance, he could hear howls begin to sound. The others had picked up Erik's trail.

"Will you please just kill me and get it over with! I'm tired of running. I won't go back to that castle! I just want it all to end!" asserted the boy.

The wolf squinted his eyes and looked over the boy again.

"I had planned to do so... I wanted to absorb whatever power it was the Erlking seemed to want so bad for myself...."

The alpha moved closer. Erik closed his eyes tight. He could hear the other wolves closing in. He opened his eyes back up just in time to see the alpha wolves hurling towards him. He clinched his body up preparing for the piercing of the wolves teeth. Instead the collar of his shirt tightened and he was being flung onto the wolves back!

"Hold on!" the alpha shouted back to him.

The massive wolf jumped and weaved through vines and twisted trees. His pack close on their tail. The wolf ran as fast as he could. He ran until the rotted vines on the ground started to turn to bright green grass. The sun had come up and ran even with them. As they came upon a cliff the wolf finally stopped. He took a moment to catch his breath. As he did Erik looked down into the chasm. It was quite the drop.

"Now what?" he asked as he looked down.

The wolf looked back at him.

"You jump!"

"What!? Are you mad? I could never survive that jump!"

"Well, didn't you ask me to kill you just a moment ago anyways?" the wolf said with a grin.

The alpha stared into the tree line. He couldn't see them but he knew his pack was close.

"They're almost here! You have to jump now. You've made it this far. A fall isn't going to be the end of you. You clearly have much more to do in this world before you leave it!"

Erik stared down. It seemed to get further away the more he looked at it. He knew he had to jump though. Just before he did he turned to the alpha wolf.

"Why are you helping me?" he asked.

"I've worked for the Erlking longer than I can remember. Raised from a pup to do his bidding. I've done things I can never take back. Never forget. All in his name. If he wants you so bad then that means you're important. That he's afraid of you. And if he's afraid of you then that may just mean you have the means to defeat him. Even if you don't know what it is yet. After all I've done to this world the least I can do is help make a new one. A better one, one free of the Erlking and his madness!"

"Traitor!" sounded a voice from the edge of the forest.

The second in command of the wolves stepped out of the woods. The rest of the pack followed. All of them have teeth showing.

"Stand down!" ordered the alpha.

None listened. They began to surround the alpha and the boy. The wolf looked back and growled at Erik.

"GO, NOW!"

As he barked his order at Erik his former pack attacked. As Erik jumped, he could see the wolves all jump onto their previous leader. He fell fast and hit the water hard. As he came up to the surface several dead wolves fell into the water around him. The water wasn't very fast, but it was deep. Erik, not being the strongest of swimmers, grabbed one of the dead wolves that floated by and used it to help him get down river.

The Hidden Spring

He floated on and on for hours. The land on either side of the river changed several times. The current stayed steady and calm for most of the trip. Between the calm waters and the warm sun on his back he was actually somewhat relaxed. He crossed his arms and laid his head down on them for just a moment.

Next thing he knew he was bobbing up and down quickly. He could feel the water rushing around his legs. The water's current was picking up! Quite rapidly at that! Ahead he could see white waters rolling over the tips of rocks. He knew he had gone as far as he could safely go. Before the water got too intense for Erik to swim he let go of the dead wolf and grabbed onto an out hanging branch. As he tried to lift himself up the current grabbed hold of his legs and shot them forward.

Smashing his knee into a rock near the edge of the water, splitting it open.

He pulled himself onto the shore and hobbled away from the river. A trail of blood followed him. He made his way back up the river where the water was more calm and began to wash off his knee. As he did he could see just how bad it was. Every time he lifted his knee from the water it would begin to bleed heavily again. Erik realized he had to figure out a way to close the wound fast or he may be in big trouble.

He began to look around at his surroundings. He had gotten off in a strange, but beautiful place. There were several flowers around of all shapes and sizes. There were vines and moss, but unlike the vile forest they were vibrant green. Several types of mushrooms grew next to the trees and along the shore.

"What a unique place," Erik thought.

Erik figured it did him no good to just stand there in the water and bleed out. So he tore the sleeve off of his shirt and wrapped it around his knee as tight as he could.

"That will have to do for now." He said out loud to himself.

As he walked through the rainforest he was amazed at its beauty. He had never seen many of the plants he was seeing. The deeper he wandered into the forest the larger everything began to grow. While he ran his hand across what he thought was a tree trunk that turned out to be a stalk of a mushroom he couldn't help but wonder if he were shrinking like Alice! He stopped a moment and fully took in everything around him. The forest really did make him feel tiny. Everything towered over his head. Even the flowers were bigger than him.

The bewilderment had almost completely distracted him from his busted knee, but as he began to walk again he could feel blood dripping into his shoe. He looked down and saw that his shirt sleeve had completely soaked through. Real panic began to set in. The wound wasn't healing itself! It was too deep! He was about to be in a lot of trouble. He quickened his pace and kept a sharp eye out for any sort of civilization or something of use.

His knee began to hurt at every bend it took. Erik could see that his leg was swelling and it was turning red all around the wound. It was already getting infected! His walk had now turned to a limp. He wouldn't be able to make it much further like this.

Ahead, he finally saw a sight of relief. A small creek gathered into a pool. It looked to be a spring.

"At least I can clean my wound," Erik thought.

He took off his bag and shirt and waded into the pool. As he did so several little eyes began to watch from the surrounding brush.

Unlikely Ally

The groundhog opened her eyes. She laid upon Teddy's wide shoulder. She had fallen asleep as the three of them made their way through the Vile forest. To her great surprise they had come quite a ways into the forest and they still hadn't run into any trouble.

"Hmmm...." she thought out loud.

"What is it?" asked the bear.

"Something is off... the Erlking hasn't sent anyone or anything after us. I expected a fight by now..."

"Maybe he hasn't seen us yet?" suggested Enbarr.

"This is HIS forest. He sees all. Something has distracted him and drawn his attention elsewhere."

"Well, that's good news for us then right?" replied Teddy.

"Good for us perhaps... maybe not so good for Erik.... I need a moment. Stop here," ordered the little groundhog.

They all stopped. The groundhog climbed down and walked away from the others. She sat upon a nearby stone in complete silence with her eyes closed. She stayed like this for several minutes. Suddenly her eyes jolted open. The green one glowed bright when she did.

"The boy is not at the castle anymore!" she blurted while still in somewhat of a trance. Her eye still glowing bright.

Enbarr and Teddy seemed more than shocked not only at the revelation but how she had come to that conclusion. All the years Teddy had known her he had never seen anything even remotely close to what she did. As she seemed to come out of the trance-like state Enbarr approached her.

"Can you see things? Things that have happened? Things far away?" asked the horse.

"Not see so much as feel. The boy is no longer in the castle. I know that much... but I have no idea as to where he's gone," she answered.

A strange voice growled from the shadows nearby as she finished her sentence.

"My guess is he's about to the white waters by now. That is if you're talking about the mid-world boy. Which I'm sure you are. He's a very popular subject these days."

A wolf covered in wounds and bite marks yet seemingly unfazed stepped into the open. He continued to talk.

"The horned king himself rides the mighty Fenrir south in search of the boy. The boy has about a day's start on him. He will be okay for the time being. Though it won't be long before Fenrir finds him. The great wolf is the best hunter there is."

The groundhog approached the wolf with great curiosity.

"How do you know the boy is from the mid-world?" she asked.

"Because he told me so, in a roundabout way..."

"You've seen Erik!?" exclaimed Teddy.

"If the mid- world boy's name is Erik then yes, I've seen him. I helped him get that day's head start I spoke of."

"You're one of the Erlking's generals, Alpha... are you not? Why help the boy?" Asked the groundhog.

"Guess you can say I had a change of heart. The boy is special... I've put my head on a pike by helping him. At least I can die with a little honor now."

"How is it that the Erlking has left his castle?" Asked the groundhog in a worried voice.

"The spell has grown weaker. Between one of the king's deaths and the powers he seems to be drawing from the boy his determination drives him forward. He is not fully himself. Only a shell for now."

"Then now would be the time to kill him!" Enbarr chimed in.

The wolf simply laughed at the horse's remark.

"Which king has fallen? And how?" Teddy asked the wolf.

"King Ailill, and at the hands of the Erlking himself."

Teddy's heart sank. Ailill had died for helping them. He was sure of it.

"We have to move quickly," started the groundhog.

She stopped for a moment and looked over at the wolf.

"Being a general, or ex-general if you will, wouldn't you rather die in battle than by execution?" she asked him.

"I suppose If I could choose, yes."

"You helped the boy, but as you said, he is far from being safe. He won't be safe until the horned king is destroyed and he has returned to his home... We need a guide to lead us south. Go with us. Help us save the boy. Help us fight. If you fall, there will be no greater death!"

It didn't take much convincing for the wolf. He nodded his head and motioned for them to follow.

"So then we head South."

The Mighty Hunter

The Erlking rode the monstrous wolf swiftly down the riverside. The Ellerkonge close behind on a boar, a fitting mount for the piggish man.

Any normal wolf would not have been able to track a scent so strongly through water, but Fenrir was no normal wolf. He stood at least ten times the size of even the largest dire wolf. His nose was so keen he could smell for miles through water or wind. His tracking skills and pure brute strength was unmatched. He was a god among the other wolves.

With Fenrir on his trail Erik surely wouldn't make it far. As the water's pace quickened the shore became more dense. Just before they left the shore Fenrir got an extremely clear whiff of the boy's scent. He began to search the surrounding area. It didn't take him long to find a rock that was smeared with Erik's blood.

As he licked the rock his eyes jutted open. The taste was sweet unlike anything he had tasted.

"It's the boy's blood. I'm sure of it!" he growled.

He looked on the ground at the trail of blood that led into the woods.

"This will be easy," smiled the wolf.

The Forbidden Spring

Tiny eyes watched as Erik cleaned his wound in the pool. As he washed away the dried blood, he could see the surrounding redness begin to disappear.

"That's odd," he muttered out loud.

The more he cleaned the wound the more it began to heal! Before he knew it the gash in his knee was completely gone!

"What in the world!?" he exclaimed in disbelief.

One of the watching eyes couldn't take it anymore. She flew out next to Erik's head.

"I'm glad you're happy! You've ruined our sacred spring!" A small angry voice shouted.

Erik looked to his side and saw the fairy hovering close to his head. Her face was red with temperament. Other fairies began to emerge from the surrounding bushes looking equally pissed. Many of them started shouting obscenities at the boy.

"I... I'm sorry! I had no way of knowing!" Erik pleaded with them.

"You've washed your filthy blood in our pool!" one shouted.

"We can't drink or bathe in it now!" shouted another.

This went on for a moment. It was clear Erik wasn't going to get through to them, he began gathering his things and tried to walk away. Still apologizing the whole while. As he tried to walk away they began surrounding him like a swarm of insects. Some even began to grow aggressive and began to poke and pull at him.

"What do you want from me!? I said I'm sorry! I can't undo what I've done!" Erik shouted as he tried to duck away from the swarm.

"You must pay for your crimes!" shouted several of the fairies.

This seemed to rally them. They all started to grow even more aggressive. He began to feel sharp jabs in several parts of his body. He began to flail his arms about in self defense. The more they came at him the harder he began to swing. As he swung his arm back he felt it strike something quite hard. He had batted one of the attacking creatures into a nearby tree! All of the fairies immediately stopped their assault and went to attend to the young fairy that had been struck down.

"You've killed him!" an angry fairy screamed.

Erik's heart sank at these words. He had hunted and fished, but never had he killed something in cold blood. Even if in his mind he was just trying to get away. He felt awful. He walked to the fallen Fae and picked him up in his hands. All the while fairies still screamed at him.

"Put him down, you monster!" many screamed.

Tears began to swell up in his eyes as he looked at the little lifeless being in his arms.

"I'm so sorry," cried the little boy.

More fairies had now begun to show up and surround Erik. One fairy who looked to be wearing some sort of armor hovered in front of him.

"You have committed two unforgivable crimes in our kingdom! You will answer for both!" said the armored clad Fae with a stern voice.

Another armored fairy flew up and blew a strange powder into Erik's face.

The King to the South

Iubdan was an arrogant, boastful, hot-headed king. He ruled over almost the entire Southern Hemisphere. His fairies were well organized and highly militarized. He backed down from no fight and made sure that everyone knew it!

He had slick dark hair and thick eyebrows. He was smiling with his mouth perched to one side as Erik opened his eyes.

"You've gotten yourself into quite the mess, haven't you?" the king asked.

Erik looked around. He was in an eloquent throne room with topaz and gold everywhere. He had clearly been talking to whatever king the fairies at the spring served. All of the fairies had grown to full size much like Ailill had done. He knew he was in trouble.

"Please sir! I didn't mean to! It was all an accident!" Erik begged.

"Yet, it still happened, correct? Mistake or not. The fountain is tainted and one of my people... dead. Am I correct?" the king said matter-of-factly.

"Yes sir."

Erik had to admit, the king was right. Even if it wasn't on purpose the laws had still been broken. Erik had still taken a life. He lowered his head and didn't speak anymore .

The king walked around the boy looking him over. A smile began to emerge. He could feel the powers radiating off of Erik.

"Hmm... we will discuss your sentence and settlement over a meal, shall we?" invited the king.

King Iubdan ordered one of his assistants to take Erik to a room to await dinner. Erik entered a wonderful room. Everything inside of it was quite exquisite. A giant window overlooked the beautiful teal ocean. This wasn't the room he would expect as an apparent prisoner. He turned from the window to see his massive bed. On it laid a splendid outfit pressed and ready to go. It looked to be Erik's size. The assistant closed the door and returned to the king. Erik was very confused by the situation. "Maybe the fairies didn't have prison cells," he thought.

Nevertheless, he was going to take advantage of the moment. First, he ran to the massive window with the breathtaking view. As far as he could see in any direction was the ocean. Next, he took the nice clothes and threw them onto a close by chair and began to jump on the soft plush bed. He eventually belly flopped down into it. Sinking into it like a ball of cotton. The sheets were cool and relaxing. The blanket was warm and inviting. Erik laid there cuddled into the covers. He wasn't tired, but he still didn't want to leave the bed. He eventually fell asleep and was woken up by the assistant.

"Sir, dinner is served. Please change and join the king and queen in the dining hall in no more than ten minutes." He swiftly turned and exited out of the room.

"Full of personality that one," Erik spoke under his breath as the assistant stepped out.

Erik changed clothes and made his way down to the dinning hall. The room was massive. At least six chandeliers hung above the elongated table. The table looked as if it could seat an entire town almost! King Iubdan and his queen sat at the far end of the table. They looked to be ants at the end of the table. It was so far away. Erik nervously counted chairs as he walked through the room towards them.

Next to the king sat his beautiful wife. She had long red hair with a crown made of shells. Her eyes were soft and welcoming, nothing like her husbands. She smiled a radiant smile. Erik was taken back by her beauty. He lost count of the chairs and even stumbled a little as he walked.

"Two hundred and one," The queen said with a smirk on her face as Erik sat down.

"Mam?" Erik asked.

"I saw your eyes rapidly moving as you walked past the chairs. I assume you were counting them."

"O,.. um yes my queen. I was, thank you. I lost co..."

"Anyways," rudely interrupted the king.

"You owe us a great debt. In my kingdom both offensives you made are punishable by death," continued the king.

"Death!" panicked Erik.

"Dear, he's only a child!" cut in the queen.

"Child or not he committed unforgivable crimes... I want him to know the severity of what he's done!"

"But Tolith didn't even d.." the queen was hushed by the king mid sentence.

"YOU have no part in this judgment my love. Now quiet please." He continued on.

The king rose from his chair and walked behind Erik, putting his hands on his arms.

"Lucky for you... I'm a forgiving king... in a forgiving mood." He smiled and leaned down to Erik.

"Give me whatever powers you hold, and we can call it even."

Erik let out a sigh of frustration.

"I don't have any powers! Not that I know of. If I did I would gladly give them to you and be done with this burden!"

The king snarled and pushed off of Erik's chair in frustration.

"I thought we could make this easy.... Why must you lie to me boy? I felt them as soon as you stepped into my domain! ... YOU CAN NOT LIE OF YOUR POWERS TO ME! YOU WILL NOT DENY ME SUCH POWER!"

Queen Bebo had never seen her husband act so rash before. She leaned back in her chair utterly confused and quite frankly a bit frightened.

"My love! what's gotten into you!" she hesitated.

She received no answer, only an evil stare. It was as if he was possessed.

The mad king returned his hands to Erik's shoulders. This time gripping them much harder.

The king's trance was broken by the sound of his kingdom's alarms sounding. Almost immediately after his assistant came barging into the dinning room with a worried look on his face.

"Sir! the Erlking is almost at our gates!" he panted. It was clear he had run all the way there.

"The Erlking! What!? How? Why?" He panicked then stopped and looked at Erik.

"He wants the boy!..."

All castles are made of sand...

The king quickly made his way to the gates with his army. Erik and Queen Bebo stood at the window and watched. Erik had not realized until he looked out front that they were on a small island. The only way to the castle was a narrow bridge. A bridge which the Erlking and his lackey the Ellerkonge now stood upon with their mighty mounts. They watched as Iubdan walked out onto the bridge to greet his visitors.

"Ahhh, what a surprise to see you out and about! What brings you all the way here great horned king?" he spoke as he approached them, fake smile applied.

Fenrir bowed down to allow the Erlking off. He drew a sword as he dismounted.

"You speak to me as if we are allies... we are far from so."

He held his sword to King Iubdan's neck now.

The king's men began to approach. As they did Fenrir crouched into attack position. The Erlking continued to speak as the soldiers froze.

"You look scared, Iubdan."

"You can't kill me. You can't just kill one of the kings!"

"Just imprison them! Lock them away! You claim I cannot kill one of the kings...you want to know HOW I'm able to stand here before you?"

The Ellerkonge reached into a bag that hung on the side of his boar. From it he pulled a round object and threw it. King Iubdan watched in horror as King Ailill's head rolled to his feet.

"Please! Please! I'm sorry for what we did! We were afraid of your power! Jealous even! Please, I beg you, let me live! I'll give you anything you want! My kingdom, my treasures, my wife!" Iubdan begged.

"You do have in your possession what I seek though...," the Erlking looked straight up at the window where Erik was standing.

"The boy!? So you've felt the powers too! We could share them! I'll help you defeat the other kings! They would never suspect me!" groveled Iubdan in a last attempt to please the Erlking.

"And why would I need your help with that? I was able to walk from my castle walls and broke one part of the spell by killing ONE king... I'm interested to see what more I can do after two."

"NO!" Iubdan screamed as his head flew from his shoulders.

Queen Bebo stood in shock as she watched her husband's head fall to the ground. She instantly turned to Erik.

"We have to get you out of here! Now!"

As she grabbed the boy and ran, all hell broke loose at the gates. In a rage the fairy army attacked The Erlking and his companions. The Ellerkonge pulled out an enormous axe and began swinging it, clearing the bridge with every swipe. Behind him Fenrir and the boar finished any Fae that had flown over. The Erlking didn't even raise his sword. He began to walk towards the castle. Dead fairies falling all around him.

The queen's plan had been to get Erik to the treasure room where there were several items that could be of use. One being a pair of shoes the king had owned that could walk on water! With the bridge compromised this seemed like a brilliant plan and best hope at escaping.

As they ran by the front doors they swung open. There stood the horned king. His eyes glowing bright yellow from within his dark hood.

"Go, RUN!" ordered the queen to the boy.

Erik continued on as fast as he could. The Erlking began to go towards him in pursuit, but was stopped in his tracks by the queen.

"You will meet the same fate as your husband if you do not move aside," the Erlking said in a calm yet annoyed voice.

"Then I will be with him again soon, for I will not move," she sternly answered back.

The Erlking drew his sword and in the same motion tried to come down onto the queen. His attack was stopped by a small dagger the queen had pulled from behind her. She wasn't going to go down without a fight!

The horned king swung his sword and again he was deflected. The queen was quick and very skilled with her blade. Before the Erlking had brought his sword back from his blow the queen had stabbed him twice in his side! He angrily swung again! Yet again, he was blocked and countered. Two more quick sharp jabs hit his side. He began to stumble back. Bebo stood solid and fierce with her blade up ready to strike again.

"Seems like you've underestimated me!" said the queen with a smile.

The Erlking began to laugh as he continued to back away from her. An eerie green fog began to cover the floor. He could feel his powers growing.

"And it seems you've forgotten who I am!" laughed the horned king.

The fog spread behind him across the bridge over all of the dead fairies. The fallen Fae began to reanimate and rise back up. Once on their feet they began to walk towards the entrance of the castle. The Erlking backed out of the door and the undead fairies began to storm through.

The Great Escape

Erik had almost reached the treasure room when he heard the Queen scream in agony. He stopped for a moment and almost turned around for her. He looked back towards the main door waiting to see the Erlking walk down the hall towards him at any moment. The fear seemed to freeze him. He stood staring at the door at the end of the hallway opposite of him now. As if he had manifested it, the door in front of him slammed open. Two armored fairies backed through the door. They were locked in combat with the Ellerkonge!

He swung his axe down. Cutting one of the warriors clean in half! As the other attempted to fight the beast of a man Erik had to make a decision. Either run past the Ellerkonge into the treasure room or try to sneak out and make another way off of the island. As the Ellerkonge peeled his axe out of the other guard's head

Erik quickly entered a close-by room. He had hoped maybe the Ellerkonge hadn't seen him.

He wouldn't be so lucky. The rank smelling man kicked open the door. He had a wild look on his face!

"You won't escape me this time! Your luck has finally run out. All of your friends are dead. You are alone! Trapped!"

The Ellerkonge backed Erik into the corner of the room. His giant arms outstretched both ways. Erik quickly scanned the room trying to see a way out. The ogress man now stood over him. He really was trapped! Thinking fast Erik squeezed behind the wardrobe next to him. The Ellerkonge, enraged, began to tear at the furniture. Throwing the doors across the room.

Erik pushed as hard as he could and managed to knock the wardrobe onto the Ellerkonge. Though it wasn't much to the mammoth of a man, he merely threw it off to the side. Still, it was enough to buy some time for Erik. The Ellerkonge looked to the window as Erik's feet slipped out.

There was no way for the massive man to follow him! Erik was safe from him for the time being, but he didn't know what he was going to do next. His escape plan had been to simply walk across the water with the king's magic shoes. It was clear that was no longer an option. He scaled down the side of the castle down to some rocks below. The land that surrounded the castle and ran into the sea on the island was much like the area around the spring. It was full of giant flowers and mushrooms.

Erik ducked under one and began to try to map out a plan to get off of the island while he was hidden. He couldn't see what was happening in the castle above but he could hear it. Screams echoed through the halls and out the windows.

Erik could see land in the distance, just below the horizon. If he had been a stronger swimmer he may have tried to swim the distance. He knew that wouldn't be an option for him.

He put his head in his knees trying to hold back his tears as he heard the screams above. The overwhelming sense of failure quickly took hold of him. So many people had died helping him. "For what?" he thought to himself. Though the darkness surrounded him in his head a small flame grew with every heartbeat. Brighter, brighter. He heard the voice in his head telling him once again not to give up. Though Erik couldn't see what it was, it was clear he had something special about him. Something the Erlking was willing to kill for and that others were willing to die to protect.

Erik began to feel hot heavy air on the back of his neck. He turned his head slowly. There above him with mushrooms crushed in his feet stood Fenrir. Drool dripped from the beast's jowl onto Erik's feet. He frantically tried to get to his feet but stumbled backwards. He began to roll down the hill towards the water. He began to grab anything he could to stop his fall. The wolf ran close behind him. Breaking through anything in his way.

Finally, Erik was able to grab a hold of a mushroom stem. As he did Fenrir tried to make an abrupt stop and stumbled over loose rocks. He too then began to tumble towards the sea.

The mushroom stem couldn't hold the weight of the boy and ripped in two only seconds after he grabbed it. Erik continued to fall down the hill, only a bit slower than before now. The cap of the mushroom rolled like a wheel parallel with Erik all the way down.

The water had already been broken by the mighty wolf's body. Giant waves crashed against the bottom of the hill. Erik crashed into the raging waters below. As he hit he could already see Fenrir emerging. He and the mushroom cap landed only a few feet away. The waves from the gigantic wolf surfacing rushed over top of Erik. Every time he would swim to the surface the water would pull him back down before he could get a good breath. The salt water burned his eyes and even though he was able to get a small gasp of air from time to time he was mostly swallowing water.

The giant wolf had now gotten back on to the shore. The waves began to settle. As they did Erik could see the undertow had pulled him out further than he had thought. He was now a ways from the island. He began to panic and looked around him. There, only a few feet away the giant mushroom cap floated perfectly with the tide. He climbed over the cap and climbed onto it. Almost as soon as he did the wind picked up and the mushroom began to move with the waves across the open sea. The wolf watched in disbelief as the mushroom cap sailed away with Erik on it.

The Long Road

Stories of the Erlking's return to the surface world spread quickly. Many had seen him riding the fierce Fenrir across their lands. Fear began to overtake many. With his stories though the stories of Erik seemed to grow too! How he had escaped the horned king on several occasions. To counter those with growing fear many started to have growing hope that Erik's tales gave them. With each town they passed Teddy and the others would hear a little more. Some even recognized Teddy from the tales!

The hike south was long and tedious. They had to weave back and forth over the great river. Their hopes to find a boat to go down seemed to dwindle after each town. It looked as if they'd have to walk the entire way. Which put them several days behind Erik.

The last news they heard had not been anything good. It was said that Erik had been caught in the forbidden spring and king Iubdan held him at his castle on the sea. The Erlking was headed in that direction as well.

Teddy and the others had walked for almost two days straight. It was beginning to get hard to keep his eyes open. They happened across a small quiet town next to the river. Everything in him wanted to keep going, but he knew if they didn't rest they would be no use in a fight. They began to approach a little inn.

They were soon greeted by a short hefty badger. He seemed to know the groundhog as he came to her with open arms.

"Gloria! Glory it's Gloria! It's been ages!" greeted the innkeeper.

He spoke as if he were from deep in the hills. They all had a certain sound to them.

"What in tarnation brings you this far south?" he asked.

"Looking for an old friend," the groundhog answered.

"You mean other than me?" he laughed.

"Well, maybe I can help ya. What's this friend look like?" he continued.

"A young boy, about twelve in age...," she started.

"Shhh shhh... lower your voice... you're not talking about that boy the Erlking is after are ya?"

He could tell by the look on her face that it was indeed one in the same.

"Come inside, we'll talk more," the badger said as he ushered them into the inn.

He curiously looked over the fellowship the groundhog had gathered as they walked in.

"Quite a unique group of companions you travel with these days."

Everyone made themselves comfortable in the lounge of the inn. Gloria and the badger sat down at a table by themselves.

"You don't seem like the bounty type. So why are you and this band of misfits looking for the boy?" asked the badger with great curiosity.

"Bounty?" Gloria gasped.

"Shh... yes, the Erlking has put a pretty big reward on the boy's head," whispered the badger as if someone was listening.

"How do you know about this?" asked the groundhog.

"I run an inn, dear. All sorts of people come through here. I hear all sorts of dealings and plotting. The boy is a big subject round these parts as of late. His reward, what he is, heard everything from him being Fae to him being a damn wizard! Seems to be quite the character. Lots of bad people after him and his associates.... So my question is. What in the world are YOU doing looking for the boy?"

"My business is my own," replied the groundhog, sternly.

The badger was shocked a bit by her response. He had never seen her quite so blunt.

"Well, as I'm sure you've heard in one way or another the boy is at king Iubdan's. Seems the Erlking wasn't the only fairy king interested in your... friend."

"Yes, that's where we were heading unless we heard otherwise."

"Well, what do you intend to do when you make it to king Iubdan? Especially since the Erlking's said to be headed that way too."

"You ask many questions, old friend. Just know I intend to help the boy. We've simply come for a good night's rest so we are ready for whatever tomorrow brings us."

"Ahh, you're right you're right. Good for you. I specialize in such things. I will have four bedrooms ready for you in no time at all."

The groundhog thanked her old friend. When she turned to tell the others of their rooms she saw Teddy and Enbarr already asleep in their chairs and Alpha asleep on the ground. She gently woke them and led them to their cozy warm rooms. Everyone was fast asleep again in no time at all. Especially Alpha who had never slept on a bed before. The groundhog took a little longer, but she too finally fell fast asleep.

Two tiny black eyes watched through secret peep holes as the last of the visitors finally went to sleep. A grin reached from ear to pointy ear on the sly badger's face.

The First Shroomboat Adventure

As the wind blew the mushroom cap sailed over the waves with ease. The castle had sunk in the horizon. Erik had made it to the landmass he had seen from the shore of the island, but it wasn't quite what he had hoped for. It was much smaller than was thought. He could almost see it from end to end. He knew this would be no place to hide if the Erlking would pursue him into the ocean.

The stop on the island would not be wasted though. He scoured over the entire island gathering up anything he could. He gathered up some wild berries from the center of the island and also managed to find a small wrecked life boat. He thought at first it may be his ticket out but the more he pulled away the growth and sand he saw it was far from any floating condition.

He sat on the seat of the lifeboat and looked out over the wild ocean. He had to figure out a way to get to the next island. He looked over at the giant cap that had brought him all this way that had also floated to shore. As he stared at it the wheels began to turn in his head.

He picked up the two oaks that were attached to the lifeboat. One of them had broken in half, but that was fine, Erik could still make use of it. He ran over to the mushroom cap and jabbed the broken oar into the remaining stem. From there he took off his over shirt with a missing arm and tied it open on the makeshift mast.

Erik pushed the mushroom back into the surf and jumped on top of it with the other oar in hand.

The sun had been down for quite some time and the stars shone bright in the sky. The calm water reflected the scene above and made Erik feel as if he were floating in space. Stars above and below. The beautiful black backdrop went on forever.

Being surrounded by the heavens Erik could help but think of all the loved ones that were out there watching him. At first a comforting feeling he then started to become sad. All the bad emotions began to fill in his head. It turned like a movie wheel highlighting each person he loved and lost, and how he let each one of them down. The stars seemed to dim at these thoughts. The darker his thoughts became the darker it seemed to get. Until soon even the moon was covered in clouds.

Erik began to come to when he noticed everything had grown so dark. The ocean didn't seem as peaceful anymore. The endless stars had turned to endless nothingness.

Erik began to try and calm himself and take deep breaths. He hadn't exactly had the best of luck when it came to the dark. Especially in this world. He awaited anxiously for the Erlking to somehow appear like he had seemed to do so many times before. He sat and waited, but nothing happened. He simply floated in the nothingness for what felt like hours.

A cloud began to move to the side and one single ray of moonlight shined through. Almost directly where the moonlight shined, something was floating in the water. Something big! Erik couldn't quite make out what it was until he was almost right up on it. The sight was sad and horrifying. Pieces of meat floated about in the water. A giant whale floated on the surface of the ocean with its insides spilled out in the surrounding water. Her smell was bad but not rotted just yet. Whatever had happened hadn't happened long ago. As he paddled by he could see a giant hole right through the side of it. It was no other animal who had done this!

As he slowly paddled by looking at the carnage he heard a splash come from behind him. There was something else in the water with him! He of course began to think of sharks coming to finish off the rest of the whale. He looked out onto the black sea just in time to see a fin break the surface of the water. It was coming right for him! He raised his oar high in the sky ready to strike.

Where the Magic Cannot Follow

The Erlking slouched in Iubdan's throne drinking from a skull assumed to be the fallen king's himself. Bebo sat in her usual place next to the king. Only now her skin was pale and she had glazed over eyes. The Ellerkonge sat at a close by table. They all seemed to be waiting on something or someone. As Fenrir entered the room the Erlking sat up in his chair.

"Well?" the horned king asked.

Fenrir did not have a pleased look on his face.

"He's made it to the outer isles.... Our crows can't fly out to them. We have no spies there... you have no power...," Fenrir was cut short.

"Do not tell me what I have and don't have mongrel!" angrily replied the king.

He sat back into the throne. He hated to admit it but the wolf was right. The fairy magic, light or dark, only seemed to work on the mainland. Once off of the island the Erlking would be powerless. It didn't take the foul king long to conjure up a new plan. He may not have power in the islands south, but he knew who did.

"Send for the pirate lord," the Erlking ordered.

Aegir

Just before Erik came down with the oar he saw a small yellow head pop out of the water. It was a baby whale! His eyes were big and full of worry. The moonlight shined off of his teary eyes. He seemed hesitant to approach Erik at first.

"You... you're not with the bad men are you?" the young whale asked.

"No little fella. I'm a friend," Erik said with an outstretched hand.

"A friend? What's that?"

"Well,... umm... a friend is someone who looks out for you."

"O. My mommy is my friend... her and daddy..."

"Yes, they are the best of friends...," Erik paused for a moment, thinking of what to say.

"So, friend. My name is Erik, what's yours?" he went on.

"My parents call me Aegir!" the whale replied.

"Well, hey Aegir... do you know what happened here? Are you all alone?" The boy tried to ask as timidly as possible.

"The bad men came. They took my dad and tried to take me! My mom fought them... then there was a loud boom,... after that she stopped swimming. She told me goodbye and that she loved me... but she hasn't gone anywhere. I don't understand what's happening."

The poor little whale looked up at Erik with his giant eyes. He hoped maybe he had all the answers. The little whale didn't realize Erik was just a child himself. Erik took a deep breath as he thought of what he might say.

"There seems to be a lot of things happening. A lot that doesn't make sense to you now, and may not for a long time..."

The moon and stars begin to poke back through the clouds. Erik walked to the edge of the mushroom and put his feet in the water. As the whale got closer Erik began to rub his head which seemed to calm him a bit. Erik continued to try to explain what had happened the best he could.

"I'll start with the hard part I suppose... though there is not really any easy part... your mother told you goodbye because she WAS leaving. Not physically, but her spirit was going to another place."

The baby whale looked at Erik perplexed. "Spirit?"

"A spirit is what's inside of all of us. It's the real us. Every living thing has one."

"Well, why did her spirit leave then?"

Erik sighed. Part of him wanted to tell the whale that the grief would never go away, and even with belief the unknowing could torment you. Of course he didn't. He chose to think all the good things he could think instead.

"Sometimes their journey in this world comes to an end....There are much bigger things than us at work. Sometimes people are taken from us before we are ready for them to be.... I like to think maybe they're needed more elsewhere... sometimes I try to think maybe when people are taken away it makes us stronger. Part of them becomes part of us and we move on stronger and better with them! I struggle sometimes to remember that... it takes a lot to remember their presence as opposed to their absence."

"Do you think my dad is with mommy? I want to be with them..."

"That's not the way it works. Your mom sacrificed herself to keep you safe. You ARE safe! So clearly you have more to do in THIS world!"

Erik looked to the distance towards where the whale looked. The direction the baby whale saw his father dragged into the distance. Erik thought about all the people he lost and how he would've done anything to be able to save them. He looked down at the little whale.

"Your dad isn't with her. Not yet. If the bad men took him off then he's still in this world... I'm going to free him. You're going to be with him again."

Now, they just needed a way to catch up to the killers. Even if the wind were to pick up it wouldn't be enough to catch them on the shroom boat. That's when Erik had an idea. He opened his bag to unroll his blanket. He could hold onto one end and Aegir could hold to the other end and pull the boat. It wasn't the most full proof plan. If the baby had been just a bit bigger Erik could simply ride on top of him. Being he wasn't though the blanket would have to work. Even if it didn't give them much space.

As Erik took out his blanket and began to twist it, something in his bag caught his eye. There sitting at the bottom of his bag was a bundle of rope! That would make things a great deal easier. The mama bird must've packed it for him. The funny thing was as many times as he had pulled things from his bag he had never seen or felt the rope in there! It was as if it had just appeared out of thin air.

Regardless of where it came from it was sure to be put to good use! Erik made a small hole in the mushroom and tied the rope through it and handed the other end to the whale.

"Ready?" Erik asked Aegir.

The whale nodded his head and looked to the horizon.

"Alright then. Let's go save your dad!"

Strange Things

The groundhog stood over the stove stirring a pot of stew. The smell of fresh made bread in the oven filled her little nose. She watched out her window as her childhood friend played with the young boy. Her friend may have been almost as old in years as she was, but he was still o so young at heart. He made the perfect companion for the boy. The perfect protector.

She smiled a grand smile as she watched the two. It all seemed so perfect.

The sweet smell of the cooking bread began to turn sour. Instead a charred smell began to fill her nose. There was no reason the bread should've burned so quickly! She turned and opened the oven. Nothing was inside! Yet the burnt smell persisted.

The little groundhog began to search the kitchen to try and find the source of the smell. To no avail. The smell just seemed to grow worse from a mysterious source. She proceeded to go open a window to try and let some of the smell out. As she did, the sight in the yard caught her eye and she immediately stopped what she was doing.

The boy now stood alone in the yard with a frightened look on his face. The sky had turned from day to dusk in a matter of seconds. As the sun set the silhouette of a man began to appear behind the boy. The darker it got the easier it was for Gloria to see the figure. She began to panic. She tried to open the door and run out but the door wouldn't budge! She ran back to the window and tried to open it. It was stuck too! She was trapped and unable to help the boy. She stood helplessly in the kitchen and screamed as she watched the silhouette pull Erik closer, until eventually he was completely swallowed by the shadow.

Her heart pounded, blood rushed through every inch of her. Adrenaline began to pump through the groundhog. Her eyes opened and she shot up straight in her bed. Only it wasn't her bed and she wasn't home.

Gloria was weak. She felt as if she had been asleep for a very long time. It took a moment for reality to start to fade into perspective. Everything seemed hazy. Including her memories.

She got up from her bed and walked towards the door. She felt lighter and her legs didn't seem to want to work the way they should. After a bit of a struggle, she made it to the door. She turned the handle, but the door wouldn't open. Around and around the knob went. After fighting with the door handle it was clear she was stuck. She began to bang on the door for help. She berated the door for several minutes, but it didn't seem like anyone was coming to her aid.

As she walked away from banging on the door she heard something shuffling around on the other side of it. She turned and could see a shadow from the crack under her door. Someone was out there! She began to call for help again. As she did she began to notice a strange smell begin to fill the air. She looked down and saw colored smoke start to come from under the door!

Gloria jumped back and grabbed a sheet from her bed and wrapped it around her face. The strange smoke began to fill the room. Even with the sheet wrapped around her head she still grew dizzy. She began to panic as her breaths grew shorter. She frantically searched the room for something of use. She slowly began to sway back and forth. Her head grew light and her vision began to blur. Just before she was to the point of passing out the door was ripped from its hinges and the strange smoke poured into the hallway of the inn.

Teddy stepped over the dead badger's body and into the room. He looked malnourished and weak. He too had been in some sort of trance. Gloria's banging on the door and her screams for help tore through his false fantasy and woke him. Next to the badger's corpse lay a pump gun much like an exterminator would use. The groundhog's old friend had betrayed them!

They broke the others out of their rooms and woke them from their deep sleeps. Everyone looked quite rough. All of them were skinny with sunk-in eyes. It was clear they had slept for much longer than a night!

As they emerged from the inn Gloria noticed the green leaves had turned to reds and yellows. They had been there even longer than she had thought. It was clear they had fallen into a trap! The Erlking's eyes and arms outstretched over all of the land now. There was truly no one they could trust. As Teddy and the others gathered their things from the inn Gloria sat quietly on a nearby rock. Once again, she tried to find Erik. Only this time she wasn't as lucky in locating him. She couldn't feel him at all! She began to feel sick to her stomach. Had she been too late? While they were asleep, had the Erlking finally gotten to Erik? Is that what her dream was about?

The four of them set off towards Iubdan's castle. The last place that they had known the boy to be. Unfortunately for them, they had no idea of the terrors that had befallen that very castle.

The Reflection

The baby whale had followed his father's echo echolocation for days. He swam like he had never swam before. After several days of pursuit and the poor whale past exhausted, they saw it in the distance! A ship full of lantern lights and torn sails. It had docked on an island! It was time!

Erik had been brave. up till this point. Now that he was closer and saw the size of the ship he began to doubt himself. During all the battles and close calls he always had someone fighting by his side. Someone helping him. This time he would be all alone. He didn't dare endanger Aegir. Erik stood and stared into the still sea. The water reflected back at him as if he were looking in a mirror. He saw the young, innocent, fresh faced boy looking back at him.

"What could I possibly do to a ship full of pirates?" he said to himself with a sigh.

A helpless pain he hadn't felt in a long time began to overcome him. The feeling grew stronger by the second. It was as if he were sinking into a hole. Overwhelming feelings of failure and disappointment began to weigh down on him. He felt like he had sand slowly piling onto his chest. His breathing grew heavier. He took a handful of cold water and ran it through his hair. He inhaled through his nose and exhaled through his mouth trying to control his breathing.

All of the bad memories and feelings rushed through his head. He was sinking into his hole deeper and deeper. He had been through so much in such a short time. Both lives he remembered seemed to be an absolute mess.

Like a locomotive, that's when it hit him. He HAD been through so much. He had fought things real and in his head that others couldn't even imagine. Yet he kept going. He was a fighter! Both lives he lived there seemed to be one outstanding constant. His will! His determination! Maybe he didn't have a giant bear to help him fight the men, but he was far from helpless! A sense of pride filled him. He couldn't forget the bad things that had happened in the past, but he could try his best to help them forge a better future.

Erik looked down into his reflection again. There was no longer a young boy looking back at him. Instead there was a young man staring Erik in the face. The young man was someone Erik had almost completely forgotten about. Someone he had been through a lot with.

"I know you," he said to his reflection.

"And I remember you," his reflection spoke back.
'

Waves began to roll over the reflection as the baby whale swam over to Erik. He had swam in the darkness of the night to go talk to his father.

"So how is he?" Erik asked on Aegir's return.

"He's tired and he's hurt. He's far too big for their nets. They're cutting into him! We have to help him, quickly."

"Did he say anything else?"

"Well, he told me to go. That you and I should leave now while it was still dark and could get away... and that he loved me very much..."

The little whale lowered his head in defeat. Erik began to rub his head, knowing that it helped calm him.

"I agree with your father," Erik said as he let out a long breath.

The whale lifted his head and looked at Erik with a worried look on his face.

"What!?"

"You see that island off on the horizon that way? I want you to swim there and wait on your father and me. If we aren't there by the time the sun is directly above your head I want you to swim as fast as you can as far as you can!" Erik ordered.

"No! I can't just leave you and him! You're my only friends! Let me help!" pleaded little Aegir.

"I promise you I will do everything I can to save your dad! But I won't endanger you! I have to know

292

you'll be far away from these men if anything bad happens!"

The whale shook his head in compliance and set off towards the isle on the horizon.

The Daring Rescue

The sun had started to come up and there was a red hue that filled the air. It wasn't quite day but no longer night. Erik had to make his move now or he would miss his chance. He paddled quietly over to the boat. Erik could hear the pirates snoring before they even laid a foot on the ship. They were all almost in unison. It sounded as if they were smuggling some sort of wild creature in their hull. As he climbed onto the ship's ladder he began to hear footsteps. He carefully eased his head above the deck and looked around.

There were two men stumbling about. Clearly, they had been drinking through the night. Neither seemed to pay any attention to their surroundings. Erik held onto the ladder and watched them closely. One eventually made his way below deck while the other found a bed among the tops of a few barrels. They were clearly going down for the count. Once the man on the barrels began to snore Erik crept onto the deck.

The sun was now level with the ship. It was day! Erik knew that made everything more risky, but he didn't care. He had promised the little whale he would do his best to save his father. No matter what that took. He carefully pulled the sleeping pirate's sword from his belt and made his way to the far side of the ship where the fishing nets entangled Aegir's father.

The netting was thick and gave only a little at a time as Erik chopped at it. He tried to slice it, he tried to chop it. Anything he could think of to try and break through the heavy rope. After several hacks he was able to cut one of the two ties that held the net.

Aegir's father could feel the ropes loosen just a bit. Enough for him to free his tail. He began to flail about to try and finish freeing himself as Erik chopped at the second tie. As Erik came down for one of his final blows his sword was stopped mid air.

A burly man with a wild mustache towered over Erik. He held Erik's sword in his bare hand without the slightest hint of pain upon his face. In an effortless motion he ripped the sword from Erik's hand.

"Not smart ta be messin' 'round wit a pirate's catch boy... specially one so special!"

As the man spoke the trapped whale twisted and turned, trying to break free with all his might. The rope holding the net had broken down to a small strand. As the captain threatened Erik all the boy could focus on was that strand. He didn't care if something happened to him or not. If he could cut that strand or if it broke on its own then Aegir's father would be free! The pirate grabbed Erik by the collar of the shirt.

"Look at me when I be talking ta ya boy!" he began to lift Erik into the air by his collar as he spoke.

"He be messin with tha wrong crew!" the pirate continued shouting.

Spit flew from his mouth as he yelled. Covering Erik's face in the nastiness. Erik calmly wiped the slobber from his face and commented on the pirate's foul breath. This enraged the captain even more. He threw the boy onto the deck.

The rest of the crew had now woken and began to surround Erik. He stumbled to get to his feet. He grabbed the closest thing he could use as a weapon. Unfortunately for him the closest thing to him was a bucket full of dirty water. He wildly swung it back and forth at the surrounding pirates. All the time keeping an eye on the tiny strand that kept the whale captive. Aegir's dad had now begun to panic as he flailed about. His motion became even more wild. The boat began to rock back and forth violently from the waves he was creating. As Erik swung the bucket the ship began to tilt almost completely on its side. Erik lost his balance and spun around before falling to the ground.

Many of the crew rolled across the deck. A few even falling over the rails into the sea. As the crew tried to regain their footing Erik lunged forward and grabbed a dagger that had fallen from a discombobulated sailor's hand.

Erik leapt onto the hanging rope and sawed at the rope like a mad man. Unfortunately the rope was now wet and even more difficult to cut through. He had almost gotten through the strand when one of the pirates swung his sword, cutting Erik across his back. The cut was deep and not in the slightest bit a clean cut. The blade was jagged and torn as it ran across his back. The pain seared through Erik. He wanted to let go of the rope, but he knew he couldn't! He clenched his teeth and continued to cut at the rope.

The rope flailed about as the whale still fought the netting. Almost flinging Erik clear off of it. Out of the corner of his eye he saw another sailor taking a swing at him. This time he was ready. He let go of the rope just as the sword was about to hit him. When he did the pirates sword sailed over the top of his head and right through the remaining stand of rope. Erik and the remaining bit of the net fell into the sea below.

Aegir's father was able to break free! Censing his son was close by he immediately headed towards the island to reunite with him. Erik watched as the whale swam to safety.

Erik tried to free himself from the netting that had fallen on top of him, but it was no use. He was too tangled and it was too heavy. Further he sank into the ocean's depths. The reflection of the sun on the surface of the water grew further and further away.

A Pirate's Life

Erik's vision began to return. He was lying on the deck of the pirate ship surrounded. All of them laughing and pointing at him. The captain stood over him with his arms crossed.

"Well, well.... Looks like our nets catch more than fish 'n whales!"

He picked up Erik by the back of his shirt and lifted him into the air as a mother dog would lift her pup. He proceeded to hang the boy on a nearby lantern hook. Erik was now eye- level with the captain. The pirate scowled at the boy.

"You cost me a LOT of money with that little stunt ye just pulled!"

Erik didn't say a word. He simply returned the scowl. The captain continued to talk to the boy who was hung up like a hog at a butcher shop.

"My men here think we outta gut ya fer what ya did."

The captain drew a knife from his waist and ran it down Erik's stomach in the motion of cutting him open. Erik didn't flinch.

"Maybe I'll just poke a few holes in ya and throw ya overboard .....Watch tha sharks finish ya!"

Erik held his silence and showed no fear towards the pirate. Even as the captain began to dig the blade's tip into the boy's shoulder he didn't move. At first the lack of response angered the captain, but as he poked and prodded the boy he began to admire him.

One drop of blood ran down Erik's throat to his chest from where the pirate had pushed his knife in just enough to break the skin just beneath Erik's chin. Still the boy stayed stoic. The captain half smiled and let out a bit of a chuckle.

"Heh... maybe we got the makin's of a pirate 'ere boys!" he boasted.

Finally, Erik decided to speak up.

"I would never join you or any pirate crew. Thieves, rapists, and murderers! The lot of you!"

"Aye, but it all be so much fun though!"

The captain lifted Erik from the hook and sat him on the ground.

"Yer a tough boy, I'll give ya that. Tough or stupid. Can't quite tell yet."

The massive pirate looked over the boy for a moment.

"Aye! I think we be keepin' em alive fer now! Take em to see tha lord. Let 'em explain to him why we be comin' in empty handed!... raise the anchor! Drop the sails! Let's take tha boy ta see tha pirate lord!"

Erik was thrown into a tiny nasty cell below deck and the pirates sailed further out into the open sea.

The Castle by the Sea

Iubdan's castle by the south sea was one of the most grand castles in all the land. The king always had great pride in his homestead. Gloria had seen it many years prior. It was one of the prettiest places she had ever seen in her life to this day.

As the fellowship approached the castle Gloria quickly realized something was off. The usual shimmering white castle by the sea looked dull. The overly manicured landscape that surrounded the castle was overgrown and dying. A dark cloud seemed to hang over the castle.

They were greeted at the door by Queen Bebo. She, much like the castle, looked drained of all life. Her usual radiant skin looked cold and gray. She didn't speak how the groundhog remembered. The strong woman now had a quiet and slow speech pattern. It was almost as if the voice wasn't coming from her at all. Like a puppet being worked by a ventriloquist.

"What brings you hereee...?" asked the queen in almost a whisper.

Gloria knew something wasn't right. She could feel an evil presence among them.

"Are you okay my queen? You don't look as spritely as usual, my dear."

At this the decrepit queen shot a vexed look at the ground hog.

"You dareee.... Insssulttt me...... youuur queeen!?" This time the queen spoke just above a whisper but with a much more aggressive tone.

"No! No! My queen! Your beauty trumps all! Just making sure everything is alright!" replied the groundhog quickly.

"Sooo..... I asssk again.... Why haveee youuu come hereee...!"

"We've come to see king Iubdan. He called for me several weeks ago. I was caught up along the way so I'm a bit late." The groundhog was sly and quick to weave a tale.

"The kinggg issss not well...." replied the queen.

"Yes dear, so I've heard. That may have been why he contacted me. He felt the sickness coming on. I've come with many ailments to help him."

The queen overlooked the groundhog's companions. Stopping at Alpha for a moment longer.

"Whaaat off your friends?..."

302

"Well, the gentle giant that is a bear is my lifelong companion and oldest friend. The stallion and the wolf are hired for protection. Little old groundhog like myself needs as much help as I can get!"

Bebo stood motionless for a moment and started off as if she were awaiting her next command by whatever puppeteer controlled her. After several seconds the queen's glance returned to the groundhog.

"Very well... I will take you to him..."

The queen turned and began to walk back into the castle. As they walked by the guards they couldn't help but notice they had the same glazed over eyes as the queen. The group of friends began to slow their pace so they could speak amongst themselves without the queen hearing.

"Something is very wrong here," whispered the groundhog.

"The smell of rotted flesh fills my nose!" huffed the wolf.

"The queen... the soldiers... they're all dead!" he continued.

A worried look appeared on Gloria's face.

"What about the boy? Can you smell Erik?" she asked.

The wolf shook his head.

"There's only a small hint of his scent. He was here at some point, but it's been a while."

"Good, well none of us speak anything about the boy. We will find out what Kind Iubdan knows and be on our way. I'm not sure what's going on but we need to get

303

out of here as quickly as possible," Gloria planned out
loud.

The wolf took in another whiff of the foul smells
in the air.

"There's more... the horned king was here..."

The groundhog stopped in her tracks and her
eyes grew big.

"That explains the undead... it can mean nothing
good."

"Do you think he took Erik?" Teddy asked.

"No, we would know if the Erlking gained Erik's
powers... the whole world would know," the groundhog
replied.

"Well, at least he's not here anymore," Enbarr
chimed in.

"He's not... but his lackey is... I almost didn't
smell him. His stench rivals that of the undead," the wolf
added.

Teddy looked forward down the corridor as a set
of guards opened the door to the throne room. There
was no turning back now.

There, sitting in king Iubdan's throne was the
corpulent fetid sluggard.

"The Ellerkonge," Teddy growled under his
breath.

The Capital of Crossbones

As the pirates approached the great ship graveyard the captain ordered for Erik to be removed from his cage. Erik was let out and escorted to the front of the ship where the captain was waiting on him.

"Not many can sail these waters. Only a true pirate can make it through to the capital city!" bragged the captain.

"Capital city?" Erik asked.

"Aye, The Crossbones Capital, home of the pirate lord and' any worthy sea-dog."

"Why are you showing me all this?"

"Cuz my boy, ye be something' special. Not everyone can stare death in the eye with such a cool and collected head. You 'av the makins of a great captain one day!" smiled the pirate.

"I would never join the likes of you! Your kind words are poison to my ears! I could never live with myself doing even half the horrible things you scoundrels do!" defended Erik.

"In a world like ours, being' good doesn't do a damn thing for ya. If ya want somethin' then ya gotta take it! It makes life o so simple my boy!"

"Who would want a simple life like that? I for one want a grand life!"

"Aye, it be grand! If yer good enough at it ye be richer than the kings in no time!"

The captain put his giant arm around Erik's shoulders. Erik quickly swooped down and out of the man's embrace.

"Your definition of rich and mine are two very different things! Materials, gold, jewels, treasures! Those are the things that you think make you rich! For me, I want to be rich with love! With experiences! Experiences I can be proud of! Things a pirate could never understand!"

The pirate scowled at Erik for a moment before looking ahead. Through a heavy fog many lights and a massive outline began to take shape.

"We be home!"

The captain smiled as he pointed ahead for Erik to look. Erik didn't want to admit it, but as the fog thinned the sight before him became quite impressive. A wall of broken ships with their jagged pieces sticking out like thorns surrounded the side of the island they were coming in on. Beyond the wall was a city unlike anything Erik had ever seen.

It stretched from the beach all the way to the top of the cliff that was in the middle of the island. There at the top of the cliff was an enormous boat! It looked like it was impaled on the tip of the cliff! Many buildings were attached to it and the side of the cliff.

The closer they got though the more menacing their surroundings became. Erik no longer focused on the grandeur of the city. He now noticed the filth and darkness as they docked the boat. Skeletons hung from ropes, blood and other mysterious fluids seemed to cover every inch of the docks. The smell of the city was awful. It smelled of sex, sweat, piss and boos.

As they exited the boat they were met by a gaggle of whores. Within the first few minutes of being ashore more than half of the crew had disappeared into the madness. The captain led Erik off the boat with no chains or shackles, only a firm grip on the back of the boy's neck. He bent over and talked into the boy's ear as they began to enter the city.

"You can try to run if ya want, but this ain't the safest place for a body yer age ta be wonderin' around. There ain't enough whores fer all the men on the island. One of these deprived sailors may just take the next best thing," the captain laughed.

Erik shuttered in disgust. He figured he'd stay with the captain for now rather than try to brave the city himself.

They made their way up the cliff towards the giant boat. Shops and houses hung from under the cliff and on the sides of the rock. Ladders and sketchy looking rope ladders connected all of the makeshift buildings. After a steady hike up the hill, they made it to the ship. It was the largest ship Erik had ever laid eyes on. Even in its condition, all broken and rotted it was still quite the sight to see.

The hull was broken in half and a new wall with a door had been built into the crack. Just above the door hung a skeleton with his arms extended. The skeleton wore a grand hat and coat full of medals across its breast. It seemed as if he had been made an example of and hung as a trophy for the pirate lord.

Inside the boat sat the pirate lord in his throne made of bones and skulls. Every inch around the throne was stacked high with gold and piles of jewels several feet high. One little path led straight through to the throne. Everything else was engulfed in the sea of gold.

As Erik and the captain got closer to the pirate lord Erik got a better look at him. He was nothing like he had expected. The pirate lord was tall and lanky. In fact he was so skinny he almost blended in with the other skeletons that made up the throne! His face was sunken and dark circles surrounded his eyes. His hair and long beard was dreaded and tangled.

When Erik was close enough to the pirate lord to see well he instantly sat up in his throne. He began to laugh an eerie laugh that filled the room.

"I don't believe it!"

The pirate lord smiled a dingy yellow and golden plated smile.

"That was easy!"

The Bear and the Pig

As Teddy and the others entered the room the Ellerkonge's face went flush at the sight. He immediately shot up from the broken throne. He couldn't believe his eyes.

"YOU!! BUT HOW? YOU'RE DEAD! I KILLED YOU!" he shouted.

Teddy started to lunge forward but the little groundhog held out her arm in front of him.

"Wait my dear," she told him.

Once he saw the bear was restrained for the time being, the Ellerkonge looked over the group before him.

"So.... A rat, a mule, a traitor and a walking corpse... quite the little rag tag group you have here! What brings you to my castle?" he laughed.

Gloria stepped forward. Even though she was only about to the Ellerkonge's knee she showed no fear towards him. She walked past him and climbed to the top of the queen's throne so she was closer to eye level with him.

"You know why we are here sluggard! What has become of the boy?" she inquired.

The Ellerkonge smiled.

"What's the matter witch ya? Can't feel him anymore?" he replied with a smirk.

"We came here for answers. Who better to ask than the man who's always just a few steps behind him at all times?"

This comment seemed to have struck a nerve in the Ellerkonge.

"I HAVE NEWS FOR YOU, WITCH! I DID CATCH HIM! YOU CAN'T FIND HIM BECAUSE HE'S DEAD! EATEN BY THE WORMS BY NOW!"

At this, the little groundhog slapped the Ellerkonge across the face as hard as she could.

"You are a fool if you think I believe that for even a second! You and your master don't even know what you seek. What the boy is! The power he holds! Your king would have already rid you of this world if you had what he needed!"

The Ellerkonge, enraged, backhanded Gloria as hard as he could off of the back of the throne and across the room. Before the Ellerkonge could even turn back around he was knocked through the throne. He felt as if he had been hit by a log. As he tried to get to his feet he was quickly pinned by the massive grizzly. Teddy hung over him with his claws dug deep into the man's forearms. He couldn't move from under him! Foam dripped from the bear's mouth. Fire burned in Teddy's eyes and for the first time that the Ellerkonge could remember... he was scared.

The zombified queen and her guards suddenly stood to attention and their eyes began to glow green. The door to the throne room flew back open and several decaying soldiers with the same glowing green eyes entered with weapons in hand.

Enbarr had picked up Gloria's limp body and laid it across Alpha's back. As the guards entered the room, he drew his guns. The horde of undead moved like a wave towards the adventurers.

The Ellerkonge tried to use the distraction to break free, but it was no use. Teddy had him firmly pinned to the ground.

"We need to go! Now!" Enbarr shouted as the room quickly filled with the undead.

The steed unloaded his pistols into the quickly approaching horde. Though many fell, more and more began to pile through the door. Alpha and Enbarr began to back into a corner as the room filled.

Teddy looked over towards them and saw Glorias body laid across Alpha's back. A rage like no other overtook Teddy. He began to pull the Ellerkonge's arms in opposite directions as hard as he could. The vile man screamed as his arms began to tear from his body.

RRRIIIIPPPP.

His arms flew from his body into the sea of undead soldiers.

The Ellerkonge screamed in agony.

"Please! please don't kill me. I'll tell you anything!" he pleaded.

Teddy looked again at Gloria's limb body.

"SHE was the one asking questions! I don't care what you have to say! I only care about cleansing this earth of your stench one and for all!"

The Ellerkonge watched helplessly in horror as the bear bit down into his neck and tore away at it. Blood sprayed over the bear's face. The grizzly rose from the disembodied carcass with a wild look in his eyes.

He turned towards his companions that were backed into the corner trying their best to hold off the wave of undead. Enbarr and Alpha fought valiantly but were quickly overwhelmed. Teddy roared a great roar that shook the entire room. He began violently slashing his way through the horde towards his friends.

Enbarr, now wielding one of the fallen fairy's swords, swung it wildly at the mass of attacking dead men. More and more began to eclipse him. Before long he wasn't able to swing the sword anymore because they had gotten so close.

They stabbed their swords and spears at him and the wolf. The wave of soldiers began to engulf him. He dropped the sword and turned his back to shield Alpha who was now huddled around Gloria. He began to feel the sharp points of the spears slowly break the skin on his back.

Just as they began to dig in deeper, the pain stopped. A gust of air rolled across Enbarr's back. He turned his head to see the undead fairies ripping clean in half midair. Teddy stood behind them, wide eyed and covered head to toe in blood. Pieces of undead were scattered from the throne to where he stood. Enbarr grabbed back up the sword and Alpha placed Gloria back onto his back. The two followed behind Teddy as he barreled through the rotting soldiers.

The three of them made their way out of the throne room. But there waiting on them stood the undead queen. She didn't seem as unresponsive as the others. In fact she seemed very aware of her surroundings.

"You won't leave here alive!" spoke the queen, her eyes glowing bright.

The Pirate Lord

The pirate lord circled around Erik like a vulture circles a cadaver. He moved slowly and unnaturally. He almost seemed to float around Erik like some sort of wraith.

The captain who had brought Erik in watched as the pirate lord examined the boy.

"Do ya know tha boy?" the captain asked.

"Aye.." the pirate lord answered in a drawn out tone.

Erik looked the eerie pirate up and down. He was certain he had never seen the skeleton of a man before. The pirate lord could see the confusion on the boy's face.

"Don't cha' worry boy, yer not crazy. We've never met in person. I just know who you are through... a mutual friend. Through stories and tales if you will," he cackled.

Erik took a deep breath, trying not to panic. He could only think of one person the pirate could be talking about when saying they had a mutual friend. Somehow the Erlking had contacted the pirate lord.

"I will take the boy from here... you have unknowingly just brought us the biggest payday of our lives captain... good job... very good job," he smiled.

The pirate lord put his boney fingers over the boy's shoulders as he talked.

"What's so special 'bout that there boy?" asked the captain.

"I'm not sure, but clearly somethin'. There be higher powers at work here. Can't ya feel it... of course ya can feel it! Otherwise ya wouldn't of brought tha boy here! Somethin' bout this here boy led ya ta bring em to me! He be special indeed. Nough so for tha horned king ta pay an absurd amount of his gold to us! Ahahaha."

The pirate lord walked Erik out onto a balcony that stuck out from the captain's quarters of the wrecked ship. From there they could see the pirate city in its entirety and the surrounding wall and ocean. It was an impressive view to say the least.

The pirate's demeanor changed when they walked outside. He took a deep breath of the warm salty air before he spoke.

"I've known the horned king fer a long time... we've always had a bit of an arrangement if ya will. He's added quite a bit a gold to tha pile.... All these years an I've never seen him so desperate... so wanting... the offer he's put on your head is like nothing I ever saw.... So what be so special about ya boy?"

The old pirate didn't look as menacing outside in the light. Inside he was a ghoulish figure with dark eyes and a skeleton's shadow hanging over his face. Now he just looked like a feeble old man. His face was dry and leathered. Wild white whiskers jutted from his chin and cheeks. His eyes were so covered in fog they looked to be white.

Erik sighed at the pirate's question. He had grown tired of answering why the Erlking wanted him so bad. Especially because he really didn't know. He knew he had some sort of power, but other than that he really had no clue.

"I really wish I knew. I know I have something special inside of me and that many people have died trying to protect me. The Erlking has hunted me my entire life trying to get whatever power I hold."

"You seem to have evaded him fer some time... that be no easy task. How 'av ya managed?"

"Luck,.. Luck and lots of friends really..."

"Well maybe ye luck be yer special powers. Seems ta be keepin ya out of trouble this far."

"Maybe."

The pirate lord stared out towards the vast sea. He seemed to go into a trance as he looked out. A grin began to run across his face. He thought of all the many adventures he had been on. He had lived several lives since he was the boy's age. He looked Erik in the eyes, but he didn't see what he had expected.

"You've looked to 'av lived quite a long life fer ya ta be so young son.... Your soul be old... yet your heart be

317

young. Still warm and inviting' like that of a child... ya really are a special..."

Erik was taken back by the kindness of the old pirate. When he was told he was meeting the pirate lord this was not who or what he was expecting.

"You're not at all like I thought you would be," Erik said as he joined the man and leaned on the balcony.

"Expecting a cut throat terrible scoundrel, were ya?"

"Well.... Yes, sort of."

"Maybe a life or two ago I was. The worst of the worst. The most vile of scoundrels... then the sea, she broke me...."

"What do you mean?"

"When ye be crazy enough to challenge Mother Nature she's not too shy ta humble ya... I was the best damn pirate the seven seas had ever seen. Thought I could sail any storm. Cursed and taunted the seas... then one night there was a storm like no other. Waves bigger than mountains.... Winds that could lift a grown man... My crew was all lost to the sea... and my ship..."

The captain outstretched his arms.

"That's how the boat ended up here! No wonder you're the pirate lord! Surviving something like that!"

"I'm no pirate anymore boy. Just an old man surrounded by useless treasures... too afraid to even step foot in the water anymore... I wish the storm would've taken me and my ship... would've been much more fitting than wasting away to dust."

Erik wanted to hate the man, after all he was the leader of some of the nastiest, most ruthless people to have ever walked this earth, but he couldn't help but feel compassion for the old man. Even sympathy and a little admiration. So much so that he had almost forgotten the situation he had fallen into.. almost. The realization hit him.

"So... when are you handing me over to the Erlking?" Erik asked with hopes, maybe the pirate lord had changed his mind.

He wasn't completely wrong. The pirate lord had no use for the reward that had been offered by the Erlking. He had a reputation to uphold, but he had grown to the point where even that no longer mattered. In all honesty he wished to keep the boy and raise him as one of his own. He could see it all. Him back at sea with the boy now a man sailing a grand ship. Kings of the sea! The pirate's life would be so fitting.

Then the pirate began to think of all the bad he had done over the years. All of the lowlife and underhanded things he did. As he looked at Erik he knew the boy could never be those things. He would never WANT for the boy to be those things.

As he contemplated what to do with the boy he began to see several giant shadows under the water quickly moving towards the city. He had been at war with the whales for as far back as he could remember and never had they been brave or bold enough to attack.. yet here they were. He shook his head and laughed as he looked back at the boy.

"No need to worry about that boy... looks like your luck and your friendships are paying' off yet again," he smiled.

"What do you mean?"

About that time a loud *CRRRAACCCKKKK* filled the air. Erik looked out to the wall just in time to see part of it crumble into the sea!

The pirate lord got down to eye level with Erik and spoke.

"There be no doubt about it, ye got the luck of a rabbit with a horseshoe round its neck and four leaf clover shoved up his arse.... But take it from me boy, luck can run out. It's up to you ta keep goin' when it does. Find whatever it is inside you the horned king really wants and use it against him!"

The pirate lord opened the door to the captain's quarters and held out his arms for Erik to pass by him. So, Erik ran into the pirate city. The pirate lord walked back over to the edge of the balcony and watched as his city began to crumble into the sea.

The pirates screamed and shot their guns into the water at the pod of attacking whales. The mighty whales barreled through several docks and beams that supported a lot of the city. As the bottom of the city fell much of the top began to crash down too. Many pirates fell into the water and were soon dragged into the depths by their enemies.

Some of the pirates even began to fire cannons into the water, but it did no good. Many of the men ran inland and tried to take refuge at the top of the hill. Erik passed several people traveling in the opposite direction. Having to push his way through them.

Among the midst of one of the rushing mobs Erik's arm was grabbed as he tried passing through. He looked up and saw who had grabbed him. It was the captain that had brought him in!

"Where ya goin' boy?!"

"Let me go! The pirate lord set me free!"

The clearly angered captain looked towards the boat at the top of the hill and then back at the boy.

"The lord grows weak in his old age. As he said, you'll bring us more gold than we know what to do with!"

As he yelled at Erik, other pirates began to hear what he was saying and now stopped around the boy as if to help apprehend him. They began to talk amongst themselves. The news of the grand bounty had already spread through parts of the city.

"So the lord just let him go?" one said.

"Stubborn old fool!" yelled another.

"We'll just take him in ourselves!" suggested another.

The captain tightened his grip on the boy's arm and began pulling him. Erik struggled and fought but the burly brute was too strong. He dragged him back up the hill towards the broken boat.

The mob of pirates kicked open the front door of the pirate lords domain. Many of them were shouting vulgarities. Between their city falling into the seas at their feet and the release of the boy, they had had enough. They no longer felt like their leader held the same beliefs as them. They approached the captain's quarters with torches and swords drawn.

The captain that held tight to Erik's arm banged on the captain's door.

"Come out here, old man!" he shouted.

There was no answer. The brute kicked open the door and walked in - Erik still in tow. He looked around the room and out to the deck. The pirate lord was nowhere to be seen! Many of the pirates began filling their pockets and shirts with the lord's gold and jewelry.

The earth beneath them shook as the whales still bombarded the city below. Several of the pirates had now made their way to the top of the hill. Once it was known the pirates lords quarters were empty the fiends began to pile in to get a take of the treasures for themselves. More and more squeezed in and fought their way through the broken ship. As they fought amongst themselves the captain seemed to be searching for something specific. He rummaged through the lord's room like a mad man. Throwing things and pulling them apart.

"That damn old bat took it! He had to of!"

While the captain was occupied Erik began to look for this chance to run. He crept towards the door slowly as the room was rummaged.

The old boat began to creak and crack as the pirates that had fled the city now pilled in. Erik had a bad feeling in the pit of his stomach. As his heartbeat quickened he visualized his path out and sprinted out the captain's quarters and into the overly crowded treasure room. The captain had noticed his escape and followed the boy out. He shouted for someone to grab the boy, but they were all too busy quarreling amongst themselves now. The burly man shoved others to the side as he worked his way towards Erik. It was hard to squeeze through the men so Erik quickly dropped to the ground and started to crawl through the legs of the crowd. This quick thinking pushed Erik ahead of the captain and out the door.

Almost as soon as Erik had gotten out of the old boat it began to move! As the pirates fought they didn't even notice as the ship began to break from the hilltop. Slowly, then all at once the half of the ship slid off the top of the hill and off of the cliff. Down it fell to the broken city below.

Erik watched as it hit the ground. Pieces of it flew everywhere. He couldn't imagine the damage that was done inside of it. Oil and alcohol began to pour from the wreckage into the town and water. It didn't take long for one of the fallen pirate's torches to catch. The old wood the city was made of began to catch quickly.

Erik began to run down the hill as quickly as he could. By the time he had reached the bottom of the hill almost everything had caught fire. Erik weaved through the burning city, somehow not burning himself in the slightest. Finally, he came to a broken dock. He looked out into the water but didn't see anything. It seemed the fire had run off the whales!

As he stood and looked out for a sign of hope a large, burned man walked down the dock behind him - smoke still coming off of him. Erik turned just in time to see the horrific man just before he reached him. As the charred man spoke Erik quickly recognized the voice was that of the captains.

"You're comin' with me boy. Even if I av ta row ya out of here on a damned plank of wood. This ere is all your doin'! I'll stay and watch the Erlking rip your skin from yer bones after I collect my reward!"

Erik tried to maneuver around the brute of a man but was caught and lifted high into the air. The dock below them instantly gave way. The pirate's legs fell through the mutilated dock and Erik fell into the water on the far side. Somehow the pirate managed to grab hold of the edge of the hole before falling all the way through.

As the captain struggled to pull himself back up he saw Erik had already managed to get back onto the dock. The oils had now run into the water, catching it on fire too. He felt as if his legs were boiling in the water below him.

Erik had managed to get back onto the dock and watched as the pirate struggled to pull himself up. At first he thought perhaps he could watch as the man struggled until eventually he fell into the water, but after a few seconds of watching the pirate struggle he came to the conclusion he couldn't just leave him. Against his better judgment he reached down to try and help the captain up.

The captain was burned from head to toe, his legs now almost boiled. His muscles had begun to give out. He knew he had reached his time. As the little boy reached towards him for help he snatched his arm and yanked him down.

Erik fought to not be pulled in with the captain. He held onto the edge of the dock with all his might. Splinters began to jab into the palm of his hand as he squeezed. Suddenly the captain's grip loosened. The captain wore a face of horror as he was snatched and drugged down by his burnt legs. Erik watched as he disappeared into the darkness below.

Erik wasn't sure what had happened but he sat and looked towards the water. The fires had now reached the other half of the boat at the top of the hill. Erik could feel the heat trap him in. He stood at the end of the broken dock and stared into the blue nothingness as the world burned around him.

From the depths he began to see a friendly face swim up towards him. It was Aegir's father! The whale surfaced and motioned for Erik to climb onto him. Erik climbed onto the massive whale and they swam out into the ocean as the cross bone city turned to ashes behind them.

The Cleansing!

The undead queen stood firmly with her daggers tight in her hands. Teddy coming down from his natural high began to slump over. The adrenaline was leaving him and his wounds festered. Enbarr began to step forward, but Gloria who had finally come to hold her arm out for him to stop.

"You and Alpha tend to Teddy. I'll handle this."

The little groundhog jumped down from Alpha and approached the queen. As she walked towards her she began pulling things from her satchel and seemed to be speaking under her breath.

Alpha and Enbarr turned to hold off the undead that were still in pursuit of them while Gloria headed towards the queen.

The small pile of mixed herbs in her hands began to glow.

The queen spoke as the groundhog approached. Her voice now sounded nothing like her own. A low hoarse voice spoke from her mouth. It was clearly the Erlking talking through her.

"Foolish rodent. Your backwoods white magic will be of no help to you here!"

The groundhog said nothing back. She nearly kept muttering her enchantment. The pile in her hand began to glow brighter and brighter.

The overly confident possessed queen bent down to the groundhog's level with a smug look on her face.

"You... your little group of misfits... you will all die here... the boy will die... I will feed on his soul and become the most powerful being anyone could imagine. I will be truly be unstoppable..."

Gloria finally looked up from her hand and stopped the chanting. She looked past the queen's eyes into that of the Erlking.

"We all die... some of us may even die by your hand, but today is not that day... the boy WILL be the end of you. I will be sure of it! You will never have the power you seek!"

Her eyes shifted back towards that of the queens. "Be at peace, my dear."

With that she blew the glowing herbs in her hand that had turned to dust into the queen's face! A green smoke began to pour out of the queen's mouth. The fog left her eyes and her body fell to the ground. She was free. She was at peace.

As the queen fell to the ground the other undead followed suit. They had successfully chopped the head from the snake. Gloria was very weak from the counter spell. She wasn't one to use magic often even though she had known it most of her life. She knew as she cast the spell that even white magic came at a price. She began to sit on the ground, but as she slouched, she stopped and her ears perked up. A wave of adrenaline shot through her.

"Do you hear that!?" she asked.

Teddy and Enbarr looked at each other in confusion. They didn't hear anything. Alpha on the other hand was already looking out towards the water. Teddy helped Gloria to her feet and everyone walked to the water's edge.

The Looking Pieces

The Erlking stepped back from his cauldron and let out a great roar of frustration. He tipped it over in the process, and a colorful liquid covered the floor. Parts of several scenes were scattered about. It looked as if several windows had burst across the floor.

His blood boiled. Everything was falling apart. No matter what he tried, he was met with failure. Not even a day before the groundhog had eradicated him from Iubdan's castle he had gotten word that the city of crossbones had crumbled into ashes.

Wherever the boy went, destruction followed. Now, the boy was out of his reach. He no longer had an upper hand. All of the Erlking's generals had been slain or betrayed him. He could feel his powers in the over-world dwindling. Even with the spell failing and his brothers dead he still didn't have the powers needed to walk among them as himself.

The Erlking looked over the scattered pictures on the floor before we wiped them away. As he did something caught his eye. A spy remained among Iubdan's fallen castle. The scene was small and hard to make out. The Erlking scooped it up in his hands to get a better look. His spy was perched in a tree looking out towards the sea. The groundhog and her companions stood at the edge of the water looking out. The Erlking began to make out something in the distance on the water's horizon. A pod of whales swam towards the castle. There, standing on the head of the lead whale was the boy!

Reunited

Erik was prepared to bring the castle crumbling down like the city of crossbones. The whales swam in perfect formation. Erik proudly stood on top the king of the whales head with a pirate sword strapped to his side.

As the pod approached the castle Erik could see four silhouettes standing on the shore. As they grew closer to the shore Erik couldn't believe his eyes. He thought for sure it was some trick being played by the Erlking. Teddy, Enbarr, Alpha.... All together. It didn't make any sense. He continued to think it was a trick until he saw the fourth person standing there. The smallest of the four. A little groundhog. There was no way the Erlking had ever known anything about her. Simply seeing her began to calm him.

He jumped down from the whale with great excitement. His eyes were swelled with tears as he ran towards Teddy first. He hugged the giant bear with all his might.

"How!? I thought the Ellerkonge.... Well... I thought you were gone! I'm so happy to see you!"

The grizzly smiled and lifted the boy in the air as he hugged him back.

"Glad to see you again too!"

Teddy returned Erik to the ground, and the boy looked upon the fellowship before him in confusion and amazement.

"How? How is it you have all come together?" Erik asked.

They all turned towards the little groundhog with two different colored eyes.

Erik's eyes lit up as he looked her over.

"I know you!"

The groundhog smiled at the comment.

"Indeed, you do! and I you!"

Erik reached down and picked up the little groundhog. Gloria gave him a long hug. The hug warmed Erik to his very core. Somehow it gave him the feeling that everything was going to be okay from then on. A relaxing and calming wave flowed over him.

"Come sweet boy, we have much to discuss."

The five of them set up camp on the beach. It was the calm before the storm. Everyone laughed and reminisced. Those who hadn't met became acquainted. The whales all stayed close to shore, especially little Aegir and spoke with their new friends. They told Teddy and Alpha of the brave little boy and how he saved the king of whales from the clutches of the dreaded pirates and the falling of the cross bone city. Erik told his friends all he had been through and they did the same.

As the night wound down and everyone began to fall asleep Gloria pulled Erik to the side to talk to him alone.

"Do you remember anything before this world? Anything from when you were a young child?" asked the groundhog.

"I'm not sure... I have bits that I remember that seem like they're from somewhere else, but others that seem to be from here. Like I have lived in two worlds my entire life!"

"That's not crazy in the least bit! Tell me what you remember of both worlds. Do you remember the first time we met? Where it was?"

Erik thought hard for a moment.

"I... I think so... but you didn't speak then!... it was the night that..."

He paused for a moment, seemingly hesitant on what was next to come out of his mouth. Almost afraid to say what he was thinking.

"It's okay dear, the bad memories are just as important as the good ones sometimes. They still make up our past. Help define our future. It's okay to think of them. To remember the pain. It's okay to hurt, to be sad sometimes."

"It was the night that my grandmother passed away... I was so little, so terrified. I had run into the woods with my teddy. I remember seeing you and your two colored eyes. I remembered thinking how crazy it was that you had the same two colored eyes that she did. It gave me comfort in a strange way... I didn't know much about death then... in my mind I thought that maybe somehow, someway you were her...."

The groundhog smiled a warm smile and put her hand on Erik's shoulder.

"And now? You're an expert on death are you?"

"Well... I guess not, but I've been through it a lot more. I don't know that I've grown to know it more or grown more numb to it."

"Who else have you lost, sweetie?"

The memories began to overcome him. Like a tidal wave crashing over the top of him. All the loss, all the pain. He seemed to have forgotten so much of it since he had been here. He remembered both of his aunts and Mr. Luthor. This time as he thought of them though, with all the bad started to come the good as well. He began to think of the vision he had had at Luthor's funeral. He could perfectly remember the warm air on his face. The feeling of freedom and peace in his soul when he saw that stallion running in the fields with his family. At this thought Erik opened his eyes and looked to Enbarr.

The little groundhog giggled a bit.

"So.. so you still think you know more about death now than when you were a small child?"

Erik was bewildered by the conversation they were having. He looked bath and forth between Gloria and Enbarr.

"So, is he? And are you...?"

"People live on in many different ways, my child. I'm not here to tell you what's what. Only to help you on

334

your way. You've been lost for a very long time dear. Hold close to all of those you love. Let them help you find your way back."

"Back? Back to where? ... the other world? To my aunt's house?"

"Your aunt's house is just that. A house. You have to decide where your home is. Where your heart is."

The groundhog gave Erik a hug, smiled, and laid down into a little ball. Erik covered her with his blanket and stared into the fire.

No More

Little by little the fire turned to embers as Erik watched the fire. Darkness now surrounded him. He knew what was to come next. Only this time was going to be different.

He looked up to the glowing yellow eyes glaring at him. No goosebumps ran up his arms, no shortage of breath, no uncontrollable urge to want to run. Only confidence and readiness resided in Erik now.

"Welcome back boy.... Have you finally accepted your fate?"

"I've accepted that none of this will end until I face you."

"HA! Face me!! Hahaha. I'm the Erlking! You're just a boy! What chance do you stand against me!"

"You've stopped at nothing to get to me. To take my powers. I may not know what they are, but I know there's something you want, and something you fear! Just like you fear me!"

"FEAR YOU!? I AM THE GREAT AND POWERFUL ERLKING! KING OF THE FAIRIES! LORD

OF THE UNDEAD! I FEAR NO ONE! ESPECIALLY SOME CHILD!"

The Erlking in a fit lunged at Erik and tried to grab him by the neck, but as he did he simply passed through him like a ghost. It seems the little power he had gained on the surface world was quickly dwindling. The Erlking stepped back. He felt weaker than he had ever felt before. As if passing through the boy drained him somehow.

"What is this? What magic have you, child! Damn you!" the Erlking demanded.

"I told you... I don't know what my powers are exactly. Just that I'm going to use them one way or another to stop you. I'm no longer afraid, and I'm no child!"

The Erlking took another step back, almost tripping over his robes. Before him stood a young man. Fearless and empowered, ready to fight. He slowly continued to back away from Erik.

"Your power! Your soul! It will all be mine!" shouted the Erlking as he retreated into the darkness.

The darkness surrounding Erik began to lift. The dawning sun began to peak over the horizon. Erik took in a fresh breath of the crisp morning air. It was like he was taking a breath of new life.

Saying Goodbye

Everyone began to wake. As they did they were shocked by Erik's appearance. No longer was he a little boy, but a strapping young man! He stood to Teddy's shoulders and had hair on his chin. He was the man he was at the beginning of his journey and more.

As everyone began to prepare for their day they quickly noticed one of them was not up with the others. Usually the first to rise, Gloria laid curled in a ball covered in Erik's blanket. Teddy knew right away something was wrong. The bear went to the little groundhog and scooped her up in his arms. She looked at peace.

"She must've gone sometime in the night. She used a lot of energy yesterday to save all of us, probably more than she had to give," said Enbarr as Teddy walked by with her.

"She lived a full, long life. Full of love. She looked after us till the very end." Teddy began to tear up as he spoke.

Erik walked over to Gloria and gave her a kiss on her head.

"I'm glad I got the chance to see her one last time. Have one last conversation with her."

They took the morning to bury their friend there on the edge of the ocean on a hilltop. It was a beautiful spot for a final resting place. As they laid her to rest they all said kind words. Teddy, knowing her for the longest, had the most to say. It wasn't sad per say. There were tears, but they knew she had had a fulfilled life. She had lived a long life. She had done what she set out to do.

Most of the day was silent. Everyone was deep in their own heads. As they finished packing up the camp they began to talk amongst themselves about the next step.

"The boy is safe and with us. So what do we do next?" Alpha asked Teddy.

"The boy is a man now. Yet he will never be safe. So long as the Erlking hunts him. Maybe we could sail away to the islands. Live there. Out of the Erlking's clutches," the bear replied.

They looked over to Erik who had waded out into the water and was speaking to the whales. As the three companions tried to make a plan to keep Erik safe he had come up with a plan of his own. When he returned from talking with the whales he had a very serious look on his face.

"The Erlking is weak. Now is our time to strike!" he said as he approached his friends.

"STRIKE!? You speak as if you have an army! The four of us and a few whales are no match for him! You have no idea what awaits in his kingdom!" Alpha growled at the ill-advised plan.

"I've been in the Erlking's castle! It's just another castle by the sea. We can drop it into the ocean just as we had planned to do to this one! I didn't see anything but trolls when I was there!" Erik said very matter-of-factly.

The wolf laughed madly at Erik.

"HA! You naïve fool! You weren't in the Erlking's castle! Not the one he hails in anyways. You were held in the ruins of his castle from when he walked the earth. His true domain is far beneath the earth. In the world of the dead!... he has the might of a thousand armies at his disposal. We will be heading towards our doom!"

"Then what will we do Alpha!? Run? Hide? Wait around to see what powers the Erlking can get ahold of later down the line!? Gloria told me I would find a way back home. I'm sure the only way I will ever find my way is if I face the Erlking!"

Teddy wanted to tell Erik no, tell him they were going to go to the islands and live out their life, but Erik wasn't a boy to be bossed around anymore. Teddy knew he wouldn't be able to change his mind. That he couldn't convince him to run. Not only that, but Teddy knew deep down this wasn't the world Erik belonged in. Not the way he was there now.

"I will be by your side until my last breath. If you choose to go to the Erlking... then I will go with you," Teddy assured his friend.

Erik hugged Teddy and turned towards the whales and the others.

"I won't run any longer! I don't blame anyone who doesn't want to fight. We may very well be heading towards our doom! But if not now then when? He is weak, he is scared! If there were ever a time to rid this world of his darkness, then now is that time!" he spoke with assertiveness and confidence.

"Why would the Erlking be scared? After killing his brothers he's grown more powerful than before! What do you know that we don't?" questioned Enbarr.

"He came to me last night after everyone had gone to sleep. He tried to grab me and passed through me like a specter. When he did something happened.... I felt a surge of power... after that he seemed afraid."

"So we just have to get you past all demons, banshees, and goblins and god knows what and you can kill him!" said Alpha in a somewhat sarcastic tone.

"We can do this! It sounds crazy, but I know we can!"

"If we do this, then we need to do it right. We're going to need help. We're going to need an army!" Alpha exclaimed.

"Do you know of such an army?" Erik asked.

"The Erlking has many enemies. I will go into the old woods, not all great beasts hold loyalty to the horned king," Alpha assured.

"I will return home and find anyone willing to fight," Enbarr added.

"You saved my son, and you saved me. I am forever in your debt. If you call us. We will come!" complied the king of the whales.

They all agreed on the plan. They would wait one month exactly to attack the Erlking's castle in full force. Alpha and Enbarr said their goodbyes and went on their way. The pod of whales went back out to sea, leaving a conch to blow when the time had come.

The Shroomboat

Teddy and Erik walked through the surrounding shroom forest. This time Erik was able to spend even more time ogling over the beauty of it all. The two of them came to a spring that ran into the river and decided to stop for a drink. As they sat on the shore they both remained silent. Both thinking of the weeks ahead.

"How will we get to the Erlking's kingdom you think?" Teddy finally asked.

At first Erik had no answer. He picked up a small mushroom by his foot and began to examine it and play with it. He began to gaze into the water as he played with the fungi. At that moment it was like a lightbulb went off.

"I have an idea!"

He took the mushroom and flipped it upside down and sat it in the water. They both watched as it calmly braved the river. Erik thought of the mushroom cap and how far it had gotten him.

"We're going to need some help though."

Over the next few days Erik and Teddy managed to gather a small work force. It was made of four beavers, two opossums, and an old brown bear - all of who would come to serve a special purpose.

They all went into the heart of the forest where the largest of the mushrooms grew. Once there they picked the strongest looking one and cut it down! Though proving to be a bit of a hassle, they were able to get the mushroom into the river and down to the sea. On the way down the river everyone simply sat on top of it unharmed. The mighty mushroom even passed through the white waters with ease. They all began to see then, maybe Erik wasn't as crazy as he seemed.

The next three weeks everyone from around not only came to see the incredible structure, but to lend a hand in its construction. Some brought lumber, others brought cloth. Some brought food and supplies for the journey north.

The plan was simple enough. Create a proper ship out of the mushroom. They would hollow out just a bit of the shroom to make the hull. Add a deck, masts and sails and it would be good to go!

The beavers cut the wood for the ship. First, was the underneath - a perfect wood square for storage and protection. Next a deck for the ship that would protect the gills of the mushroom. It was the finest wood and crafted eloquently, because everyone knows beavers are master woodworkers. From there they built the rails and finally the wheel. They were done with their part.

The opossums were excellent craftsmen. It so happened the two opossums were both very special. One had mastered an art of sewing with silk from small silk worms. Another had found a way to work cotton into a heavier material that would catch more of the wind. The handy workers crafted two of the most seamless and efficient sails one had ever laid eyes on!

The old bear tied the knots to everything. In his old age he had learned to tie knots that no one had ever heard of. Knots that tighten like no other. Others that were easy to unlatch but sturdy to anchor down. His wisdom and steady hands provided the security the ship needed.

Many had come together and in no time at all Erik's idea had come to life! There before them was the Shroomboat! One enormous mast jutted up from the stem and another just behind it. It looked like a ship had been placed on top of the upside down mushroom almost. It was a glorious sight to behold.

The night of the completion many forest creatures celebrated in festivities. From all around they came to see the Shroomboat and the man named Erik. Word had spread and he and the ship were now like a beacon of hope. Talks of rebellion and upheaval filled the mainland. People were no longer quite as afraid of the Erlking!

The Hooded Figure

Bards had already made songs of Erik's adventures of past and to come. Everyone seemed to be in high spirits. Everyone but Erik. He had sparked the fire, but he still had a bit of self doubt. So many now counted on him. He didn't have a plan. Not really. An army gathering and a ship made, but what would come next? Sail to the old castle in hopes he pokes his head up? As the others celebrated Erik took a walk along the shoreline.

Idea after idea raced through his head. He just didn't know enough about the Erlking's kingdom. He wished more than anything Aplha was there to help him plan. Especially since he was the only one who had ever really seen or been to the under-realm at all.

The fires from the celebration were now but a blip in the distance. After a while Erik had stopped thinking so hard on a plan. He walked and didn't think of anything perplexing or stressful. He even began to hum a song to himself.

The moon was bright and the sand was a beautiful white. It was the first time Erik could remember that he had walked at night and been at peace. The woods parallel were silent and as he closed his eyes all he could hear was the wind and the waves gently crashing into his feet.

He walked until the sand began to turn to rocks before the ocean ran straight into cliffs. He sat upon the rocks with his feet in the water. Watching the waves rolling across the top of the sea. Erik stayed here for quite some time.

On his way back the moon was still bright. The water had risen, but not too high. As he walked Erik noticed something floating out on the waves. As he grew closer he could make out that it was a rowboat! It was full of holes and broken wood, Erik was puzzled as to how it was still even floating.

Not too much further up shore Erik could see footprints across the sand and into the mainland. The ones at the end of the shore in the shallows of the water were still there, meaning they were still quite fresh. He followed them towards the forest.

It didn't take long to find the source of the footprints. As Erik looked down following the prints a pair of old rugged boots came into view. Erik quickly looked up. A tall man in a hood stood at the edge of the beach. Erik met eyes with him. A crooked yellow and golden smile grinned at the young man.

"Ye be lookin' a bit more like yer self now boy!" the pirate lord exclaimed.

Erik was taken back by the surprise. He looked at the pirate lord perplexed. He was amazed the old man recognized him without a bit of hesitation. As if he knew who he really was all along. Not only this but Erik wasn't the only one who had gone through a change in his appearance.

The broken, beaten, and scared skeleton of a man looked to be at least twenty years younger! He still had the same sharp features and pointy nose. He looked similar but cleaner. His beard was braided and hair tamed. Under his robe several things began to shine in the moonlight.

"What are those?" Erik asked.

The pirate lord pulled back his robe to reveal a naval coat full of medals. It was the one that had hung above his door! Erik had thought it to be an enemy, but the pride that the old sailor had when he wore it made it clear it was his.

"I wasn't always a bad guy. The sea set me upon that mountain when I needed her the most. When I was lost... I had fallen so far from grace, so far from myself. I had created a whole new me and hated it as the real me watched from the inside... when that city fell to ashes behind me as I sat upon a boat in the water for the first time in nearly forty years... something Rejuvenated within me. As I put my hand in the salt water it was like my soul returned to me. That the me I had created died in that fire and I was born again. The stories of you have spread far and wide now... If the whales will have me, if you will have me, I would gladly sail into the depths of hell with ya!"

"I'll have to talk to the king of the whales, but as for me I would love to have a sailor such as yourself aboard my ship."

"O, I won't be aboard your ship. I'll be sailin' next to ya in me own ship."

Erik looked out towards the little torn up row boat.

"Haha, no boy, you forget I'm the lord of the pirates. My ship should promptly be here two days from now..... I just came here ahead for the party!" the old pirate laughed.

As the two walked back Erik began to confess about his lack of a plan to the pirate. The old man didn't seem in the least bit worried.

"Well, as I told ya before, I've had dealings with the horned king for many a years now. I know a thing or two about the old pixie and his creepy castle," he smiled.

Full Speed Ahead!...Below?

One month had passed. Erik at the wheel of his shroom boat. Now equipped with canons that shot from below deck. It was an easy addition that the pirate lord helped with, including the donations of the canons themselves. Next to Erik sailed a massive ship. Ten canons lined up each side of the ship. Three massive sails pushed it along. Standing at the front of the ship was the proud pirate lord. Around and below them swam at least fifty whales.

He could see what he once thought to be the Erlking's castle in the distance. The real castle was just below it. All he awaited was a signal from the inland that the others had arrived. They had kept in touch with messengers and planned it all perfectly. Or at least

Enbarr had. Alpha hadn't been seen since the night he left.

Enbarr began to stack a pile of wood and pour oil over it. He had searched all through the dry lands trying to find allies. Unfortunately, not many came to the call. He stood firm with no more than twenty men at his back. He grasped the torch tight in his hand.

Enbarr hoped that at any moment he would see Alpha and a slew of wonderful creatures to come to their aide. He waited and waited until he couldn't wait any longer. No reinforcements were coming. Erik was waiting for the signal. The day they had agreed on was coming to an end. There was no turning back. They had come this far. They at least had to try. Enbarr held the torch to the woodpile and a fire ignited.

Erik saw the signal and immediately let down the sails to the Shroomboat. They sailed at great speeds towards the castle.

"So what's the plan to get to the actual castle?" Teddy asked as they sped towards the old ruins.

"Well... it's going to sound a little crazy,..." Erik laughed.

With this he began throwing ropes over one side of the boat. Teddy noticed the pirate's crew was doing the same.

"The castle is under there right? Just make sure you hold on to something!" Erik joked.

Teddy's eyes widened.

"What! You can't be serious... Please don't tell me we're about to do what I think we're doing!" Teddy said as he looked over the side of the boat.

As he saw whales take the ropes to their mouths he quickly realized his worry was well warranted.

"Well,... looks like you've got it covered up here. I'll just be below deck if you need me," said Teddy as he was already backing down the stairs to the lower deck.

"Perfect! Ready the cannons! We have no idea what madness we are about to sail into!"

"If we make it there," the bear muttered to himself as he went below.

The Gate

Meanwhile, back on land, Enbarr and his small group had begun their assault on the ruins. Many goblins and trolls resided within their walls. Though great in numbers the goblin's clubs and axes were no match for the hot steel that shot from the dry-landers guns.

They made quick work of the first wave of guards. Enbarr split his group in half. Sending half to finish clearing the ruins above ground and the other half went with him further into the underbelly of the old castle. He had heard rumors of a gate within the walls that led to the underworld. He hoped they were true.

Enbarr's aim was slow and steady. He made sure every shot he took counted. He and his group followed several corridors deeper and deeper into the earth. After several turns a glowing green light began to shine at the end of one of the halls. Several strange sounds came from the same direction. The closer they got the more they could make out the sounds. Several growls and snarls echoed out into their hallways. They weren't sure what they were about to walk into, but they knew it wasn't good.

Enbarr was the first to round the corner into the green room. His guns at the ready he quickly turned into the room. The stallion wasn't easily scared. He had seen many things, but the sight before him made him shiver to his core. His muscles all froze.

A giant green portal glowed before him. Goblins and demons crawled out of all sides of it in droves. It looked as though an ant hill had been poked and all of its inhabitants were swarming out of it! As soon as Enbarr regained control of his body functions he stepped backwards into the hallway with the others. His breath was heavy.

"What? What is it?" asked one of the dry-landers.

Enbarr held his finger up to his lips. He took a deep breath and poked his head back around into the green room. The room was quickly filling with more and more creatures from the portal.

The curiosity of one of the dry-landers, a sand cat fittingly, got the best of them and he stepped around the corner to see for himself. When he did he let out an enormous gasp and a bit of a scream before Enbarr was able to cover his mouth.

The horse stood there holding his hand over the sand cat's mouth. Hundreds of gnarly faces staring right at them. The walls, floors, and ceilings all began to move at once like the shadow of a door closing out a light. Enbarr slung the cat behind him and drew his pistols.

"Go! RUN!" he shouted to his allies.

Not being any sort of soldier or lawmen like the stallion, they quickly turned tail and ran back the way they came. Some even dropped their guns in the process. At the end of the hallway the sand cat stopped to look back. He could no longer see Enbarr. Only a wall of goblins and demons coming straight towards them.

The sand cat quickened his pace. As he rounded the corner though he was met by the back end of a jackrabbit. One of his fellow dry-landers. The whole group that had come down with Enbarr stood still in awe.

A grand elk wearing fur and bones as armor stood before them. On each side of him a buck with similar armor. All three wielded swords bigger than most of the dry-landers. The sand cat and the others dropped any remaining guns they had. Surrendering to the cervids. The elk in the middle moved to the side. As he did, a giant wolf ran through and jumped clear over the dry-landers.

"Move cowards!" Alpha roared as he cleared the tops of their heads.

The wolf ran fearlessly towards the wall of creatures. Close behind him followed an enormous moose who's antlers stretched the whole width of the hallway. Behind him the bull and stags followed. The dry-landers stayed against the sides of the hallway as they all passed.

Enbarr stood in the middle of the enormous green room. Only now he could only see rays of green as it shined through the multitude of bodies. They swarmed around him, constantly moving. He felt as if he were in a cyclone made up of monsters.

By some miracle he was still alive! Even though he shot wildly as they came at him it seemed every bullet found its target. Not only that, Enbarr was moving at speeds unheard of. Almost as soon as he was opening the cylinder to reload it was full again. As he passed his guns under his bandolier it was as if the bullets just fell off right into the guns!

Enbarr had begun to think he was untouchable! Until he reached for his gun belt and felt only one bullet left.

He thought for a moment what might be the easiest thing to do with that bullet. Surely it would be better than being torn apart by these things that swarmed him. He loaded the last bullet into the gun. Time seemed to slow down around him as he brought the gun to his head. He looked around and saw several demons jumping towards him. One was particularly close. He looked the demon in its cold black eyes as it inched his way forward.

As he pulled the hammer back time instantly sprung forward. Before Enbarr even realized what was happening he was firing his last bullet at a demon across the room striking it in the head. The one that was close to him was gone. Alpha knocked off the dead demon from on top of him and spit another from his mouth.

A bright green light shined through as the moose broke through the wall of demons. More light began to shine through as the rest of the cervids cut their way to them. Alpha shouted across to Enbarr.

"We have to get through the gate! The boy will need help! They can handle this!"

They ran to each other and made their way towards the gate. Enbarr grabbed a club from a fallen goblin for his new weapon.

"How will Erik get into the world of the dead?" Enbarr asked in a concerned voice.

"The vale is thin here. He's a special young man. He'll find a way!" Alpha smiled.

Just as the two of them were about to step through the gate a massive beast emerged from the portal, almost stepping on them. It was the mighty Fenrir!

The Below

Erik held tight to the wheel as the Shroomboat began to turn on its side. The whales pulled hard on the ropes. He stared ahead. Down, down towards the castle. Down towards the Erlking!

Soon the boat capsized. Further down the whales pulled the upside-down boat.

They passed through a cold glowing green cloud. As they exited the strange fog they were still upside down. Only now the clouds had turned to the sea and the sea (and) the sky. The whales swam as if they were still in water. The air was thick, but Erik could breath like he was on the surface.

He and the pod of whales made their way towards the castle. It hung in the distance like a stalagmite from the clouds. As they grew closer several ships that looked to be made of shadows began to descend from around the castle.

The Shroomboat stayed its course. The approaching boats began to open fire on them. Erik did his best to maneuver through them. Teddy immediately jumped into action and began firing back. The damned ships dropped easy enough, but were great in multitude. They seemed to just keep coming out of the fog the castle hung from.

The shadow ships began to now get on both sides of the Shroomboat. The undead crew loaded the cannons to destroy the invaders. Before they were able to fire they began to get bombarded by a reign of canon balls.

The whales pulled the Shroomboat down and in its place between the ships sailed the pirate lord and his ship. They lit up both lines of ships that surrounded them. The whales released the pirate's ship and off he sailed into the madness, canons ablaze.

A massive ship, even larger than that of the pirates, began to emerge from the fog. It sailed right towards The Shroomboat. Not having a way to fire forward, Erik and Teddy were in trouble. The massive ship's crew began to roll two canons to the bow of the ship. The whales saw this and dropped the ropes pulling The Shroomboat and darted towards the enormous ship. They shot at the enemy ship like massive torpedoes.

Just before they made contact with the boat several long tentacles jutted from the fog and wrapped around the whales. Several giant squids began to swim from the fog. They were fierce and frightening creatures. They began to bat the whales away from the ships. The two whales that had pulled The Shroomboat sank into the depths still wrapped in the arms of the squids.

One of the giant squids had latched onto the king whale. He fought hard, but eventually the squid was able to wrap his arms around him. The cephalopod tried its best to break the bones of the king whale. He could feel his ribs beginning to crack beneath the pressure of the monster.

Suddenly, the squid let go and released ink everywhere. The king whale could see a severed tentacle floating down. Teddy reloaded his cannon in an attempt to finish off the beast. As he went back into position he could no longer see the beast. He could no longer see anything. The ink had spread in the water and the area around them was pitch black. More squids began to come down from the fog.

It was too inky to see anything around him, but Erik hoped for the best and sailed forward. He could hear the cries of the whales as they sailed through the blackness. As the ink cleared the nightmare before him was revealed. Several whales had been ripped to pieces by the giant squids.

Teddy began to fire on anything he could. Explosions of ink filled the air. While he fired on the squids more ships began to emerge from the green cloud. As Teddy turned to look forward he could see there now stood almost an entire armada between them and the castle!

Erik dropped down his sails and continued full speed ahead towards them. A barrage of canon balls came down onto The Shroomboat like a meteor shower.

The Beast

Alpha stood his ground as the wolf at least ten times his size stood before him. The demon wolf surveyed the room. Picking out in what order he would make his kills. He looked down in front of him to the snarling dire wolf.

"A traitorous fool. I shall take great pleasure in killing you first," Fenrir bellowed.

He bit down at Alpha with his massive mouth. Alpha quickly jumped out of the way and slashed four small scratches over the beast's nose.

"I will not die easily!" the dire wolf said as he landed back on his feet.

He crouched down ready to try and strike the great beast again. Fenrir smashed down his mighty paw... missing his target again.

Out of the corner of his eye Alpha could see Enbarr running to his aid.

"NO!" The wolf shouted.

"I'll hold him off! You HAVE to get to Erik! He's all that matters now! GO!" Alpha continued to scream.

Enbarr shook his head in compliance and jumped through the glowing green portal.

Fenrir turned to follow the stallion through the door but Alpha grabbed hold of his ankle and pulled with all of his might. The beast's leg didn't budge at first, but as the skin and meat began to tear from the bone it made him take a step back.

When he did, the elk plated in furs and bones swung his massive sword at the bits of exposed bone on the back of Fenrir's leg. It was a mighty swing. One that could cut down an old oak in one swing. Unfortunately the demon wolf's bone was dense. The elk's sword wedged itself deep into the ankle of the beast. Fenrir jolted his head back and snatched the Elk into the air. Swallowing it whole with little effort.

Alpha jumped for the other rear leg but was swatted midair by one of Fenrir's massive paws. Alpha jumped back to his feet and prepared to attack again. He ran to Fenrir's head. The beast looked down at Alpha and smiled with his massive sharp teeth. The dire wolf and the demon wolf looked into each other's eyes. One was unrelenting, the other unamused. Alpha knew he couldn't win the fight, but it didn't matter. He only needed to live long enough for the boy to finish what he set out to do.

As he tried to quickly come up with his next plan of attack Fenrir bit down towards him. At first he was going to dodge it, but as he looked through the beast's legs he could see an ally. The bull moose had managed to free himself from the demon horde and was running straight towards the beast's wounded tendon with his head held low ready to ram.

Alpha smiled as Fenrir bit down over him. He could feel the hot breath surrounding him as the beast's mouth engulfed him. Just before it closed down on him it quickly shot back open as the wolf screamed out in pain.

The great beast fell to his ass as his back leg folded underneath him. The moose had finished breaking the bone in half and the weight came crumbling down. Fenrir shuffled back to his feet. His back right leg hung down like a wet sock hanging from a clothes line. If it weren't for a small piece of skin holding it together it may have been completely severed.

Fenrir roared in anger and slammed his front paw down onto the moose, turning him into a pile of mush. Alpha tried to bite into the other back leg , but was thwarted. Fenrir now knew what Alpha was trying to do and was sure to stay facing the dire wolf at all times.

Again and again he tried to bite at the beast's legs, each time missing or being swatted away like a fly. Blood dripped from the dire wolf's mouth. He looked down at himself. His adrenaline had been pumping so hard he hadn't felt anything during the fight. Yet, as he looked at himself he quickly realized Fenrir had bested him. Alpha's skin had been torn away from his ribs. Parts of his intestines even hung from an opening in his stomach. Fenrir could see the realization hit Alpha and began to laugh.

"I must admit, you put up quite the fight, but you should've known you stood no chance against me. You will die here alongside all of your new found friends. You've chosen your allies poorly. You could've sat next to the great king when all of this is over. Instead you're going to lay here on the cold ground as your innards slip from your body!" teased the demon wolf.

Alpha began to slowly droop down. He stood in a pool of his own blood. Fenrir looked at him in disgust as he walked by him into the portal, leaving him there to die a slow death. Fenrir proudly limped through the door.

On the other side was a small path leading all the way to the castle of the damned. He could see the stallion not far ahead. As he started down the path Alpha leaped from the portal onto Fenrir's back. It didn't take much for the massive wolf to lose balance on the small walkway and with only three legs.

They wobbled from one edge of the path to the other. As Fenrir leaned to the side with the gimp leg Alpha saw his moment. He grabbed hold of the back of Fenrir's neck and flung his body to the side Fenrir leaned. As he did, the beast's remaining legs lifted from the pathway. They both fell to the chasm below. Stalactites shot up through the demon wolf in several places. Alpha laid only a few feet away. He too had several spikes jutted through him. He didn't mind though.

As he saw the fire of the great Fenrir's eyes burn out he knew he had done his part. He knew his warrior spirit could now rest easy. He could die a worthy death. He looked above him and saw The Shroomboat fighting its way through a mass of ships. Alpha smiled and closed his eyes. He knew Erik would soon bring the downfall of the Erlking and the world would start anew.

Falling Stars

Erik floated down towards the stars. Explosions went off all around him. He looked around as he sank. Almost all of the whales had been slain. Pieces floated around. Far above he could see the pirate lord's boat blown clear in half. Debris fell down from the wreckage. The Shroomboat floated overhead with its sails on fire. His pride and overconfidence had gotten the best of him. All he had managed to do was lead all of his friends to their doom.

The stars grew closer. Some even seemed to move. It looked like a swarm of fireflies descended down into the water. As the dark world began to get brighter Erik quickly realized the stars were falling through! Several hundred stars shot through the floor of the strange land. Several latched themselves to one of the giant squids. There right after the squid sank into the abyss.

When the stars were right on him Erik could now see they weren't stars at all. They were fairies! As one flew by he grew to full size and grabbed Erik by the arm.

366

Together they floated over to the main entrance of the castle. Everything finally seemed to flip right side up as Erik's feet touched the ground. He turned to his rescuer.

"Thank you! Who are all of you? Where have you come from?" Erik asked excitedly.

"We serve the one true fairy king, the great Oberon. The might of the king's army is at your command, Erik the brave." The armored Fae answered as she bowed to the young man.

Open the Gate!

The castle was unlike any place Enbarr had ever been to. Stairs went in every direction. Gravity or logic didn't seem to have a place amidst these walls. Everywhere that Enbarr looked it seemed more like an extended dungeon rather than a castle. Skeletons and rotted bodies lined the walls. Several lay twisted and contorted from strange torture devices.

The halls were quiet and the echo from Enbarr's hooves carried far through the corridors. At first he thought the sound would give him away and something would jump him out of nowhere, but the further he got into the castle he began to realize the bottom few levels had been emptied.

"Maybe the Erlking sent his entire army out to fight," Enbarr thought to himself.

Knowing though, that was very unlikely. At every corner he passed he waited for a trap to spring. Enbarr crept his way through the eerie twisted castle all the way to the main floor. He could hear voices but couldn't see anyone. Ahead of him he could see the front gate.

Still not running into any trouble. As he approached the gate he could hear the madness on the other side of the gate. The gate was heavy and clearly made for more than one person to open it. He managed to crack open the top of the gate and when he saw what was unfolding outside he knew he had to get it all the way open!

He dug his hooves down into the old stone floor and pushed the wheel connected to the gate as fiercely as he could. As the gate fell open Enbarr could fully see the war that raged outside. Shooting stars seemed to be falling up from the sky below, decimating anything in their path. Great beasts floated around in the air fighting one another. His attention was quickly reeled back in as one of the stars grew brighter and was heading towards him. It looked to be carrying something!

Erik and a full-sized woman covered in armor now stood at the end of the opened gate where the star had just crashed. Other stars began to crash on the gate behind Erik. Soldiers in glorious golden armor rose up in perfect form and fell into formation. Erik and the golden army marched into the front door of the castle. Enbarr ran to Erik.

The two embraced. Though the moment of good spirits was short lived as Enbarr looked back to the fallen gate. Dozens of skeletons and undead pirates fell from above. As they landed on the gate they began returning to their feet and inching towards the gate.

As the golden Fae followed Erik up the stairs, Enbarr walked out onto the gate. The skeletons were slow and clunky. One at a time he would have no problem disposing of them. Enbarr was no master of blunt weapons, but he knew enough to keep himself alive. The problem was they weren't going to be coming at him one at a time. The mass at the end of the gate piled higher. Skeletons and undead crawled and pulled themselves from the pile and moved towards Enbarr.

He readied his club. Just as they were about to reach him three cannon balls, one right after the other shot through the gate right in front of him across in a line. The farthest side of the bridge collapsed into the abyss below, taking several undead and walking skeletons with it. Enbarr looked up just in time to see The Shroomboat speed over him and plow full force into the castle wall, canons still smoking.

Erik and the Fae army had just reached the top of the stairs when the wall behind them exploded. Through the debris The Shroomboat came barreling into the old castle. Its sails burnt to nothing and the mushroom itself full of holes.

Erik ran to the boat and began to remove debris hurriedly. Just before Erik began to really panic, Teddy crawled from the wreckage from below deck.

"You know how damn hard it is to steer the ship and shoot the cannons at the same time!?" he joked as he crawled from the pile of burnt shroom and stone wall.

"Quite the entrance," Erik joked back.

They laughed together. The laugh ended slowly before it was complete silence as they both sat there. They knew very well that could be the last laugh they ever had. They appreciated the fact they were even able to muster up a laugh given the circumstances.

"You ready?" Teddy asked.

"As I'll ever be," Erik answered as he shook his head to the side.

Erik and Teddy approached the throne room doors.

The Portal

Enbarr started up the stairs behind the others at first, but the more he thought about it the more he began to worry about the way he had come. It was only a matter of time before the Erlking called his hordes of demons back to the castle. One way to the castle was destroyed. Now he had to find a way to destroy or block the other one! He knew this would trap him and the others, but they all knew what they were signing up for when they came here. Everyone did. None expected a return journey.

He knew he had to buy Erik and the others as much time as he could. He ran back through the castle and back out onto the pathway. Luckily nothing had come back through the portal yet. He began to run towards the gate but stopped halfway as something enormous below him caught his eye. He paused and looked down to the deadly chasm below. There, impaled on several pointed rocks laid the mighty Fenrir. Not far from Fenrir lies Alpha.

"You did it.... You stopped the demon dog... and you got your warrior's death... Thank you for all you've done. May your spirit go where it finds peace." Enbarr nodded his head and tipped his imaginary hat at his fallen friend.

Enbarr looked up at the portal. He didn't want to think about what had unfolded on the other side. The way they had crawled out in droves. There wasn't much chance of anything making it.

The horse examined the structure holding the portal. It was almost as if the portal was keeping the large stones in place as they floated around it. Enbarr took the goblin club and swung it as hard as he could at the gate. It shot out several feet before springing back into its place like a piece of metal to a magnet. He tried several times more. Each time ending with the same result.

He began to feel the ground around him shake and the sounds of growls grow louder. They were coming back through!

Enbarr took a few steps back and stood ready. Several goblins came running through the portal as if they were being chased. A few were looking behind them with frightened looks on their faces. Before they were all even fully out of the portal they were all run through with one massive spear like a shish-kabob. Other goblins ran through but were dropped only a foot or so from the gate. Enbarr couldn't even see what killed the goblins. It moved so fast. After the last goblin fell the attacker finally stood still.

There stood an enormous deer. Even the moose warrior paled in comparison. She was dressed in armor like that of a Viking warrior. Axes and swords hung on her sides and back. She wore enormous golden antlers on her head and her feet looked to be made of bronze. She was a magnificent creature indeed.

The Ceryneian Hind walked over to Enbarr and handed him one of the several swords that hung from her.

"This will work much better than a stick," she said, smiling before facing back towards the portal.

A handful of cervids ran through and quickly posted up next to the golden antlered deer. It was clear something wasn't far behind them! The ground shook to the point where it was hard to keep your footing. At least for Enbarr. Then, as if a dam had busted, demons and goblins poured out of the portal onto the pathway.

It's a Trap!

Erik and Teddy led the golden army through a long corridor of pillars leading the throne room. The pillars were all sculpted to look like demons and gargoyles. Whispers filled the room, but no one could be seen. Teddy began to become uneasy. About three quarters of the way through the corridor the doors to the throne room slammed open. A horrid stench began to seep into the long room. An enormous shadow could be seen standing in the doorway. The bright green light shining from behind him.

The dark room began to brighten as the surrounding flames almost doubled in size. Through the green light Teddy could make out the figure that guarded the door.

The oversized walking corpse wore a metal plate on half of his head. His neck and arms looked to be held together with twine. His eyes burned red. He smiled as he made eye contact with Teddy.

"Now YOU get to see how it feels to fight someone you thought to be dead! Ahahaha," the Ellerkonge laughed.

As he did, black blood poured from his mouth and the openings in his neck.

"You've got one foot in the grave already. Shouldn't be that hard to get the other one back in there!" Teddy retorted.

As the two of them went back and forth the golden army stood ready to attack. All but one of the soldiers who gazed upon the mesmerizing sculptures that surrounded them. He looked at all the details. As he stared at one of their eyes his heart skipped a beat as the eyes looked down to him.

"They're alive!" the young soldier screamed as he lifted his shield in vain.

The stone creature stepped on the Fae soldier, crushing him underneath his shield. Several other gargoyles began to step down from their podiums.

The general turned to Erik with a serious look in her eyes.

"You have to defeat The Erlking. If you do, all of his magic,.... All of this... will cease to be. Our king believes in you. I believe in you. We all believe in you. Now believe in yourself and do what needs to be done!"

The golden army clashed with the gargoyles as Erik and Teddy ran towards The Ellerkonge and the door. When they reached the brute Teddy tackled him as hard as he could onto the ground, allowing Erik to slip by into the throne room.

There Erik stood face to face with the Erlking. Before, fear would paralyze him. His heart would beat so fast it made him feel like he was about to pass out. Now, his heart beat fast, but rather than be overwhelmed it flooded his body with adrenaline. He drew his sword.

A Last Stand

Enbarr and the cervids made a wall across the pathway. The goblins crashed against them like waves onto rocks. They were quickly slashed to pieces or thrown over the side. Wave after wave fell to the defenses. The demons, being a bit less dim witted than the goblins, watched as their comrades fell. They dug their claws into the ground and began to crawl beneath the path!

The demons began to emerge on either side of the pathway next to Enbarr and the others. They began to fill in behind the heroes. Enbarr and the cervids were slowly getting boxed in. It was not long after they descended on them that many of the cervids fell. Before long only Enbarr and the Ceryneian Hind stood. It wouldn't be long before they too were overwhelmed.

Enbarr swung his sword back and forth, but there were too many. In only seconds several enemies piled onto Enbarr and began to scratch and bite at him. As he helplessly sank into the ground from the weight of the demons he began to hear a crack coming from beneath him. He felt as the path began to give.

The great hind had been brought to her knee, but she refused to go down. Demons hung off of her like clothes on a drying rack.

"The bridge is breaking!" Enbarr managed to yell across the snorts and growls of the demons and goblins.

More creatures pulled onto the stone bridge. The cracking noise grew louder. Next thing Enbarr knew he was being pulled from the pile of demons and whisked down the path towards the castle. The golden horned hind was quick and agile as she made her way down the path. Clearing the path with her spear along the way. Only as soon as a section was cleared would it fill right back within seconds. It took quite an effort just to get them through the masses.

The demons were fast and close behind them when they reached the entrance. It wouldn't be long at all before they were inside! The hind let go of Enbarr and turned back towards the oncoming wave.

"Don't let them get into the castle," she shouted back to Enbarr.

She turned her spear to the side and held it with both hands as she sprinted back towards the horde. They began to pile in front of her. Unable to push her back. The pile began to grow over her head as they crawled over one another and dropped down behind her.

Enbarr could now see the cracks he had been hearing form underneath them all. Several cracks began to run across the path. As a crack ran across in front of him an idea struck.

"Hurry! Come on!" he yelled to the hind.

But it was too late. She had been completely engulfed by the demons. They mulled over her lifeless body and towards Enbarr and the castle. Enbarr lifted his sword high into the air with the tip pointed towards the ground. He drove the sword down into the crack with all the power he had left in him.

As he did, the crack widened and the bridge began to crumble. The demons clawed at the air in desperation as they fell. The entire bridge fell to pieces bringing the armies of demons and goblins down with it. After Enbarr watched the last of the bridge fall into the chasm he collapsed to the ground from exhaustion.

Face to Face

Before, Erik saw fear, death and the very face of evil when he looked at the Erlking. Now, he only saw a scared, power-hungry shell of a king. The Erlking stared at Erik with his yellow eyes. There was no laughing or snide comments as usual. He sat quietly as Erik approached the throne.

Banshees and specters flew around the top of the room. They circled around Erik like sharks circling their prey. The young man paid them no mind. He knew if he could simply run his sword through the Erlking's black heart it would all be over. Erik grew closer with his sword held steady. Just as he was about to plunge the sword into the horned king's heart the Erlking finally spoke.

"Don't you want to know the truth? Don't you want to know *what* you are?" he asked.

Erik paused with his sword held inches from the Erlking. His hand began to shake. He wanted so badly to just end it. He was so close, and yet his curiosity gnawed at him. If he killed him he may never know what "powers" he had or what made him so special. He would never know why he had to run or hide all these years. He slowly lowered his sword.

The Erlking closed his yellow eyes and let out a small sigh, perhaps relieved.

"You are one of my many children. A changeling. A Fae." He paused for a moment as if to see Erik's reaction.

However, there wasn't one at all. Erik stood there unblinking with his sword still gripped tight in hand. The Erlking continued on.

"But you, you are extra special!... you're more powerful than I could've ever imagined."

"Then why have you tried to kill me or convince me to take my own life for all these years!?"

"I was afraid. Changelings are usually vile little creatures. I didn't want to imagine one running around with powers matching that of the great kings!... I see my mistake now. You are so much more than a changeling. You are my true son. Not some magical creature!... I see now all these years I should've asked you to be by my side!" The Erlking tongue was sly and quick thinking, even almost convincing.

Erik began to laugh a wild laugh.

"HA! You expect me to believe any of this? I've been told many times I was no Fae... You tried everything you can to kill me and now that I'm here and you realize you can't. Now you beg for your life and try to make false alliances... Do you take me as such a fool? You're afraid of me! You're afraid to die!"

The Erlking, enraged, grabbed Erik by the neck with both hands. He squeezed as hard as he could, but as he did he began to feel his grip loosen. The longer he held onto the young man the more his power seemed to drain from his body. His hands even began to burn as he tried to stay clasped on.

The horned king let go and looked down at his hands in shock. He said nothing. Only looked as smoke rose from his burning hands. Much like The Ellerkonge it seemed The Erlking could no longer touch Erik.

"This is MY home! You don't have any power here! How! How are you doing this!"

The monster's glowing yellow eyes began to look a lot more human. The fear in them began to show. Erik sheathed his sword and grabbed the Erlking's face. Steam began to pour from under his hood. The Erlking managed to jerk his head back. As he did his hood fell. Two burnt in handprints laid upon each cheek of a long forgotten face. The man snarled at Erik, smoke still seeping from the handprints.

"Who are you!" Erik demanded.

"You know who I am. The Erlking. The horned king, the king of the damned. Which name do you prefer?" Aggravated The Erlking.

"No! Who are you *really*!? I know that face! How do I know you?" Erik asked again.

"I told you already," The Erlking said as he smiled.

Erik angrily grabbed the man's face again. He could now feel the skin melting away as he squeezed.

383

The Erlking screamed in agony as he did so. Soon his screams were drowned out by the screeches of the banshees above. They flew wildly above Erik's head. It was almost like they could feel the Erlking's pain.

Erik let go of the king's face and backed away. The banshees began to swirl around him. Their screams were deafening. Before long Erik began to feel blood running down his neck from his ears. Soon all he could hear was a high pitched ringing.

A headache that felt like a knife stabbing him in the top of his head overcame Erik. He closed his eyes and clenched his teeth. He wanted nothing more than for the banshees to disappear. For the headache and ringing to end. Then, as if he had magically snapped his fingers, the ringing stopped.

Erik opened his eyes and looked around the room. The banshees were no longer there! They had just disappeared. The Erlking had a look of shock on his face as he looked up to where the banshees had been. He quickly gathered himself and looked Erik in the eyes.

"I see all the hate in your eyes boy... that's what created me... that's what will kill me... any moment your anger will bust through and end me.... Only it won't end there. No... YOU will become me! YOU will continue the cycle!"

"What in the hell are you talking about!? I would never become anything like you!"

A loud roar filled the room. Erik looked back and saw Teddy standing in the doorway. Pieces of the reassembled Ellerkonge now torn to even smaller pieces spread across the floor. Teddy walked to Erik's side.

"Ahhh... and there it is," The Erlking said with a sly tone as his eyes followed the grizzly.

"And to think. Before you were corrupted by all the boy's anger you were his safety, his protection," The Erlking continued to taunt.

"What the hell are you going on about!?" Erik shouted to the Erlking.

The cloaked man said nothing back. He simply looked at Erik and then back at Teddy. Erik looked up to the bear as the Erlking stared and gazed at him. Awaiting death at any moment. The grizzly's hair was matted with blood and his eyes glowed red just as the Ellerkonge's had. Full of hate and anger. He growled with his sharp teeth showing and saliva dripping down his chin. Erik's heart began to sink. This was not the Teddy he remembered. Had he turned him into this beast? The Erlking seemed to see the revelation happen as he looked back at Erik.

"Now I believe you're beginning to understand."

Erik looked long and hard at the burnt face of the cloaked man before him. It was a face he had buried a long time ago. A face he had feared.

"I hate you," Erik said in a low voice.

"What's that? I can't hear you... boy!" teased the Erlking.

"I HATE YOU!!" This time Erik screamed it at the top of his lungs.

The horned king leaned in closer.

385

"So end me," he whispered.

Teddy roared again. His dripping jowls only inches from The Erlking's head. He opened his mouth wider as if to take the head off the man in one swift bite. The Erlking could feel the beast's hot breath on his burnt cheeks. The grizzly's jaws hung open ready to slam shut like a bear trap and end The Erlking's life. Teddy seemed to be reacting to Erik's emotions solely. Just before the jaws shut, just before it all ended, the bear abruptly stopped and looked towards Erik.

Erik stood there with tears in his eyes.

"I hated you,... but I forgive you. I see your face... and I know who you are, and I forgive you. All of these years I blamed you for so much.... You're not going to be the bad guy in my story anymore."

The tears began to run down Erik's cheeks now. The castle began to shake violently. The Erlking said nothing. He only looked at Erik in disbelief. It was nothing like he had imagined would happen. He thought for sure the darkness, the anger, the hate, would consume his son as it had him.

The castle walls began to collapse around them and the floor cracked beneath their feet. The old man smiled as a single tear ran down his face as he looked at Erik. It wasn't the ending he had foreseen, but it was the ending he could never have. It was much better than anything he thought. The new world would be in the image of this young man that stood before him. He was the architect, the creator and he didn't carry with him the same baggage he had, not anymore.

The floor opened, and the throne and The Erlking with it fell into the nothingness.

As the earth opened wider, Teddy began to lose his footing and he too began to fall into the opening. Erik dove for him and held tight to his arm with both hands. Teddy knew he was too heavy to be pulled up. He also knew his time here was over. He had done what he set out to do. He looked up to Erik and smiled.

"It's okay."

"NO! NO! I won't let go!" Erik screamed as he tried to pull the massive bear up.

"It's okay, I promise. You have to let me go. You've let go of your hate, now let go of your anger too."

"No! You're so much more than that! You're my best friend!"

"And I always will be. Let go of me but hold on to all those good things. Hold on to the real me!"

Erik couldn't do it. He couldn't let his best friend, and sometimes only friend fall to his death. He pulled with everything in him, but it was no use. The bear was too heavy.

"It's okay. I'll always be with you. We ALL will. Now go home!"

Teddy slipped from Erik's exhausted grip and fell down into the black abyss. Erik screamed as he fell.

In the White Room (Part Three)

Erik's screams began to turn to a strange high-pitched noise. He closed his eyes and the castle crumbled down onto him.

When he opened his eyes again he was in a white room. Several tubes and wires ran from him to machines. A familiar face lifted his head at the sounds of the machine's noises. His eyes grew wide as they made contact with Erik's. It had been many years, almost his whole life, since Erik had last seen his father. His hair was white and his skin loose. His eyes filled with tears as Erik began to sit up from his hospital bed.

"I'm sorry.... I know you could probably never forgive me. I nev-" the man started but was interrupted by Erik embracing him.

He wrapped his arms around the tiny old man and held him tight. Erik's father squeezed Erik tight, as tight as his feeble old body would allow. Tears ran down both of their faces. Tears of joy, tears of thankfulness, tears of forgiveness.

In the End… There is a Beginning

Over the next two years, Erik spent every moment he could with his father. They moved back to his aunt's old house. There he repaired and refurbished the entire place with his father's help. (Mostly as the supervisor.)

The more the two got to know each other the more Erik began to learn. His father knew all about his aunts and even the friends Erik had. He had secretly talked with the aunts on occasion. He knew of Luthor, Sam, and even Amelia. He seemed to always be watching Erik from the shadows. Erik learned it was his fathers own hate and anger that had kept him from making contact all these years. His hate for himself. His failure as a father and all the bad choices he had made. The anger he had towards Erik's mother for leaving them so soon.

It wasn't until he received a call from a man named Henry he had met at a feed store that he was able to put the past behind him. Henry had called him and told him Erik had fallen from a three story balcony and was in critical condition. He was told he may want to come say his goodbyes.

As he sat by Erik's side. Watching his son cling to life he began to think. Think of all his choices. How things may have been different. At first he had grown even angrier at himself, but as he sat he began to think of Erik's mother.

He chose to let go of his anger for her that had plagued him all these years. He chose to remember the love she had and try to understand the pain she felt. He chose to accept his own pain and stop hating himself for it.

They both grew over those next two years. They both loved like neither thought they ever could before. They loved themselves and each other as a father and son should. As Erik and his new family sat by his side in his final moments he was joyful as he looked over them. He let go with his burdens left behind and only love in his heart and a smile on his face.

Epilogue

A little old white haired man walked out onto a cliff overlooking the ocean. A small cross was stuck into the ground next to him. Across the middle of the cross was the name "Gloria" etched into it.

"That was my mother's name!" he thought to himself.

Next to the cross was a little ragged teddy bear. He had played with that very bear several times when he was a child. As he held the bear he looked out over the ocean and took a deep breath of fresh air.

Not far from where he stood and looked laid an old castle that had fallen to rubble. There, in the middle of the ruins grew a garden unlike any other. Full of unique flowers and plants. In the middle of that garden lay the skeleton of a mighty bear. Vines and flowers covered it from top to bottom. As a tiny butterfly landed on top of one of the flowers the earth beneath it began to move...

Erik put down his pen and paper and headed into town.

The Shroomboat Adventures: The World Beyond

Lucy

A black crowd of tearful mourners stood on top of what was once the most green and beautiful hill in the entire town. Rain poured down and the curtain of umbrellas looked to create a cloud on the hill. One little girl stood out from the others. In the cloud of black she wore yellow and held a yellow umbrella above her head.

No tears ran down her cheeks, no look of sadness in her eyes. Instead, her eyes stare unblinking down into the ground at her best friend's casket. Some said it was because she was too young to understand what was happening, that she'd understand when she was older.

As Lucy gazed into the ground something ran across the corner of her eye. She looked to the nearby bushes and saw a little white rabbit looking at her. It even looked like it was smiling!

She couldn't help but smile back.

Mark Lynn was always a little odd. Creating things was always a passion of his, from drawing to writing to playing pretend. His imagination was his sanity. No matter how tough things would get growing up, he always had his stories and imaginary worlds to escape into. All things fantasy or fairy tale called to Mark. After seeing several characters over and over in his head and in his drawings, a world of his own began to form. Before long the silly drawings came to life and the stories turned into books.

397

Printed in the USA
CPSIA information can be obtained
at www.ICGtesting.com
CBHW010035250224
4616CB00009B/26

9 781733 467025